Safe
HARBOR

Praise for Radclyffe's Fiction

"...well-plotted...lovely romance...I couldn't turn the pages fast enough!" – Ann Bannon, author of *The Beebo Brinker Chronicles*.

"...well-honed storytelling skills...solid prose and sure-handedness of the narrative..." – Elizabeth Flynn, *Lambda Book Report*

"...a thoughtful and thought-provoking tale...deftly handled in nuanced and textured prose that is both intelligent and deeply personal. The sex is exciting, the story is daring, the characters are well-developed and interesting – in short, Radclyffe has once again pulled together all the ingredients of a genuine page-turner..." – Cameron Abbott, author of *To the Edge* and *An Inexpressible State of Grace*

"With ample angst, realistic and exciting medical emergencies, winsome secondary characters, and a sprinkling of humor...a terrific romance...one of the best I have read in the last three years. Highly recommended." – Author Lori L. Lake, Book Reviewer for the *Independent Gay Writer*

"Radclyffe employs...a lean, trim, and tight writing style...rich with meticulously developed characterizations and realistic dialogue..." – Arlene Germain, *Lambda Book Report*

"...one writer who creates believably great characters that are just as strong as mainstream publishing's Kay Scarpetta or Kinsey Milhone...If you're looking for a great romance, read anything by Radclyffe." – Sherry Stinson, editor, *Outlook Press*

SAFE HARBOR (Second Edition)

ISBN 1-933110-13-9

This Trade Paperback Original Is Published By
Bold Strokes Books, Inc.,
Philadelphia, PA, USA

First Edition: Renaissance Alliance 2001
Second Edition: Books Ends Press 2003.
Third Printing: November, 2004 Bold Strokes Books, Inc.
Fourth Printing: December, 2004 Bold Strokes Books, Inc.

Credits
Editors: Stacia Seaman and Laney Roberts
Production Design: J. Barre Greystone
Cover Design By Sheri (GRAPHICARTIST2020@HOTMAIL.COM)
Title Page Art: Judith Curcio

By the Author

Romances

Safe Harbor

Beyond the Breakwater

Innocent Hearts

Love's Melody Lost

Love's Tender Warriors

Tomorrow's Promise

Passion's Bright Fury

Love's Masquerade

shadowland

Fated Love

Honor Series

Above All, Honor

Honor Bound

Love & Honor

Honor Guards

Justice Series

A Matter of Trust (prequel)

Shield of Justice

In Pursuit of Justice

Justice in the Shadows

Change Of Pace: *Erotic Interludes*
(A Short Story Collection)

Acknowledgments

This book will always be special to me because it is set in the place where my heart is happiest and my soul most free. Every time I visit or write of Provincetown, I am reminded of how wonderful it feels to be one among many, and not alone amidst legions. A day may come when we are all simply one, but even then, this beautiful haven on the edge of the world will be a safe harbor for me.

Laney Roberts did an excellent job of editing the first edition, and Stacia Seaman provided her usual superb skills editing the second edition. Jane Chen also proofed the final version and, as has been true before, picked up a few things we all missed. They are innocent of any remaining errors, which belong solely to me. Many thanks to my friends and beta-readers, Athos, JB, and Tomboy, and to HS and all the members of the Radlist, for constant encouragement, support, and inspiration. I took the cover photograph of the lighthouse on Long Point this summer, and Sheri turned it into an unforgettable image that reflects the soul of this story. I am ever grateful for the gift of her talent on these covers. Lee's love and patience make all this possible. *Amo te.*

Radclyffe 2004

Dedication

For Lee,
For Sanctuary

CHAPTER ONE

Provincetown's newest deputy sheriff pulled her cruiser to a stop in the parking lot overlooking Herring Cove. It was six a.m. on a clear, crisp morning in May. Other than a Winnebago parked at the far end of the lot, she was alone. To her right stretched the curve of sand leading to Race Point, and in the distance, she could make out the figures of a few early-morning walkers. Seagulls swayed low over the ocean, searching for their breakfast, their shrill calls echoing on the wind.

The water reflected the color of the nearly cloudless sky, iridescent blues and greens slashed through by the frothy white of the churning waves. The air carried the damp mist that hovered over the dunes, chilling her skin. Despite the cold, she had rolled the windows down, allowing the scent and sounds of the sea to flow through the vehicle. A coffee cup sat on the dash, tendrils of steam drifting off on the breeze. Unconsciously, she shifted her wide leather belt, settling her holstered automatic more comfortably against her right hip.

Reaching for her coffee, she let her gaze idly follow a trawler far out on the bay. Her mind held no distinct thoughts, only the impressions of the timeless forces of nature that surrounded her. She felt totally insignificant—yet completely at peace—and more at home than ever. That fact should have been surprising, considering that she had only called this tiny town on the curving finger of land thrust arrogantly out into the Atlantic Ocean *home* for a few weeks. She had moved across the country to a place she had never even visited before and left behind a life that had shaped her since she was a child. Nevertheless, it felt right to be here now, in this place, at this point in her life, and she accepted it with the equanimity with which she had been trained to face all the circumstances life presented.

A flash of color close to shore caught her attention, and a red kayak with a bright yellow racing stripe slid into view. The powerful rhythmic strokes of the kayaker propelled the craft swiftly over the water, but rather than disrupting the quietude, the churning arms and slicing paddle blended with the motion of the waves, harmonizing with the bay's pulsing tides. She watched until the craft was just a dot on the horizon before starting her engine and pulling slowly away from the water's edge.

❖

Sheriff Nelson Parker glanced up as the door to the station house opened, admitting a small gust of wind that rustled the papers on his desk. The sheriff's department was one large room. There was a small waiting area just inside the front door. Beyond that, on the other side of a low railing with a latched gate that squeaked when opened, was a section that contained several desks pushed close together and the dispatch center. In an adjoining room, at the rear of the building, were two holding cells that rarely saw any use. The sheriff himself was a hardy man in his early forties whose thick dark hair was free of gray and whose sharp eyes were winter gray.

As his deputy entered on the tail of the draft, he was surprised once again by the slight disquiet he felt whenever he saw her. Maybe it was her height—she was damn near as tall as he was— or maybe it was the ramrod straight way she carried herself, no matter what the situation. Broad shouldered and firmly muscled, she was in better physical shape than any of his men. The trim fit of her crisply starched, flawlessly pressed khaki uniform reminded him once again that he needed to work off those extra twenty pounds that seemed to have settled all too unyieldingly around his waist. Maybe it was only that she seemed totally unaware of how imposingly good-looking she was. She certainly *seemed* oblivious to the appreciative glances she got when the two of them were out walking the streets—especially from the women. *Jesus. I think I might be jealous. Damned idiot.*

"Morning, Chief," she said, heading for the small corner counter and the coffeemaker. A frown creased the sculpted features of her angular face as she tilted the pot to skeptically survey the two inches of dark liquid in the bottom. "Last night's?"

"'Fraid so, Reese," he answered with a shrug. "I just nuked mine and chewed it."

"Jesus," she muttered, dumping the remains in the nearby sink. "That looks worse than the sludge from my old duty office. And I wouldn't even drink *that* unless I was half dead." She started a fresh pot and settled behind the desk that was situated across a narrow aisle from his. There were a few reports from the night shift stacked in the bin, and she picked them up to review.

"Anything I should know?" she asked.

"Nothing out of the ordinary. A few traffic stops for speeding, one DUI, and a couple of bar brawls down at the Governor Bradford."

She glanced at the calendar displayed in one corner of the bulletin board. It was less than two weeks until Memorial Day weekend. She had not yet experienced the transformation that reportedly befell the tiny fishing village with the onset of the summer season, but she'd heard about it many times already in her short time in Provincetown. From the end of May until after Labor Day, a flood of tourists would swell the normal population of several thousand to many times that number. Most of the townspeople depended on the influx of visitors to support their economy, despite the constant complaints by the year-rounders of the hectic crowds and unmanageable traffic.

"Not much happening until the big weekend, I expect," Reese observed.

"Nope," the sheriff agreed. "But after that, you can expect a lot of traffic, both vehicular and foot, more accidents, more nightlife, and more drunk and disorderlies. Four months of nonstop pandemonium, and then eight months of deadly quiet."

Reese filed the reports silently, envisioning the upcoming weeks of work.

"Think you'll be able to stand the off-season?" Parker asked. "By December, you'll be able to see the length of Commercial

Street without a car blocking your view. You'll walk down the street and the only footprints in the snow will be yours."

Reese looked up in surprise, her blue eyes questioning. "Why should that bother me?"

He shrugged, curiosity warring with his sense of diplomacy. She'd been working for him for almost a month, and he didn't know word one about her personal life. She never mentioned her past or spoke of any family. He found it hard to believe that someone who looked like her wasn't attached some way. Still, she never left any room for those kinds of questions, and he often found himself fishing for some clue to her, beyond the impersonal data in her resume. "Well, it's probably not the kind of life you've been used to."

Reese fiercely guarded her privacy. Not only was it instinctual, it was also learned. She fought the urge to leave his unspoken question unanswered. This man was her boss and likely to be the person she would spend most of her time with in the coming months. In his own way, he was trying to be friendly. She reminded herself she had nothing to hide. "The life I was used to was military life, Sheriff. It can be *very* boring in its own way. It hasn't changed much in two hundred years."

"You know, you're way overqualified for this job," he continued. "I knew that when I hired you. I just couldn't *not* hire you, what with your experience as a MP and a law degree thrown in."

Still struggling with her unease at casual conversation, Reese contemplated how much she wanted to share. Her social interactions were molded by a lifetime in the military, a rigid hierarchical world where relationships were defined and shaped by rank and politics. There were rules determining where you ate, where you slept, and *with whom* you could and could not sleep. There were ways around those rules, if you were careful and so inclined. Reese had never found the need to challenge them, but she was far from naïve about the consequences. Revealing your thoughts, and certainly your feelings, could be dangerous and, in some instances, deadly. As a young officer candidate she had been taught there were only three acceptable answers to any question or request put to her by a superior—*yes sir, no sir,* and *no excuse, sir.*

But this was not the Marines, it was a new life. She took a breath. "After fifteen years, I found I was getting a little cramped in the military. I had to make a decision to stay for the rest of my life or make a move. I didn't like practicing military law, but I liked upholding the law. This job gives me the chance to do that."

Trained to provide facts without revealing her emotions, she didn't even try to explain the unrelenting restlessness she had felt the last few years; she didn't understand it herself. Whatever it was, it had been strong enough to make her walk away from a brilliant career that also offered financial security and a familiar structure. Looking at her life to that point, she couldn't fault it—yet still she had left it behind. Now she was here, and she was content with her decision.

Nelson regarded his second intently and wondered what she wasn't saying. For a moment she'd seemed to let her guard down, and a hint of what might have been sadness had flickered across her face. But now she regarded him impassively once more. Apparently, he had all the answers he was going to get. Gruffly, he added, "Well, I'm glad to have you. And for Christ's sake, call me Nelson."

"Sure thing, Chief," she responded, suppressing a grin. She brushed the lock of jet-black hair from her forehead with one long-fingered hand, a tiny smile deepening a single dimple to the right of her mouth. Her deep blue eyes were laser-like in their focus. "You want the first circuit through town or do you want me to take it?"

He shook his head, trying not to laugh. "You go ahead. I'm waiting for a call about next year's budget from the county office. God, I hate the paperwork. I should never have run for sheriff. I was much happier as the deputy sheriff."

"Too late now," Reese rejoined, "the job's taken." Then she settled her hat over her thick, neatly trimmed hair and snapped the brim with a practiced motion to secure it over her deep-set eyes.

For a second, Nelson had the urge to salute her. "See you later."

"Roger." Grabbing her keys, Reese headed happily for the door. She loved to be out on patrol, simply observing the day-to-day activities of the community she was making her own. Once in the cruiser, she headed east out Route 6 toward Truro and then turned back on 6A when she reached the town limits. She'd nearly completed her slow tour through the still-sleeping village when the radio crackled to life.

"Reese?"

"Here," she answered, thumbing the mike.

"They need you out at the medical clinic on Holland Road. A break-in."

"Two minutes," she replied tersely as she wheeled her cruiser up one of the narrow side streets that crisscrossed the main part of town, while flipping her lights on with one hand. "Is there a suspect on the scene?"

"Negative. But keep an eye out on your way. The doc just got there, so we don't know how long the suspect's been gone. And Reese? The doctor is inside the building."

"Roger that," Reese replied curtly. *Perfect.*

A civilian in an unsecured building could easily turn into a hostage situation. At the very least, it made her reconnaissance more difficult because she had to be on guard for innocent bystanders as well as the possible perpetrator. She did not use her siren. If anyone was still on the premises, it was best not to broadcast an alert. For the same reason, she did not want an army of police cars barreling into the scene. Not that there *was* an army of patrol cars in the small Provincetown force. "I'll call in when I've checked the area. Hold the backup for now."

She saw no one suspicious as she traveled the short distance to the East End Health Clinic, and when she pulled slowly into the small parking lot, it was empty except for a Jeep Cherokee with a kayak roped to the top. She recognized the red craft she had seen an hour earlier on the bay. Angling her cruiser across the drive, she effectively blocked the exit. Once on foot, she drew her automatic and quickly circled the building, noting the shattered window at the rear of the small one-story structure.

Moving cautiously to the far side of the clinic and around to the front again, Reese was on full alert as the front door slowly opened. In the entryway was an auburn-haired woman in a white lab coat, leaning slightly on a burnished mahogany cane. The lower end of a leg brace was apparent below the cuff of her creased blue jeans. When she saw Reese, automatic in hand, crouched in a shooter's stance at the foot of the steps, her hazel eyes widened in concern. "What—"

"I'm Deputy Sheriff Conlon, ma'am. I'll need you to step outside." Reese lowered her weapon slightly as she spoke. Then she quickly ascended the short flight of stairs, took the other woman firmly by the elbow, and maneuvered her out through the door onto the small porch. "Please wait in the patrol car while I check the building."

"There's no one here," the woman replied. "I've already looked."

Reese nodded, her eyes already scanning the interior of the clinic. "Just the same, you need to wait outside."

"Of course," the doctor replied. She stepped down off the porch, but then turned back. "Patients will be arriving in a few minutes."

"Just keep them in the parking lot," Reese instructed as she moved cautiously into the waiting area. After she checked the offices and examining rooms, she returned to her cruiser and called Nelson. "Chief?"

"Go ahead, Reese."

"No one on the premises. I'll be here for a while getting the details."

"Okay. Let me know what you get."

"Will do." Reese turned to face the woman beside her. "Let's go inside so you can fill me in."

"Can it wait until later? I have a full schedule, and my office hours are due to start soon."

"Just some routine questions," Reese assured her. "I'll be as quick as I can."

"All right. Let's get it done." As they entered the building, the doctor extended her hand and said, "I'm Tory King, by the way. I'm the clinic director."

"Reese Conlon, Doctor." Reese took the offered hand, returning the firm grasp. "Can you tell me what you found when you arrived?"

"I opened up at my usual time—seven a.m.," the doctor said as she led Reese down a corridor to a room at the far end of the building that was apparently her office. A bookcase nearly covered one wall, framed photos and diplomas covered the opposite one, and a broad, dark wood desk sat in front of a window which looked out on the dunes. "I didn't notice anything amiss until I opened exam room one."

She grimaced slightly, adding in disgust, "You probably saw the mess for yourself when you searched the building."

"Yes."

Leaning her cane against her desk, Dr. King sat behind it and folded her hands on the scratched surface.

They were steady, Reese noted.

"I called the sheriff immediately. Then I looked around."

A brave but dangerous thing to do. Reese's face revealed nothing of her thoughts. "Did you see anyone walking on the road before you got here or a car—anything—that seemed out of place?"

"No, but then I wasn't looking for anything."

Reese studied the woman carefully, noting the strong forearms exposed by the rolled-up sleeves of her white coat. Under that, she wore a simple deep blue polo shirt and pressed blue jeans. She appeared to be in her mid-thirties and was lightly tanned, with a smattering of freckles on her cheeks that only added to her attractiveness. She had the well-toned look of an athlete, despite the cane at her side. Raising an eyebrow, Reese asked, "Your kayak out front?"

Tory ran a hand absently through the short layers of her shoulder-length hair, shrugging slightly as she did so. "Yes," she expelled on a breath and waited for the expression of disbelief that usually followed. Most people looked at her leg and assumed she couldn't manage anything physical. She had come to expect it, but it still angered her.

"Do you do that every day?" Reese asked pointedly.

"Yes, why?" Tory replied defensively.

"Because in a town this small, any local would know that," Reese responded evenly, giving no sign that she had heard the edge in the doctor's tone. "And they would also know when the clinic was empty."

"Oh, I see," Tory murmured, feeling a little foolish at her own reaction. She wasn't usually so quick to judge, but she found the severely professional woman across from her oddly unsettling. As a doctor, Tory was used to establishing rapport easily with people, and now she felt a little off balance, because the deputy sheriff was so remote as to be unreadable. Why was her cool, controlled manner so disconcerting? *Her precise, impersonal approach reminds me of some surgeons I've known—excellent technicians but no feel for people. Perhaps that's it. She reminds me of K.T.*

"Are you all right, Doctor?" Reese asked quietly. The clinic director's tension was obvious and seemed to be increasing the longer they spoke.

Tory jumped, startled to find her focus wandering. She had obviously been more affected by the violation of her clinic than she had realized—a fact that apparently had *not* escaped the notice of the observant sheriff. Tory blushed, embarrassed to appear less than capable in front of this woman, and then quickly wondered why she should care. After taking a deep breath, she let it out slowly. "Yes, I'm fine, thank you. I'm usually much better in a crisis."

"I'm sure that you are, but I don't imagine you deal with this sort of thing very often." Reese smiled.

Tory's breath caught at the sudden transformation of the sculpted features that accompanied the brilliant smile. In an instant, the sheriff's face was suffused with not only compassionate warmth, but also stunning beauty. It was like watching a work of art unexpectedly come to life. What had been remotely perfect before suddenly became something much more affecting. Blushing again at her completely unanticipated visceral reaction, Tory hoped that she wasn't as transparent as she felt. *God, I never react this way to anyone.*

Gratefully, Tory observed that, at the moment, the dark head was bent over a small notepad balanced on a crossed knee. Taking herself firmly in hand, she replied calmly, "You're right, this is the first time anything like this has happened here. What can I tell you that will help?"

"What's missing, for starters?" Reese looked up, noting a less guarded countenance and a softening of the doctor's elegant features.

"I have no idea." Tory raised her hands in an open gesture. "I'll have to inventory all the examining rooms and the pharmacy before I have any idea."

"What drugs do you have here?"

"Let me think—antibiotics, a lot of pharmaceutical samples, AIDS meds—"

"What about narcotics?" Reese interrupted, still taking notes.

"Not much. I don't dispense drugs here, but I need a small quantity of a variety of medications in the event of emergency. I'm the only full-time doctor for thirty-five miles. I have a limited supply of codeine, Percocet, methadone."

"Injectables?"

"About a dozen ampoules of morphine. All of the narcotics are locked in the drug closet."

"Was it broken into?"

"I didn't have time to check."

"Let's do that now, please."

They both stood, and Reese followed the doctor into a small room at the rear of the building that was little more than a walk-in closet. Shelves held linens, sealed surgical packs, IV solutions, and other supplies. A cabinet with a built-in lock was tucked into the corner of the room.

The doctor sighed with relief when she saw that the door to the drug locker appeared sound. After inserting a key, she opened the front and scanned the interior. "It looks okay."

"Good," Reese replied. "I'll need a list of all the employees, the cleaning service, and anyone else who has access to this building. Who owns the building?"

"I do." Tory grasped Reese's arm as the sheriff turned to leave the storeroom. "There's no way anyone who works here would do this."

Reese faced the doctor and kept her expression carefully neutral. "I'm sure you're right. It's just routine."

After Tory prepared a preliminary list, Reese folded it into her notepad. She studied the doctor for a moment, not missing the slightly distracted look in her eyes. "Are you sure you're all right?"

Tory extended her hand, squared her shoulders, and lifted her chin. She was very aware of being appraised by the cool blue eyes that searched her face questioningly. "I am. Thank you, Sheriff."

"Ma'am." Reese shook the offered hand, touched her fingers to her cap in brief salute, and left.

CHAPTER TWO

"Tory! Where are you? Tory?"

"In here," Tory called. "In the procedure room." She looked up from where she was kneeling, sorting and cataloging supplies, to greet the clinic's head nurse. "Hey, Sal. God, am I glad to see you."

"What's going on? Are you okay?" Sally Long asked anxiously, surveying the mess on the floor.

"Yeah, I'm fine. Somebody broke in last night."

"I saw the cop out front. She's a new one, isn't she?" Sally retrieved several unopened boxes of surgical gauze from the floor and stacked them on the counter. "What a hunk. Did you catch the body? Jesus."

"God, you never miss a thing, do you?"

"Not when it comes to women," Sally laughed. "And not when they look like that. I suppose *you* didn't notice she was drop-dead gorgeous?"

Yes, I noticed. Irritably, Tory ran a hand through her hair. "I was a little bit busy here, Sal. I wasn't watching her."

"Huh." Sally raised an eyebrow but decided not to push. "So, are we seeing patients or what?"

Tory rose slowly to her feet, trying to ignore the cramp in her leg. "I think we'd better reschedule the morning ones. We need to clean this place up and figure out what's missing."

"Okay." Sally sighed. "I'll start calling. Come out when you can and tell me about this morning."

"You mean tell you all about the deputy sheriff, don't you?" Tory questioned sharply. She wasn't sure why, but she didn't want to talk about the remote, albeit attractive, sheriff. She would rather forget about her all together.

Even though she knew that the sheriff had simply been doing her job—calmly, cooly, and entirely professionally, there had been something about her attitude of command that had taken Tory by surprise. No one had ever managed to set her emotions so on edge from a single encounter. And no woman had captured her attention so immediately in more years than she could count.

Sally was surprised by the strain in Tory's voice. She had never known anything to upset Tory's usually imperturbable demeanor. In fact, sometimes Sally wondered if her reclusive friend wouldn't benefit from a little disruption in her life. From her point of view, Tory's life was altogether *too* safe and predictable. In the four years they'd worked together, she had never known the other woman to date anyone or even show interest in doing so. Instead, Tory worked longer and longer hours, refused to consider taking on an associate, and even when she could be coaxed out to a party, usually made an excuse to leave early. Sally had made any number of attempts to set her up with friends, but Tory always smiled and firmly declined.

"You don't like her, do you?" Sally queried. "And she's so hot she should be illegal. So, tell me what she did to piss you off."

"I don't have any opinion of her, one way or the other." Startled by the observation that was too close to true, Tory blushed. "I hardly know her."

"Okay, okay," Sally cried, raising her hands in mock surrender. "So don't tell me what she did to make you so touchy."

Tory stared at her in total exasperation. "Just go, already. Call patients." She turned resolutely back to her checklist, determined to put the tall, handsome officer from her thoughts. *I don't dislike her. I just don't trust women who are that sure of themselves, or that good-looking.*

❖

"So, what have you got?" Nelson asked before Reese even reached her desk.

"Amateur break-in. Rear window was smashed, cabinets rifled, stuff thrown around." She pulled a blank report form from a stack in the file cabinet and settled into her chair. "They didn't get to the drug cabinet, which means either they weren't locals or the doctor surprised them before they had finished searching the place."

Reese reflected on the clear strong features of the clinic director—her rich auburn hair and porcelain skin—and the way her green eyes sparked fire when she was provoked. The thought of Tory King walking unexpectedly into a bungled robbery made her uncomfortable. She had a feeling the doctor might have tried to handle the situation on her own, and she knew how quickly such things could become violent. Dismissing the disconcerting image and unfamiliar disquiet, Reese methodically filled out her report.

"What?" Nelson asked when he saw her frown. He could tell something was on her mind; she had that distant look in her eyes again.

"If Dr. King had walked into the middle of that, it might have been a disaster," Reese said quietly. "She doesn't look like the type to back away from trouble, and she could have gotten herself hurt."

Nelson snorted. "Don't bet on it. The doc has some kind of black belt in one of those martial arts. Plus she's strong as a horse. I've seen her lift a grown man onto a stretcher without blinking. That leg slows her down some, but it sure doesn't stop her."

"I'm glad to hear she can take care of herself," Reese said, bending her head to her paperwork, ignoring the strange lingering unease. There was no point thinking about something that hadn't happened. She had work to do.

Nelson stared at her, aware that he had been dismissed but at a loss to know why. *Damn, she's a hard one to figure.*

When Gladys Martin, the sole department secretary, dispatcher, and general all-around manager, showed up for her nine-to-five shift, she found them both silently typing. She wondered, not for the first time, how well the chief was going to adjust to his new second in command. It wasn't so much that she was a woman as the fact that she *wasn't* so much *like* a woman. Gladys had a feeling that he hadn't had much close experience with this type. Plus, the girl was so private it made you all the more curious.

And God knows, Nelson Parker is too curious as it is. But anyone with a smile like that young one has—the kind that breaks your heart whether you are "that way" or not—is worth getting to know, even if it does take some work.

"'Lo, Gladys," Nelson called.

"Ms. Martin," Reese said with a nod.

"Good morning, you two," Gladys answered, settling behind the reception desk and message center. "Why is it you both look busy? The president coming?"

Nelson grunted, and Reese grinned as she tilted back in her swivel chair.

"I thought he only went as far as Nantucket," Reese joked. "Not civilized enough out here."

"Then it must be the excitement out at the clinic." Gladys's tone was exaggeratedly casual. "Everything okay out there?"

"How do you know about that?" Nelson asked in surprise. *Is there anything she doesn't know about?*

"You forgot about my scanner, Chief," Gladys replied smugly.

"Don't call me Chief," Nelson replied automatically. "Reese is on it. Break-in."

"Is everyone all right?" Gladys asked in genuine concern.

"You can relax. Everything's fine."

Reese stood up and stretched, grinning at the friendly banter. "I'm going to make another tour, Chief," she called, already anxious to be out of the cramped office.

Gladys waited until the door swung closed before turning to the sheriff. "How's she doing?"

"About like you'd expect, considering her resume. She's the best officer I've ever had."

"Quiet, isn't she?"

Nelson eyed his old friend speculatively. "Just what is it you want to know, you old busybody?"

"Ha! Like you aren't nosey." Gladys held up a finger, listened to a radio request, and spoke softly for a second. Then she continued without a break, "I worry why a young woman like that would come to this town out on the end of nowhere. Could get mighty lonely."

"She doesn't seem lonely to me," Nelson mused. "Just solitary—like she's used to being alone."

"That can get awfully close to lonely," Gladys observed.

"Maybe. But I wouldn't worry about her too much. Looks to me like she won't have any trouble finding company, no matter what kind she's looking for."

"As if it ain't plain what kind of *company* that would be," Gladys commented dryly.

"Now don't go making assumptions, just because this is Provincetown," Nelson remarked, irked that Gladys always seemed to know more than he did.

"Oh, Nelson. You could put that girl anywhere in the country, and she'd be turning women's heads."

"Yours, too, Gladys?" he joked.

"If I weren't so old and twenty years married to George, she just might at that."

Nelson stared at her, finally at a loss for words.

❖

Reese left the cruiser idling outside the deli while she ran inside for a sandwich. The two women who ran the tiny gourmet market in the center of town greeted her warmly. Though still a relative newcomer, she seemed like one of their regulars.

"Tuna, lettuce, and tomato?" Carol called as the tall, trim officer entered.

Reese laughed. "I'm obviously getting too predictable. Make it corned beef today."

"Sure. How's the new house?"

"Fine." Reese hid her surprise. She hadn't yet gotten used to the easy intimacy of the year-round residents. This was definitely not the place to come if you didn't want to know your neighbors. "I'm living in it. The renovations will be done in a few weeks. Sarah's crew is really good."

Carol nodded in agreement as she wrapped Reese's order. "I envy you that view. There aren't many places left with a clear line to the bay."

"I was lucky to find it," Reese agreed, slipping bills from her wallet and handing them to the woman behind the counter.

"Here you go. Take care now."

"Thanks."

Reese opened the sandwich on the seat beside her, eating as she slowly cruised through town. There weren't many people in the streets yet, but in little over a week there would be. In addition to the tourists, many of the shop and gallery owners were returning from their winter venues and reopening for the season. She was looking forward to it, even though she knew her work would be tripled. She liked the sense of being part of the community and taking care of it in her own way. Without conscious thought, she headed back to the clinic. The parking lot was crowded as she pulled in.

The blond young man behind the counter in the reception area looked harried. Standing quietly beside a mother with two small children in tow, Reese waited while he finished making up a chart. He looked up at her expectantly, flipping his hair distractedly away from his eyes. His astonishingly beautiful face was set in an anxious frown.

"Can I help you?"

"Any chance I could see Dr. King?" Reese queried.

"Oh, please. I'd sooner be able to get you an audience with the pope." He sighed dramatically.

"Sorry, but it's important."

He had the longest eyelashes she had ever seen. If he were a woman, she'd call him pretty, but there was still something decidedly masculine about him that belied that description.

"Let me see where she is, okay? We're way behind, but I guess you know why."

Reese nodded, shrugging apologetically.

He returned a moment later. "Follow me. She'll meet you in her office when she gets a break. She said she'd just be a couple of minutes."

He led Reese to the office she had left just a few hours previously, then hurried away. While waiting, she perused the walls. There was just the one diploma, announcing that Victoria Claire King had received her medical degree from McGill University in Canada. Of much more interest were the many framed photographs of female rowers, some in squads of four or eight, many in single sculls. Reese bent closer to look at the faces. In several photos, the woman pulling the oars was unmistakably Victoria King.

The sound of the door behind her closing interrupted her study, and Reese turned to find the doctor watching her. "Doctor."

"Surprised, Sheriff?"

Reese raised an eyebrow at the challenging tone in the woman's voice. Her blue eyes met the flashing hazel ones calmly. "Why should I be?"

Tory tapped the leg brace with her cane. The metal rang sharply.

"Ah. To be honest, I didn't think about that," Reese replied, still surveying the doctor's face.

Tory returned the look steadily and finally shook her head ruefully. "You may be the only person who ever *has* forgotten about it."

"I didn't say I forgot," Reese said softly. "It just never occurred to me that it would inhibit you on the water. I saw you this morning—kayaking out on the bay. You were so much a part of the sea that you didn't even disturb the rhythm of the waves."

Tory's lips parted as a small gasp escaped her. There had been many descriptions of her rowing, but none quite so genuine, nor so eloquently spoken. She averted her gaze, swallowing hard.

"Thank you," she said at last into the sudden silence. She moved behind her desk, and the sheriff walked to face her on the opposite side. Finally looking at her visitor, who stood with her hat tucked under one arm, Tory wondered if the woman had any idea how imposing she was, or how attractive.

"Sit down, Sheriff. You're making me nervous," Tory said lightly.

Reese laughed, a deep full laugh, as she sat in the chair in front of Tory's desk. "Now that I doubt."

To her amusement, Tory was irrationally pleased at the response. A heartbeat later, she was aware of her disappointment as a serious look eclipsed Reese's smile as quickly as it had come.

"I know you're busy, Doctor," Reese said. "But have you had a chance to find out what's missing?"

"I'm afraid not." Tory sighed wearily. "It would figure today would be the day half the town has the flu. I've been going nonstop since you left. I did get together a list for you, though. A damn strange one."

Reese sat up a little straighter, her eyes flashing. "How so?"

"We are missing needles but not syringes. Some surgical instruments but not scalpels. Boxes of gauze and alcohol, and—of all things—a portable sterilizer."

"No drugs?"

"The narcotics are all accounted for. I can't be sure, because I don't inventory pharmaceutical samples, but I think there is an assortment of antibiotics missing."

"That's it?"

"As near as I can tell. If I miss anything else, I'll let you know."

Reese nodded. "Mean anything to you?"

"Not a thing. Addicts would want the syringes. I guess the sterilizer would make sense if someone wanted to reuse the needles, but what good are they without the syringes?"

"I don't know," Reese mused. "How late are you open?"

"Until six, except Wednesdays, when I see patients until ten p.m."

"Is there someone here with you the whole time?"

"Well, Randy, the receptionist, leaves when the clinic closes. My nurse, Sally, stays until we clean up. Then I usually stay an hour or so later to finish paperwork."

"Don't," Reese stated flatly. "At least not for the next few days. Leave when Sally does, and make sure you're both in your cars with the engines running before either of you drives away."

Tory looked at her in amazement, her shoulders stiffening. "Is that really necessary? I've got work that needs to be done, and I'm sure this was just some kids—"

"*I'm* not sure of that," Reese rejoined firmly. "You're fairly isolated here. There might be something else they wanted and couldn't find this morning. I don't want you here alone if they decide to come back."

Tory heard the unmistakable tone of command in the sheriff's voice, a tone that came easily and suggested that she was used to being obeyed. What she was saying made sense, but Tory resented being told how to conduct her business.

"Is there any room for negotiation here, Sheriff Conlon?"

Again, that hint of a smile. "None, Doctor."

Tory tapped her pen on the desk, trying to decide if she felt so resistant because the request was unreasonable or because she resented the authority behind the demand. Whatever the reason, this woman had an amazing effect on her. The sheriff was so certain, so sure; it made Tory want to argue with her, even when she knew what was demanded made sense.

Reese waited.

"All right," Tory conceded reluctantly. "I can manage that for a few days."

"A week."

Tory's eyes flashed fire as she prepared to protest.

"Please," Reese added.

It was Tory's turn to laugh, despite her annoyance. "You are very hard to resist, Sheriff." She immediately regretted her words. Not only did they sound flirtatious, but, she realized with chagrin, they were true. The sheriff's combination of faultless control and subtle humor was powerfully appealing.

"I understand that it's difficult, Dr. King, and I appreciate your cooperation," Reese responded dispassionately.

"I'll do the best I can." When Reese stood and tapped a finger to the brim of her hat, Tory found the gesture charming in spite of her lingering annoyance.

"Thanks for making time in your busy day. I'll let you know when I have a lead on this."

"Thank you!" Tory called as Reese left. She sat for a moment trying to gather her thoughts. Again, she had the disconcerting sense of being slightly off balance, when she was so used to having everything in her life firmly in hand. Exasperated with herself, she pushed the memory of that fleeting smile and rich laughter from her consciousness. There was plenty of work still to do, and she could count on that to occupy her mind.

❖

At the end of her shift, Reese sat in front of the station house, fiddling with her keys and struggling with a decision. Eventually, she pushed her patrol car into gear and headed for the east end of the three-mile-long street that ran the length of the town along the harbor's edge. She pulled to the curb in front of one of the myriad art galleries tucked into every available niche. This one showed evidence of preparations for the season's opening. Reese had noticed a new sign being hung above the door just the day before, and general cleanup was underway. The owners were clearly in residence after a winter elsewhere, which was why she had come.

She had been avoiding this moment ever since she arrived in Provincetown, and she knew she couldn't delay any longer. The town was just too small. Already, most of the shopkeepers knew her name. After a minute of hesitation, she headed resolutely to the tiny adjoining cottage. She rang the bell, her pulse racing.

A fiftyish woman in baggy jeans and a tattered sweatshirt opened the door and looked questioningly at the officer on her steps.

"Yes?" she queried. Then her eyes widened as she focused on the steel blue eyes and chiseled features. The resemblance was unmistakable. "Oh, my God. Reese?"

"Hello, Jean," Reese said softly.

"Kate!" the woman squeaked. Then finding her voice, she called loudly, "Honey, you'd better come here!"

"What is it?" called the tall woman who entered from the rear of the house. She halted behind her lover, stunned and at a loss for words.

"Hello, Mother," Reese said as she gazed at her mother, marveling at the sun-burnished skin, the blond hair laced with gray now, and the blue eyes so like her own. Despite her anxiety, she felt strangely peaceful. "Sorry to just show up like this."

"My God, how did you find us?" Kate exclaimed.

"It wasn't that difficult." Reese smiled self-consciously. "About six months ago, I asked a computer friend at my last posting to run a search of the National Registry of Art Galleries and Owners. He traced you through the gallery. I thought it was time I visited."

"I'd given up hoping you ever would," her mother murmured in a choked voice.

"I'm sorry...I..." Reese faltered, not knowing how to explain the years lost between them. When her mother left, she hadn't wanted to attempt contact. She had been angry, hurt, and finally, just resigned to Kate's absence. Then as she grew older, her life assumed an orderly path almost without her awareness, and the time had never seemed right.

"Don't be sorry. Just come in and tell me—well, tell me whatever you want." Kate touched her daughter's cheek gently as she spoke, then reached for her hand to pull her inside. She led Reese through the few rooms to a small kitchen that looked out on the harbor. "Please, sit," Kate said, pointing to the table in front of the windows. "Would you like tea? Or coffee?"

"Yes, thanks," Reese said, laying her hat on the table. "Coffee if you have some."

"I'll make it," Jean, who had followed them, offered.

"How long have you been here?" her mother asked, unable to take her eyes off the strikingly handsome woman at her table. If she hadn't been practically cloistered since the moment she got back to town preparing for an upcoming show, she would have known. A newcomer always attracted attention.

"Just a few weeks," Reese said, gesturing to her uniform. "I'm the deputy sheriff."

"Just can't give up a uniform, huh?"

Reese laughed, and the tension in the room dissipated. "I never thought of it that way, but I think you're right."

"And you live here now," her mother stated in wonder.

Reese nodded, uncharacteristically uncertain. "Is that all right?"

Tears shimmered in Kate's eyes, and a small sob escaped before she could stop it. Placing a hand protectively on her partner's shoulder, Jean kissed the top of Kate's head. Her own eyes were tear filled.

"'All right' is an understatement, Reese," her mother said at last. "I thought when I met Jean all my dreams had come true, and that I wouldn't get any more. I never even dared hope for this."

Reese looked away as the pain of old memories washed through her. She didn't begrudge her mother happiness, but the price had been high for all of them.

"If it could have been different, Reese, if there was something I could have done—" Her mother stopped, knowing there were no words to explain the past. Or to undo it. "I'm so sorry."

Reese met her mother's gaze evenly, her voice steady. "I didn't come here for an explanation."

Kate twisted the gold band, the one that matched Jean's, on her ring finger and said sadly, "I tried to tell myself that you would be well cared for, and loved—"

"And I was," Reese assured her quickly, meaning it. "But it was time for me to see you. Long past time."

Kate searched her daughter's face in alarm. "Are you all right, are you sick, or...?"

"No, I'm fine." Reese smiled, reaching for her mother's hand where it rested on the small table. "Better than fine. I like it here."

"So you're here to stay?"

"Yes," Reese said, feeling the rightness of her words. "I am."

Jean set a large tureen of chowder in the center of the table, saying firmly, "I have a feeling it's going to be a long night."

And they began to talk.

CHAPTER THREE

It was close to midnight when Reese left Kate and Jean's cottage. It had taken that long to sketch in the outline of the last twenty years of her life. They hadn't touched on deeply personal things; neither she nor her mother had been ready for that. But it was a beginning, and it felt right.

Still much too excited to sleep, Reese decided to drive. She turned off Commercial Street and followed the meandering turn of narrow streets to the clinic. It wasn't exactly on her way home, but nothing in the two-by-three-mile town was out of the way. She frowned when she saw the Jeep Cherokee still parked in the lot. The building was dark.

She left her vehicle on the shoulder of the highway and circled through the scrub and sand to the rear of the clinic. When she gently tried the handle, the door swung open. Gun in hand, she made her way slowly down the darkened hall, carefully opening each door she passed and quickly ascertaining that the rooms were empty.

Rounding a corner into the shadowy reception area, she sensed movement to her right. Swinging her outstretched arms in that direction, gun double-fisted, she shouted, "Police!"

Her movement deflected the already descending blow, but pain seared along her right forearm where the strike landed. Propelling herself forward, she inadvertently slammed her forehead against the edge of a short metal file cabinet as she dove. Ignoring the pain, she came up into a crouch, poised to fire on the shape backlit in the moonlight when a voice called out, "Sheriff, no! It's Tory King!"

The lights came on and Reese found her weapon trained on Victoria King, whose cane was still raised for a second sweeping strike.

"Stand down, Doctor," Reese muttered, lowering her automatic and wiping her face with one hand as she stood. Her hand came away bloody, and she swayed, suddenly dizzy.

"Sit down, Sheriff," Tory commanded, moving forward quickly. She grasped Reese around the waist, directing her into a chair. "You're injured."

"I need to secure this place," Reese protested, shaking her head, trying to clear her vision. "The back door was unlocked."

"Never mind that. Sally is always forgetting to lock it." Tory scrutinized Reese's face carefully. "You've got a laceration on your forehead that's going to need sutures."

"I need to call for backup—"

"Why? Am I under arrest? I didn't know it was you until you spoke. I heard a noise in the hall—"

"Terrific." Reese grimaced, doubly embarrassed. "First I announce my presence, then I let you take me out. Maybe *you* should be wearing the badge."

Tory smiled without humor. "This cane is nearly as deadly as that gun of yours, at least at close range. I'm thankful I didn't break your arm." She looked at Reese with mounting concern and gasped, "I didn't, did I?"

"I don't think so."

Kneeling with some difficulty, Tory grasped Reese's right hand in hers. "Squeeze my fingers."

"Can't," Reese mumbled, battling a sudden wave of nausea. *Oh Christ, don't let me vomit. I'm humiliated enough.*

"I must have hit the median nerve," Tory noted clinically. "It may be a couple of hours before you can flex your fingers, but nothing seems broken." She continued to probe along Reese's forearm, aware of the well-developed muscles under her fingers. "You're lucky you're in such good shape—your muscle mass protected you. Still, we'll need to watch for compression injuries. You're going to get a lot of swelling." She rocked back and studied Reese's face, brushing a lock of hair off Reese's forehead. The sheriff was pale, but her gaze was clear. "You've got a laceration through your eyebrow. We need to go back to the procedure room so I can take care of it. Can you walk?"

Reese nodded, holstering her gun awkwardly with her left hand, as she carefully pushed herself to a standing position. Once upright, she extended her uninjured hand to assist Tory to her feet. "Are *you* all right?"

"I'm fine," Tory said firmly as they moved to the rear of the clinic. "I can't tell you how sorry I am, Sheriff."

"It was a lesson worth learning, Doctor," Reese said grimly. "Having a gun sometimes makes you overconfident. A well-trained martial artist is a real threat in close quarters. That's what you are, isn't it?"

"Sit here," Tory indicated, motioning to the operating table in the center of the room. She was silent as she opened gloves and a suture tray. "Are you allergic to any drugs?"

"No." Reese watched her as she efficiently set up the suture tray. "Aren't you?"

"Aren't I what?" Tory asked, although she knew and couldn't understand her own reluctance to answer.

"A trained martial artist."

"Lie back. I just need to clean this up a bit." As she went about her work, she finally answered, "*Hapkido*. Do you know it?"

"Some. I'm trained in *jujitsu*," Reese replied, wincing slightly at the sting of the lidocaine injection. "*Hapkido*. That's Korean, isn't it?"

"Uh-huh," Tory responded as she placed the sutures. "It's a combination of aikido and tae kwon do. Fortunately for me, it also teaches the art of the cane."

"Well, it's certainly effective," Reese said flatly. She'd heard the sarcasm in the doctor's voice but ignored it. "You'll have to show me sometime."

"If you like. There, that's it." Tory's tone suggested that she didn't consider the request a serious one. After pulling a stool over, she sat down facing Reese. "I'll need to take these sutures out in five days."

"Fine. Thank you."

"What are you doing here?"

"I happened to be driving by, and I saw your Jeep. The place was dark." Reese lifted a shoulder in a shrug. "I was worried. You're not supposed to be here alone, remember?"

"I know." Tory sighed. "We ran so late I sent everyone home an hour ago. I had literally just finished and was heading out the door when I heard you. I am so sorry—"

"Please," Reese said, pushing herself up to a sitting position. Thankfully, her head felt clear. "I'm glad to know you can take care of yourself so well. Let's just leave it at that, okay?"

Tory stood, reaching for an alcohol swab. When she cupped Reese's chin in one hand, Reese tensed. "You've got blood on your neck," Tory said quietly, wiping the skin gently.

"Thank you," Reese murmured, her eyes meeting Tory's deep hazel ones. She was acutely aware of the warmth in the doctor's touch.

Tory stepped back quickly, averting her gaze as she broke their contact. The withdrawal was so abrupt that Reese shivered involuntarily. Tory frowned. "You need to be in bed. Come on, I'll drive you home."

"I'm okay," Reese muttered, jumping down from the table. Her light-headedness returned unexpectedly, and she reached out unsteadily toward the table for support. If Tory hadn't slipped an arm around her, she would have fallen.

"Not quite, you're not," Tory said decisively, loosening her grasp as Reese regained her balance but keeping one hand on the injured woman's back. "You may be strong, but you're not made of steel. You've had a nasty blow to your head and with that impaired arm, you're not fit to drive. I mean it."

"I can't leave my cruiser on the road," Reese protested.

"Then *I'll* drive it. I know the house you're fixing up and it's not that far. Come on."

❖

"Go get into bed," Tory said as she followed Reese into the living room of her partially renovated home. "I'll get some ice for your arm. Kitchen through there?" she asked, indicating with a nod of her head.

"Yes, but I can get it—"

Patience at an end, Tory rounded on Reese, her eyes flashing. "Look, Sheriff, you can save the butch routine for the bad guys. I *know* you can get it. The point is that I want you to lie down, so *I'm going to get it."*

Reese stared at her, an uncomprehending look on her face. "I...I'm not trying to be butch. I'm just used to doing things for myself."

"Yes, I'll bet you are." Tory's features softened, and a smile curved her full lips. "But tonight you don't have to. Now go on. To bed—please."

A few minutes later, Tory found Reese in her bedroom, awkwardly attempting to hang her gun belt and uniform in the closet. The sheriff's right arm was still uncoordinated and visibly swollen. She had managed to pull on a faded green cotton T-shirt, USMC stenciled over her left chest. Her legs were bare below the hem of the shirt. Tory tried not to stare at the expanse of smooth skin and tightly muscled limbs, finally deciding she couldn't avoid looking at her unless she suddenly went blind. Taking the hanger from Reese's fumbling grasp, she said firmly, "Bed."

Then Tory folded the trousers carefully and hung them up in the precisely ordered closet. Shirts and pants were neatly segregated—dress clothes to the left, casual clothes to the right. She stared thoughtfully at the crisp judo *gis* and the carefully folded *hakamas* on the top shelf. *The mysterious sheriff is more than a casual martial artist.*

Turning, Tory observed Reese propped up in bed, her injured hand resting on the sheets that covered her to the waist. She was watching Tory carefully, her face inscrutable. Tory stared back at her, thinking that this woman spoke volumes with her silence. Softly, Tory asked, "What?"

"I was watching you study my closet with such interest. Are you always so observant?"

"Occupational hazard," Tory chuckled. "Being a doctor is a little like being a detective—you have to learn not to overlook the subtle details. How about you? Always so neat, ordered, and controlled?"

Reese laughed. "Yes. Fifteen years of the Marine Corps will do that for you. However, it might be hereditary. My father is career military."

"And your mother is an organizational systems manager?" Tory joked.

Reese grew suddenly still, her expression thoughtful. "No, my mother is an artist. I'm afraid I didn't inherit anything from her."

Tory sensed that personal subjects were clearly off limits, and once again, a vast distance settled between them. "Here," she said, approaching the bed with the plastic bag of ice in her hand, "hold out your arm."

When Reese complied, Tory wrapped a towel loosely around Reese's forearm, then applied the ice pack and secured it with another towel. "Keep this on for as long as you can. If you have more pain during the night or the numbness worsens, call me. It's unlikely you'll have a problem, but I don't want to take any chances."

"Uh-huh. What's your phone number?" Reese inquired politely. She had no intention of taking up any more of this woman's time. From the outset, the whole ridiculous situation was her own fault. No one had ever taken her by surprise like that before.

"Just yell. I'll be on your couch."

Reese shot straight up in bed. "You are not staying here."

"Listen to me *carefully.*" Tory's tone was steel. "My Jeep is at the clinic. I'm extremely tired, and I'm starting to get cranky. I intend to go to sleep immediately. Don't worry; you won't even know I'm here."

"That's not the point," Reese exclaimed. "You've already done too much for me."

Tory raised an eyebrow. "And just how would you define too much, Sheriff? Is any help at all too much?"

When Reese only stared, Tory eventually smiled faintly. "Just tell me where the sheets are—I'm beat."

Reese pointed to a military footlocker pushed under the windows. "Bedding's in there, Doctor. Only what the PX had to offer, I'm afraid. I've only been a civilian a short time, and shopping off base has not been high on my list of priorities."

"It'll do for a night. Thanks," Tory said as she headed for the door. "Now, lights out, please."

"Yes, ma'am," Reese sighed, realizing she had been outmaneuvered in more ways than one that evening.

❖

At five a.m. in May on the North Atlantic coast, sunrise was still a long way off. Reese stood in the dim light reflected from the kitchen looking down at Tory King, captivated by how peaceful she appeared. The doctor slept on her side, arms wrapped around the pillow. Her tousled auburn hair framed a face soft and youthful in sleep. Though her clothes were tossed haphazardly over a nearby chair, she kept her leg brace and cane leaning within arm's reach.

Before Reese could move away, Tory rolled onto her back and opened her eyes, moving from sleep to full wakefulness almost instantaneously. She saw the curiosity in Reese's face before all expression fled. "What?" Tory asked. "Is there something strange about the way I sleep?"

Reese contemplated her for a moment, aware that Tory was naked under the light covering. The curve of hip and the slight swell of breasts were subtly outlined in light and shadow. Realizing she was staring, Reese forced her eyes to Tory's face. "Well, you don't just sleep. You seem to embrace it, as if it were nourishing you."

Her voice trailed off. She had no words to express how beautiful the woman had been. "I didn't mean to disturb you," she finished awkwardly.

Tory sat up, holding the sheet to her chest with one arm. With the other, she brushed her hair back from her face. "I think I felt you in my sleep, but it didn't disturb me."

Tory looked at Reese uncertainly. She was sure the sheriff hadn't touched her, but her skin tingled with the sense of a lingering caress. Abruptly, she swung her legs to the floor. This was getting ridiculous. Too much turmoil in the last twenty-four hours had her imagining things. "I need to be up anyhow," she said, more sharply than she intended.

"Right. I'll let you get dressed." Reese quickly turned away, nonplussed by the abrupt change. "Coffee?" she asked as she retreated quickly to the kitchen.

"Please," Tory called after her.

She joined Reese in the kitchen a few moments later. Taking in the details not noticed in her earlier quest for ice, she found the room a pleasant surprise. It was newly renovated, modern, and equipped with professional appliances. "What a great kitchen. You must cook."

"A secret vice." Reese grinned, ducking her head shyly, and handed Tory a steaming cup of freshly ground French Roast.

"How ever did that happen? Weren't you forced to eat in the mess hall or something?"

Reese laughed, warming Tory with the rich timbre of her voice. Tory relaxed, leaning against the large center cook-island that dominated the space. She sipped her coffee as she examined Reese in the early morning light. The sheriff was in uniform again, the creases in her sleeves and trousers razor sharp, her tie knotted exactly under a crisp collar. Her shoes sparkled with a flawless shine. *She* seemed flawless, too. Her black hair was trimmed precisely around her ears and above her collar. The full front fell rather dashingly over clear blue eyes. The nose was straight, the chin bold and strong. She was handsome and beautiful at the same time, and warning bells began clashing in Tory's brain.

Women this good-looking generally knew it, and that, she had learned from experience, always spelled trouble. The years had not quite erased the pain left behind by someone nearly as heart-stopping as this. She forced herself to concentrate on what Reese was saying, reminding herself that she would never make that mistake again.

"I lived mostly off base. Learning to cook gave me something to do with my down time, since I've always lived alone."

"Always?" Tory asked. It was hard to believe that a woman with her appeal wasn't attached.

"Yes, always," Reese replied quietly.

Once again, Tory sensed a door closing as a distant look settled in Reese's eyes.

"How is your arm?" Tory asked, retreating to neutral ground.

"Better. Stiff, but the sensation has returned."

"Can you handle your weapon?"

Reese looked surprised. "I think so."

Tory shook her head. "You have to be able to, or you can't work. Seriously, Sheriff—"

Reese held up a hand. "Please, call me Reese. You can't keep calling me Sheriff in my own kitchen."

"And I'm Tory," Tory said with a laugh. Then, serious once again, she regarded Reese's slightly swollen hand critically. "Now, draw your weapon."

Reese studied her for a second, recognizing the determined set to her features. Reaching behind with her right hand, she set the coffee cup on the counter. In the next instant, she had pivoted away from Tory, her automatic in both hands, crouched in a shooting stance. The tailored uniform stretched taut against coiled muscles, the gun unwavering.

Tory caught her breath, surprised by Reese's speed and grace. "You pass," she said lightly, aware that her throat was dry and her pulse was racing. She had to admit the combination of physical beauty and controlled power was compelling.

Reese straightened, holstering her automatic. She smiled faintly and saluted Tory casually. "Thank you, ma'am."

She wasn't sure why Tory was staring at her so curiously, but she liked the way the doctor laughed. For some reason, the laughter made her happy.

CHAPTER FOUR

After driving Tory to retrieve her Jeep from the clinic parking lot, Reese circled through town to the station house. Nelson was at his desk, frowning over yet another voluminous report he had to complete. When he saw the bruise on his deputy's face and the fresh stitches on her forehead, he blurted, "Jesus, Conlon—what happened to you?"

Reese shook her head ruefully, tossing her hat on her desk. "If I told you the truth, you'd fire me."

"Try me," he ordered. He was laughing by the time she finished the story. "I told you the doc could look after herself. Just be glad she's only got one good leg, or she really might have hurt you."

They stared at one another as he grimaced in disgust. "Oh hell, I didn't mean that. It's a damn tragedy, and here I am joking." He shook his head in discomfort.

"What do you mean?" Reese asked quietly.

"I guess it's not a secret—as if anyone in this town has secrets. She was a rower. Did you know that?"

"I know she rows," Reese remarked, recalling the photographs in Victoria King's office.

"She *did* row. She rowed for the Canadian Olympic team. She was their big hope for a gold medal in the '88 Olympics. Another rower hit her scull in a trial heat just before the Games. Cut her boat in half and nearly took her leg off with it. She hasn't rowed since."

Reese turned away, her chest tight. "Is this stuff last night's dregs again?" she asked gruffly, snatching the coffeepot from the burner.

Nelson gaped at her in surprise, wondering if he'd ever understand his new second in command. She closed up faster than anyone he had ever known, men included. But he respected her moods, so he just grunted as he returned to the endless paperwork on his desk.

Reese focused on making coffee, forcing the painful image of Tory lying injured in a shattered boat from her mind. Unexpectedly, she flashed on the way Tory had looked asleep that morning, remembering the still beauty of her form beneath the light covering. The image was inexplicably calming. Reese took a deep breath, her emotions under control once again, and turned back to the chief.

"I'm going to start my tour."

"Sure. Hey, grab me some donuts, will ya?"

❖

Instead of turning right into town, Reese went the opposite direction to Route 6 and Herring Cove. The fishermen and women were out in numbers, casting in the offshore depths for the plentiful sea bass. Reese parked at the water's edge, searching the horizon.

Sunlight shimmered on the cold blue-gray morning water, two forces of nature meeting. There, off to the right, cutting swiftly and surely toward Race Point, was the red kayak. The tension in her chest eased as Reese watched Tory fly across the surface, unfettered and free. Soothed by the sight, Reese wheeled out of the lot to continue her day.

After her second pass through town, she headed east on Route 6, the main highway that ran the length of Cape Cod. A hundred yards ahead, a rollerblader caught a wheel on something in the road and flew off onto the shoulder. The skater didn't get up. Reese pulled up nearby, lights flashing, and ran to the prone figure.

"Take it easy, son," she said as she bent down next to the wiry youth with short-cropped dark hair. "Oops, sorry," she amended as she looked closer, realizing the skater was female. "Are you hurt?"

"Jammed my knee pretty good," the young woman muttered, grimacing as she straightened her injured leg. She had been skating in tight shorts without gear, and the length of her thigh was badly scraped and bleeding. She bit back a groan as she tried to get to her feet.

"Don't put any weight on that leg," Reese cautioned, slipping an arm around her waist. Bending slightly, Reese got her other arm behind the young woman's legs and stood, lifting her easily. "Come on. I'll take you to the clinic."

As Reese walked the few feet to her cruiser, the injured skater protested, "I'm okay."

"That may be, but we'd better make sure." Reese pulled the rear door open and slid the girl gently onto the back seat. "What's your name?"

"Brianna Parker," came the quiet reply. Reese looked at her carefully. Her hair was very short and spiked; she wore no makeup. She had a small silver ring through the corner of her left eyebrow, a tattoo encircling her right upper arm, and a wide silver band on the middle finger of her left hand. At first glance, her appearance was typical teenager, but on closer examination, the girl had a haunted look.

"Sheriff Parker's daughter?"

"Uh-huh," she admitted reluctantly.

"I'll radio him," Reese said as she slipped behind the wheel.

"Aww, man. Do you have to?"

Swinging around in the seat to face her young passenger, Reese asked, "How old are you?"

"Seventeen."

"You'll need your dad's permission to be treated—"

"Uh...can't we wait to see if I *need* to be treated? He's going to be so pissed. He doesn't want me blading out here. Besides, I'm supposed to be in school."

Reese considered the request. Nelson was likely to be angry if she didn't call him right away, but there was something in the girl's face that swayed her. She could wait a bit.

"I'll have to call him, Brianna, but let's check the damage first, okay?"

"Yeah," the young woman sighed. "And you can call me Bri. Everybody does."

Reese pulled into the clinic lot just ahead of Tory's Jeep and climbed out of her cruiser. "I'll be right back," she said to Bri.

As Reese approached, Tory regarded her questioningly, pleased to see her again so soon. With a smile, she said, "Hi."

"Good morning," Reese replied, her voice warm. "I'm afraid I brought you some early business. The chief's daughter took a header out on Route 6 on her rollerblades. Banged up her knee."

"Damn," Tory muttered, already mentally planning what needed to be done as they walked to Reese's car. "Neither Sally or Randy is here yet. I guess you can handle a stretcher, can't you?"

Reese didn't reply as she opened the rear door of her patrol car and leaned inside. To Tory's surprise, Reese straightened up with the young woman in her arms. Automatically, Bri threw one arm around the tall officer's shoulder for support.

"Lead the way, Doctor," Reese announced.

Tory merely nodded, deciding that she should get used to being surprised by the seemingly totally self-sufficient sheriff. She led Reese through the building to the treatment room, where the sheriff gently deposited Bri on the treatment table.

"I'll wait," Reese said. "I'm going to need to call her father."

"Fine," Tory answered distractedly as she bent over her patient. Then as an afterthought, she asked, "Think you can make some coffee?"

"Absolutely," Reese replied with a grin. She found the tiny kitchenette and soon had a pot brewing. She was just pouring two cups when Tory appeared.

"She's fine," Tory answered to Reese's questioning look. "A pretty bad sprain and a few bruises and scrapes. I put her in a knee immobilizer. She'll be skating again in a week or two."

"Thanks," Reese said. "I'm sorry to have bothered you, but I thought—"

"Nonsense," Tory said, stilling Reese with a touch on her arm. "You were right to bring her in. She's more worried about her father than her knee. Nelson keeps a pretty tight rein on her. Did you know she got into some kind of trouble last year? Teenager stuff."

"It's hard being that age," Reese said quietly. "I'll call him, then I'll run her home."

"Hey, you're good at this small-town policing, Sheriff."

Reese smiled, pleased. "Thanks. I don't have much experience with community life. I was a military brat, then active duty right after school." She halted self-consciously. "I'd better go call Nelson."

It took her a few minutes to calm her boss down, but she finally convinced him that he did not have to personally come to the clinic. She thanked Tory once again, then settled Bri back into the cruiser.

"Is it true you have a black belt in karate?" Bri asked as Reese pulled out onto the highway.

"Not exactly," Reese answered. "I have a black belt in *jujitsu*. They're quite a bit different. How did you know?"

"My dad told me."

"Uh-huh." It was on her resume, and Reese assumed the sheriff had noticed. She waited for Bri to continue.

"Would you teach me?" the young woman asked, her voice low and hesitant.

Reese turned her head briefly to study the teenager. Her hopeful look stirred a distant memory. Reese had been a solitary teenager in a world of adults. Her martial arts training had helped focus her aimless adolescent energy. It centered her still.

"It's a very serious commitment, Bri, and it takes a long time to learn. Why do you want to do it?"

Bri knew she was being asked an important question, and it felt like Reese really cared about her answer. She struggled to find the right words. "Because I want something that's my own—something I chose, something I earned." She hesitated and took a deep breath. "And because I'm bored. I feel restless all the time."

Reese nodded. She had been about Bri's age when she had begun her training. It had been a difficult time in her life. She didn't want to refuse, but it meant a commitment for her as well. Taking on a student was a significant responsibility. "You'd need to train at least three times a week. And your dad has to approve."

"All right." Bri's face set in determination. "When can I start?"

"Not until your knee is healed and Dr.. King gives you the go-ahead. But you can come to my house when you're ambulatory again, and I'll explain some things that you need to know."

"When?" Bri persisted.

Reese almost smiled. "A week from this Saturday."

"I'll be there."

CHAPTER FIVE

"What's this about my daughter and *jujitsu*?" Nelson asked the minute Reese walked into the station house at the end of her shift.

"She talked to you already, huh?" Reese smiled faintly. Bri was eager, and that was encouraging.

Nelson nodded. "I stopped home at lunch to see how she was, and that's all she talked about. You really want to do this?"

"She seems sincere, Chief." Reese settled one hip on the corner of her desk, regarding him intently. "It's a great way for a kid—for anyone, really—to learn self-confidence and self-control. And it never hurts for a woman to know how to protect herself. I'm willing to teach her, if she's willing to put out the effort. It's not easy, and it requires a real commitment over a long time."

Nelson walked to the front windows and stood staring out. In the short time she'd known him, Reese had come to recognize this as a habit of his when he was turning over something in his mind. She waited silently. He didn't look at her when he spoke.

"I found her out under one of the piers about six months ago with some kids from a couple of towns over—kids we'd had trouble with before. They were fooling around with drugs." He took a deep breath and expelled it audibly. "Bri swore to me that she hadn't done anything, but it scared me pretty good. She's smart, and she always did real well in school, but this past year—I don't know— something's changed. She doesn't get along with any of her old friends. She's skipped school some. Nothing real bad yet, but the signs don't look so good."

He turned and met Reese's eyes. "She doesn't talk about anything. Hell, she hardly talks to me at all. This is the first thing she's shown any interest in doing in a long time. I can't pay you much, but it'll be worth it, if you think it might help her."

Reese chose her words carefully, not wanting to offend him. "Nelson, teaching your daughter something I love is not a hardship for me. *Jujitsu* helped me when I was her age. Sometimes, I think it kept me from going a little crazy. I don't need you to pay me, but I will expect Bri to help me out in the *dojo*. There's still a lot of work to be done."

"The *dojo*? Where's that?" He was pretty sure he knew every building in town.

"Well, right now it's my garage." Reese grinned. "I'm in the process of turning it into a training space, and I could use a little help with it."

In fact, she had already done the bulk of the work, but she wanted Bri to feel that she had a part in it, too. The *dojo* was much more than a gym; it was a singular haven from outside distractions and stress. That feeling of peace was something she hoped Bri would gain from her training.

"I'll see that she understands that's part of the arrangement."

"Fair enough."

❖

Once home, Reese changed into sweats and a T-shirt and went in search of Sarah Randall, the crew boss of the women hired to finish the renovations on her house. The previous owner had left many things uncompleted or, in some cases, had done the work improperly.

"How's it going?" Reese asked the small blond, finally locating her in the basement.

Sarah grimaced. "Save me from do-it-yourselfers. The plumbing to the master bath is a nightmare. No shut-off valves anywhere you could use them, of course. And don't get me started on the wiring."

Reese smiled at Sarah's exuberant display of distress, then asked seriously, "Can you fix it?"

"Oh, sure. I might need a week more than I originally planned, though. Is that okay?"

"Fine. Just tell me where you'll be working, and I'll try to stay out of your way. If you need me to, I could move out for a while."

"Not necessary, but I'm afraid that there will be some additional costs." Sarah shook her head. "I'm sorry. I underestimated the state of things here. No one's lived in this baby for quite a while, and there was some water damage and other—"

"Don't worry about it," Reese interrupted. "Just do whatever has to be done. If you need another advance for materials, let me know."

Sarah looked at the other woman appreciatively. God, it was nice to work for someone who didn't think she was trying to rip her off all the time. And such a good-looking woman at that. Sarah had been considering asking her out, but she couldn't get a clear read on her.

As friendly as Reese was, she was personally unapproachable. She never discussed anything other than business and never gave a hint of sexual innuendo. Sarah wasn't even 100 percent sure the sheriff was gay. Just because she had a rock-hard body that looked impossibly good in a uniform and a face so androgynous it belonged on a Greek statue didn't necessarily mean that she was a lesbian. But Reese Conlon was turning women's heads all over town, and they couldn't all be wrong.

Sarah realized with a start that Reese was waiting for her reply. Blushing, she assured Reese that she would keep her apprised of the work schedule.

"Great. I'll get out of your way then," Reese said.

Sarah watched her take the stairs up to the kitchen two at a time, uncomfortably aware that just talking to her was a turn-on. She shook her head, deciding that the gorgeous cop was too dangerous to fool with. If a simple conversation could do that to her, she was afraid to think what might happen if they actually touched. She wasn't ready for anything that serious and intense, and instinct told her *everything* about that one was serious and intense.

Oblivious to Sarah's lingering glance, Reese grabbed her gear and walked the mile into town to the gym. Three or four times a week, she worked out at the woman-owned facility in the center of town. Usually she had the place to herself. Most of the tourists were sunning or shopping in the late afternoon, and the regulars tended to work out in the morning.

Reese nodded hello to the owner and headed for the free weights. Before straddling the weight bench, she placed her gym bag against the wall within easy reach. The chief had informed her that she was expected to carry her weapon at all times. Their force was small, and though serious trouble was rare, they did have recurring problems with drug use and the violence that accompanied it. Nelson said he wanted her to be available at short notice, especially since she was second in command, and insisted she keep the cruiser for quick response. Reese didn't mind; she was used to readiness as a way of life. Her gun and her beeper were as much a part of her life as her car keys. That she was essentially always on call didn't bother her either—she didn't really have a personal life beyond her job and her training. She worked, she worked out, and she trained in the *dojo*. That was the life she knew, the one she had built since the time she was a teenager, and the one with which she was content. Lifting the barbell over her head, she began to count.

Marge Price, who owned the gym, leaned against the counter and leafed through a magazine, watching the quiet one work out. That's how she thought of her: "the quiet one." She knew who Reese was, of course. Someone as exciting as a new deputy sheriff, especially a good-looking female one, didn't go unnoticed in a place as small as Provincetown. Marge had been watching her for a couple of weeks now. Moderate weights, high reps, with an occasional heavy set thrown in. The sheriff was obviously working for strength, not mass. Though from the stretch of her T-shirt across her broad chest and the muscular tone of her thighs, it was obvious she could have done heavy lifting if she'd wanted. Bulk clearly wasn't her goal, and the ease with which she stretched after every workout suggested remarkable flexibility.

Marge admired her as an athlete and was intrigued by her as an individual. Reese was always polite, considerate, focused, and completely remote. Marge wondered if she was so calm because she wasn't easily disturbed, or if there simply wasn't anything in her life to disturb her. Avoiding personal involvements also avoided much of life's turmoil, and Marge had never seen the quiet one with anyone. In fact, Marge hadn't seen her *anywhere* around town unless she was in uniform working or in the gym working out.

I wonder what she does for enjoyment? Hell, if I were younger, I might be tempted to try unsettling that one a little bit myself. I bet once she gets started, she's going to be hard to hold back. That rare flicker of a smile of hers reminds me of a fire that's been banked all night and is just waiting to flare.

At that moment, Reese approached, asking, "Can I get a bottle of water?"

"Sure," Marge replied, reaching into the small refrigerator under the counter. She twisted off the top before she handed it over.

Reese took it gratefully. "How much do I owe you?"

"On the house," Marge answered.

"Thanks just the same, but I'd rather pay," Reese said, no hint of censure in her voice.

"A dollar, then," Marge said. She regarded the other woman seriously. "We're not looking for any favors, you know, with the little handouts people are probably offering you. You do a job we all appreciate. Our businesses are our lives, and if the community isn't safe, tourists won't come. Without them, we starve. Next week, this place will go crazy, and your life will get complicated."

Reese drained the bottle dry. "I know that, and I'm grateful for your appreciation. But it's my job to keep order and see that the streets are safe. I don't need any extra perks for doing what I'm getting paid to do."

Marge stared at her. Reese looked back with a steady, unwavering gaze.

"The Boy Scouts really lost out when you turned out to be a girl," Marge deadpanned.

"What makes you think I wasn't a Boy Scout?" Reese rejoined just as seriously.

Marge laughed in surprise, and a second later, Reese joined her. As they were both catching their breath, Marge asked impetuously, "How would you like to have dinner with me one of these nights after you finish your workout?"

Reese was momentarily uncertain. She wasn't used to casual social encounters, especially with people she didn't know well.

But there was something so comfortable about this woman that Reese didn't fear the intrusiveness she experienced so often with strangers. "Okay."

"So how about tomorrow?" Marge persisted. She had a feeling her quiet one was shy, and she didn't want to give her a chance to change her mind. She couldn't say exactly what there was about the younger woman that appealed to her, but she simply liked her.

"Let me see how next week shapes up," Reese replied after a moment's thought. "Once I know what I'm in for, I promise I'll save a night for you."

Marge smiled. "I'll be waiting."

CHAPTER SIX

Tory glanced toward shore as she stroked rhythmically through the water at six a.m. There were a few anglers out, hoping for a jump on the other fishermen. And situated on the drive-off above the beach was the police cruiser. It had been there every morning for almost a week, and she felt sure she knew who was in it. She almost waved a greeting, then stopped, chiding herself for her foolishness.

There was no reason to think that Reese Conlon was there to see her. She hadn't heard from the sheriff since the day she had showed up at the clinic with Brianna Parker in her patrol car. That was the morning *after* the night they had spent together at Reese's house, she reminded herself. She flashed on an image of Reese standing nearly naked in a faded green T-shirt and, when her heart skipped a beat, just as quickly banished the thought. *Thinking about her is not a wise pastime. Chances are half the women in this town are fantasizing about her.*

Still, she had to admit she had hoped Reese might call with news of her investigation. And despite her resolve not to linger on the memory of the dark-haired, handsome sheriff, she found herself looking for the police car each day when she kayaked. And her pulse raced a little when she saw it.

A rogue wave took her by surprise, rocking the small craft and reminding her to stop daydreaming. She glanced once more toward shore, trying to make out the profile of the driver, then turned her mind to the sea and the soothing cadence of her strokes.

Reese drained her coffee cup as she watched the red dot disappear around the corner at Race Point. She sat a bit longer before she started the engine. Those few minutes each morning watching Tory King glide across the horizon were the most peaceful moments of her day. She couldn't say exactly why, but she knew what she felt and had no reason to question it. Settled and ready to work, she pulled the cruiser around toward Route 6, driving east to the town limits, then right toward the harbor to complete the circuit back down Commercial Street. At this hour, there was almost no traffic except for the delivery trucks double-parked along the narrow one-way street while their drivers serviced the many businesses that densely crowded the thoroughfare. Bikers and rollerbladers claimed the road that would be filled with tour buses and tourists on foot by eleven a.m.

With the first day of Memorial Day weekend, there would be a steady stream of cars crawling slowly through town until well after midnight. Despite the chief's gloomy predictions of chaos, she looked forward to the activity. Chances were she'd be working twelve-hour shifts, but that didn't bother her. She'd have to make adjustments in her workout schedule, but that was the only real change. Most nights after the gym she spent completing the renovations to the garage, getting her *dojo* ready. By nine p.m., she was usually in bed with a book. Up at four a.m., she ran five miles along the beach road, then showered and was ready to leave the house at 6 a.m. for work. She kept military hours, the same hours she had kept since she was fourteen years old.

Her life was orderly, routine, and predictable. Her work as a peacekeeper, first in the military and now here, provided her with a sense of purpose and satisfaction. Her martial arts training challenged her body and calmed her mind. The absence of close personal ties was not something she questioned or even considered. This was the life she had always lived, and on the whole, she was content.

She waved to Paul Smith as she pulled into the small lot behind the municipal building. Paul was one of the young officers who worked the night shift, and they knew each other only well enough to say hello.

"Quiet night?" Reese called.

"Yeah," he said as he unlocked the door to his Dodge truck. "Couple of drunks needed an escort home. I swung by the clinic a few times like you asked. The doc left at midnight. After that, it was like a tomb. It's not warm enough for much action in the dunes yet."

The National Park Rangers patrolled the dunes during the day, but at night, they left the job to the sheriff's department. As summer approached, the three miles of sand along Herring Cove would be packed with bathers and would-be lovers. The dunes above the beach and along Route 6 were favorite areas for rendezvous. The police discouraged people from traversing the dunes to deter the incidence of sex and drugs as much as to protect the habitat. Reese didn't particularly like the duty, but it was part of the job.

Since Nelson was at yet another meeting, she took advantage of the quiet to finish time schedules, make up duty rosters, and peruse recent crime reports from nearby townships. Sooner or later, whatever trouble the other towns had would filter down to her community.

She was about to brew another pot of coffee and starting to contemplate lunch when the scanner picked up a 911 call to the EMT station between Provincetown and Truro, the next town over.

"Come quick! A guy fell, out on the Long Point jetty," an anxious male voice reported. "It looks like his leg is twisted in some rocks, and he's bleeding all over the place."

Reese was up and through the door before the passerby finished giving the information to the dispatcher at the station ten miles away. She was two minutes from the scene. Long Point jetty was a curved finger of rocks that formed a protective arch between Provincetown harbor and the Atlantic Ocean. It stretched a good two miles and was a favorite tourist attraction. Unfortunately, people often underestimated how treacherous the huge slabs of rock could be, especially when still wet from high tide. A crowd was visible as Reese swung around Bradford Street, angling her cruiser across the road to prevent access to more curious onlookers. People parted for her rather reluctantly as they pushed out onto the jetty, jostling for a better look.

All she could see was another crowd milling about several hundred yards further out on the rocky causeway, presumably the site of the accident. She started toward them as quickly as she could, but her progress was hampered by poor footing on the rocks, which were slippery with the debris left by the receding tides. The jetty was comprised of angled blocks of stone piled adjacent to one another, forming a discontinuous walkway. There were large gaps between some slabs, requiring her to jump from one uneven surface to the other. She had gone about a hundred yards, moving as rapidly as she could, when she overtook Tory King, who was cautiously making her way toward the gathered crowd.

Reese was having trouble keeping her balance; navigating this surface with a cane and a leg brace was suicide. Reese slipped her hand under the doctor's elbow to guide her down the steep surface she was about to descend, saying as she did, "You shouldn't be out here, Doctor."

Tory's temper flared as she looked up at the taller woman. The angry reply died on her lips when all she found in the blue eyes that met hers was a quiet concern. There was no condescension and, thankfully, no trace of pity.

"You're absolutely right, Sheriff, but here I am."

"Why don't you let me go up ahead and assess the situation?" Reese suggested. "The EMTs should be here in five or ten minutes."

Tory put her hand on Reese's shoulder to steady herself as she pushed up onto the next rock face. "Why don't you go up ahead and get that crowd under control, so I'll have room to work when I get there," she rejoined. "I need to be sure that whoever's trapped down there isn't bleeding to death. I made it this far; I'll be fine."

Reese had to admit the plan made sense. She wasn't sure why she didn't want to leave the doctor alone, but some instinctive desire to safeguard the woman made her want to protest. Stomach tight with tension, she yielded to reason. Her training was too ingrained to allow individual concerns to interfere with logic. "Right. Just be careful, will you?"

"Absolutely. Now go."

By the time Tory reached the scene, the sheriff had enlisted a few of the onlookers to keep the others away from where a man lay twisted among the boulders. His leg seemed to disappear into a crevice between two angled sheets of stone. Reese was kneeling, her back to Tory, as Tory inched her way down the rock face toward the accident site.

"What have we got?" Tory asked. She gasped when Reese glanced up at her. The sheriff's face and shirt were streaked with blood.

"Are you hurt?" she questioned anxiously as she slid the last two feet.

"No, it's his." Reese grunted with effort as she inclined her head toward the man who lay wedged in the rocks. Blood welled up from the wound in his leg, a gaping tear, which Reese was attempting to hold closed with both hands.

"Open tibia fracture," Tory assessed as she searched for the pulse in his neck. It was faint and thready. "He's pretty shocky. We need to get this bleeding stopped."

She pressed two fingers into his groin over the femoral artery, and the steady stream of blood from the open wound slowed to a trickle. "Reese, there's a towel in my knapsack. Tear it in half and wrap the wound closed as tight as you can."

"Roger." Reese let go of her hold on the injured man's leg and turned to search through Tory's bag. As she finished the compression bandage, a siren in the distance signaled the rescue vehicle's approach. "EMTs are here."

"Good," Tory gasped. "My arm is fatiguing."

"Want me to take it?" Reese offered.

"No, you'd better go give them a hand. We need their equipment out here. And tell them we need the hydraulic jaws to shift these stones."

"I'll be right back," Reese said, unable to keep the concern from her voice. "Will you be okay?"

"I'm fine," Tory assured her. "Go."

The few minutes it took for Reese to return carrying one of the equipment cases seemed like hours as Tory crouched awkwardly in the cramped space, afraid to move lest she lose her tenuous hold on the artery beneath her fingers. She was starting to develop spasms in her own injured leg from her bent kneeling position. She gritted her teeth and cleared her mind, focusing only on the next thing she needed to do.

"I need to start an IV," she said as Reese dropped down beside her. "Can you get the line and the bag ready, then take over the compression?"

"One minute," Reese said as she tore the plastic wrapper off the tubing and saline bag. Behind her, two EMTs were trying to find a place to wedge the hydraulic jack between the rocks. "Okay," she said, placing her hands on Tory's, following her fingers down to the artery. She pressed inward so Tory could let go. "I've got it."

Tory reached behind her for the emergency kit, pulled out a length of soft rubber tubing, and wrapped it around the man's upper arm. She found a large bore IV needle and expertly slid it into the vein in the bend of his elbow. Then she attached the tubing Reese had readied and allowed the saline to run in at top speed.

"How much longer?" Tory called to the techs, a worried frown on her face. "This guy's in trouble. He needs blood, and if I don't get the fracture at least partially reduced, he could lose his foot."

"These rocks are going to shift all over the place when we activate the jack," the taller of the two female paramedics warned. "It's not safe where you are. You're going to have to get out of there."

Tory looked at the steady trickle of blood from the compound fracture in her patient's leg and shook her head. "We've only got this partially controlled as it is. If we reduce the compression, he may bleed out. Let me get back in there, Sheriff. I'll keep the artery tamponaded."

Reese looked up over her shoulder at Tory. Her face showed no trace of strain. "He's going to need you a lot more than me when they get him out of here. You'd better climb back out of the way. I'm staying with him."

A surge of fear took Tory by surprise. She had a sudden image of Reese pinned under tons of rock, and something close to panic clutched at her throat. She didn't want Reese to be the one in danger when that jack started.

"No," she started to argue.

"This is my call to make, Doctor. You worry about keeping him alive. Now climb up out of here." The tone of absolute command was unwavering. Reese turned her attention back to the injured man, the conversation clearly at an end.

Tory knew that there was no other way and no more time to argue. "For God's sake, be careful," she murmured as she carefully pulled herself up the steep rock face to safety.

"Are your legs clear?" one of the EMTs called down to Reese.

"All clear."

When they activated the power jack, bits of stone chips and sand filled the air, clouding Tory's view of the chasm where Reese and the victim were wedged. As the grating noise from the shifting rocks subsided, she peered anxiously downward. She could just make out Reese's tall form hunched over the injured man. "Are you okay?"

"Yeah," Reese gasped, "but he's slipping down into the crevice. I need a harness of some kind. Fast!"

Her arms were straining to hold up his dead weight, and she was afraid she might lose him. One of the EMTs threw a harness and a guide line to her, and moments later, they had the victim up. The techs secured him to a backboard while Tory adjusted an inflatable splint over the mass trousers that they applied to improve his blood flow.

"Take him to the heliport in Dennis," she instructed. "He needs to be air-vac'ed to Boston. Run two IVs wide open and give him whatever plasma substitutes you have. Make sure he gets a loading dose of Ancef, too."

As soon as they left, she turned worriedly to Reese, who was still bent over trying to catch her breath. "Let me check you out, Sheriff. Are you hurt anywhere?"

"I'm okay," Reese panted. "Just a little winded. I almost lost him there at the end."

"Well, you didn't," Tory replied as she ignored the sheriff's protests and quickly examined her. "You've got a lot of small cuts on your hands, but I think we can forgo sutures today."

Reese held up her hands tiredly, looking at them as if she were seeing them for the first time. "Just little nicks from the stone chips," she noted with a shrug.

Tory nodded, then handed her several alcohol wipes from her knapsack. "Clean them off with this."

"Thanks."

"Are you ready for the hike back?"

Reese got to her feet, her strength returning. "I'm ready when you are."

Tory took one step and grimaced. She wasn't going to make it without help. The muscles in her injured leg were strained from the arduous and unaccustomed climbing and were cramping badly. She didn't think she could trust her balance at this point, even on level ground.

"I'm in a little trouble here," Tory admitted reluctantly.

Turning, Reese searched her face in concern. "What can I do?"

"If I lean on you, I should be able to make it."

"All right, then." Reese slipped one strong arm around Tory's waist, holding her securely. Guiding them over the treacherous rocks, she said, "Let's just take it slow."

When they finally reached the end of the causeway, they both sank gratefully onto a stone bench provided for sightseers.

"Doing all right?" Reese asked as she removed her hat and ran a hand through her sweat-soaked hair. Her shirt was plastered to her back with moisture as well.

"Yes. Thank you," Tory said quietly. She hadn't needed nor sought assistance from anyone in a long time. Truth be known, she was amazed that Reese's assistance hadn't bothered her more. There was something about the equable sheriff that made accepting help from her easy. While Reese radiated strength and self-assuredness, there was also a simplicity about her that was not only surprising, but captivating. She saw a problem; she dealt with it. She made no judgments. Despite her competence and air of command, there was never a hint of superiority or condescension. Tory couldn't remember ever having met anyone quite like her. Certainly no one had ever made her feel so safe without making her feel diminished.

"You're getting to be indispensable around this town, Sheriff," Tory added sincerely.

Reese shrugged. "I'd like to think I'm earning my pay." She looked at Tory thoughtfully. "That took real courage for you to trek out there today. That guy doesn't know how lucky he is that you were there. How'd you know?"

Tory blushed at the compliment and spoke hurriedly to cover her embarrassment. "Ha! You forget that this is Provincetown. Probably everyone in town knows that I swim at the Inn on my lunch hour. It's just across the street, so when someone ran inside to make the 911 call, the manager came to get me. I would have gotten to him a lot sooner if it hadn't been for this damn leg."

"You did a great job," Reese remarked, plainly discounting Tory's last comment. She sighed, stretching her stiff muscles. "Can I buy you some lunch?"

"Thanks, but I'm already late for the clinic." Tory tried to ignore the racing of her heart. She was certain Reese was just being friendly. "I'm going to be backed up all evening at this rate."

"I won't keep you then. It was good working with you, Dr. King." Reese stood and settled her hat over her brow. Smiling down at Tory, she added, "I'm going to head on home to change into a uniform that isn't filled with sand and covered in someone else's blood."

"You've still got sutures that need to come out," Tory reminded her. "In fact, you should have come by a day or two ago."

Reese fingered the row of nylon stitches in her brow and shrugged, a disarming grin on her face. "Nelson has been keeping me pretty busy, especially with all the planning for the holiday weekend. They didn't bother me, and it slipped my mind. How about if I come by the clinic later?" she offered. "I'm going to be in town for dinner."

"I'm sure I'll be there." Tory smiled ruefully. "Tonight's my late night anyhow." She wondered fleetingly with whom the new sheriff might be dining, then quickly pushed the thought from her mind. Looking up at the sheriff, whose face was partially shaded by the brim of her hat, Tory found her to be an imposing figure outlined against the clear blue of the sky. She had to work hard not to stare at the taut, sleek body.

"I'll be by," Reese informed her.

"Good."

As Reese strode away, Tory couldn't resist watching her go.

CHAPTER SEVEN

Marge greeted Reese with a grin when she walked into the gym that evening after work. "I thought you might not make it."

Reese glanced up at the clock behind Marge's head. It read five-thirty p.m., exactly the same time she arrived for her workout every evening. "How come?" she asked in surprise. "I said I'd be here."

"Silly me." Marge shrugged elaborately. "I should have known that was as good as a guarantee. And of course, I never thought for a minute that you might be avoiding our dinner plans."

Reese raised one eyebrow at the gentle chiding and set about her routine without comment. She finished three sets of leg and back exercises in ninety minutes, then went to the locker room to shower. She put on pressed tan chinos, a navy blue denim shirt, and a light beige blazer that covered the holster she secured under her left arm in a shoulder rig. She checked the mirror, making sure the gun didn't show, and went out to meet Marge.

They walked down Commercial Street toward town and turned in at the Cactus Flower. It was still too early in the season to worry about reservations, but that would change within the next few days. After choosing a table at the front windows, they ordered margaritas while perusing the menu. Outside, the slow stroll of passersby provided a colorful tableau to watch as they dined.

"This isn't a date, you know," Marge announced after they had given their orders to the waitress.

Reese sipped her drink. It was strong and tart. She gazed calmly at the woman across from her. "It hadn't occurred to me that it might be."

"This is Provincetown, Sheriff." Marge laughed. "When one woman asks another woman out to dinner, it's usually a date."

"I see," Reese commented solemnly. "Then why isn't this a date?"

Marge stared back, totally nonplussed. The startlingly handsome woman across from her was impossible to figure out. She gave nothing away in her expression or her voice, and nothing seemed to surprise her or throw her off stride. Marge wondered what, if anything, could shake her calm control. She also wondered what price that kind of control exacted. Reese seemed completely without pretense, and Marge answered in kind. "It's not a date for two reasons—my expectations and my intentions."

"How so?" Reese inquired. She voiced no challenge, only honest interest.

"I'd be a fool to think you'd be interested in me. For one thing, I'm twenty years older than you."

"Hardly." Reese smiled and shook her head, studying Marge's tanned, well-developed form.

"Close enough," Marge grunted.

Reese waited while the silence grew. "And the other reason?" she asked quietly.

Marge blushed but continued boldly, "You're too damn butch to go for an old jock like me. I figure your tastes run more to the femme type."

"You do?" Reese leaned back, contemplating Marge's words, while the waitress slid their plates onto the table. Marge was the second person in as many weeks to say that to her. She had never thought of herself as butch and tried to imagine how she appeared to others. It was something with which she had no experience. Up until this point in her life, her rank and performance had determined how others related to her and how she related to them. The rules of conduct, including with whom you could fraternize, were clear. They were frequently circumvented, but not by Reese. It wasn't that she agreed with the rules so much as she had no reason to challenge them. She had spent her life either preparing to be, or being, an officer. Her professional and personal lives were one and the same.

"I'm not so sure about the butch thing, but I'm pretty sure I don't have any particular taste for a type of anything," she said after a moment.

Marge snorted as she busied herself with her food. "Trust me on this, Sheriff. If you will allow my politically incorrect terminology, you are as butch as it gets. But don't let it bother you."

"Well, whatever you call it, it comes naturally to me." Reese smiled. "So. This is just a friendly dinner then?"

"Yes."

"Fair enough."

"Since we're being all revealing here," Marge continued, "how'd you end up in our little town?"

"I needed a job, and this was the right one for me," Reese remarked.

"So you didn't come here looking for love?" Marge asked half-seriously.

Reese shook her head ruefully. "Not precisely."

"And you didn't leave anybody behind? No attachments?"

"No," Reese replied firmly. "I don't have any attachments."

"You are definitely something of an oddity around here," Marge observed dryly. "Most people come here to find someone— or to escape something."

"I'm not all that different, I suppose," Reese mused softly, surprising herself at the admission. "It's just not what you're thinking."

"And I don't suppose you're going to fill me in?" Marge prodded gently.

Just as gently, Reese replied, "Not tonight."

They finished their dinner in easy conversation and were about to leave when Marge saw Reese glance at her watch for the second time.

"You have to be somewhere?"

"The clinic," Reese answered. "I'm supposed to stop by there and have these stitches removed. The doctor said she'd be there until ten."

"Don't rush. She's always there late. I live just down the road. She doesn't seem to do much *except* work."

"It must get pretty busy, especially when you're the only doctor in town," Reese commented, remembering Victoria King's resolute determination to make the dangerous journey over the rocks to aid the injured man. Her dedication was clear and admirable.

"Sure it's tough, especially if you use it as an excuse to avoid a social life. Don't you think there are plenty of doctors who would just love to live up here during the season and work for her?"

Reese regarded her dinner companion silently. She felt a strong desire to come to Tory's defense and a strange surge of anger at Marge's criticism. Both responses confused her.

Marge didn't miss Reese's sudden withdrawal. Seriously, she said, "Hey, don't get me wrong. I like her. I always have. She's a great friend to the people of this town, and there are more than a few who would like to know her better, if she'd let them."

Marge shrugged as she reached for their check. "She just doesn't seem to trust anyone to get too close, and that's a damn shame."

"I'm sure she has her reasons," was all Reese said.

❖

Randy was on his way out the front door when Reese walked up.

"All through for the night?" she asked the receptionist.

"*I* am," he said petulantly. "The last patients are in rooms, but at the rate *she's* going, it could take her another hour. She can barely walk, and it serves her right. Traipsing out on that jetty like some macho superhero. I wouldn't be surprised if she isn't on crutches tomorrow. And it wouldn't be the first time either."

His obvious distress belied the criticism in his voice. He was clearly worried about Tory, and Reese immediately liked him for it. He continued to fuss while he unlocked the door for Reese. "Do you think she'd let me cancel patients just because *she* needs to be in bed? Of course not." He held the door open as he spoke. "You might as well go back to her office and wait. It's more comfortable there, and she'll find you when she's finished. She insisted that *I* go home on time. Could do without me, she said. *Ha!* Wait until she sees that appointment book. Good luck! Then we'll see who doesn't need me."

Reese had to smile at the slender, attractive young man's tirade, but her thoughts were of the woman who had made a selfless gesture, despite the cost. She was suddenly very anxious to see the doctor. "I'll go on back. Thank you."

Reese settled into the now familiar chair before Tory's desk and let her eyes wander over the photos of the former Olympian. Eventually, she heard the approach of slow footsteps and turned to greet the doctor. Tory looked pale and drawn, but her eyes held a smile.

"Have you been waiting long?" Tory inquired as she eased herself into the leather chair behind her desk. She tried to hide a grimace as another spasm clamped onto her calf, forcing her to gasp.

"Not very," Reese said quietly. Tory's pain was obvious, and watching her struggle with it made Reese feel helpless and uneasy. "Is there anything I can do?"

"About what?"

"Your leg."

Taken aback, Tory stared at her in surprise. "God, you get to the point, don't you? Why is it that my *handicap* doesn't seem to put you off the way that it does most people?"

Ordinarily, she never would have voiced those feelings, but she was too tired and in too much pain to hide her bitterness. She closed her eyes as another wave of cramps struck out of nowhere, causing her to gasp faintly.

"You have an injury, Doctor. *Handicapped* is not a word I would use to describe you," Reese remarked as she moved boldly around the side of Tory's desk. Softly, she said, "Now, what needs to be done here?"

"I need to get this damn brace off," Tory said through gritted teeth. "But if I do, I'm afraid I won't be able to get to my car."

"We'll worry about that later," Reese said as she knelt down. She pushed up the leg of Tory's jeans and studied the hinged metal device that extended from just below the knee to the arch of her foot. Expressionlessly, she took in the crisscrossing of surgical scars and skin grafts over the damaged atrophied muscles.

"Doesn't look too complicated," Reese said evenly, trying not to think about how horrific the trauma must have been. Her hands were steady as she reached for the brace. "May I?"

Reese's actions had taken Tory completely by surprise. She stared into the deep blue eyes that searched her face, suddenly terrified that she might cry. She was so used to fighting the endless discomfort and awkwardness alone that the straightforward offer of help almost overwhelmed her.

"Please," she whispered, her throat tight.

Reese released the velcro bindings and gently eased the brace off. Tory's leg was swollen from the calf down, and her ankle was starting to discolor. Tory gasped with pain as Reese softly massaged the injured tissues, bringing a sudden rush of blood to the area.

"I'm sorry," Reese murmured. "We need to do something about this swelling. Ice?"

"There's a cold pack above the sink in the treatment room," Tory managed, struggling with the physical pain and the unexpected emotional turmoil Reese had unwittingly provoked.

Reese retrieved the pack, snapped it open, and wrapped it around Tory's ankle with an Ace bandage she had found. "I think that's the best I can do," she said apologetically.

"It's more than enough," Tory replied gratefully once she caught her breath. "Were you a medic in the Marines?"

"Not exactly." Reese chuckled as she leaned against the edge of Tory's desk. "Military police, before law school. We had our share of minor injury calls, though."

Multitalented, aren't you, Sheriff Conlon? Tory regarded Reese thoughtfully. Reese was so easy to talk to, and the scary part was that she wanted to. She wanted to admit just once that she couldn't take it anymore, that she was just too damned tired. Realizing just how much she wanted to trust those blue eyes holding her own so steadily made her wary. Something this compelling could get out of hand. "Just give me a minute, then I'll see if I can get the damn thing back on again."

"Why?"

"I can't walk very far without it," Tory replied, trying to laugh.

"How much do you weigh?"

Tory did laugh at that. "My God. Have you no sense at all? Don't you know that's a dangerous question to ask of a woman who's not entirely in control of her faculties?"

"Huh." Reese buried her hands in her pockets and answered with a straight face, "I must have missed that in the training manual."

Tory could tell by the determined glint in Reese's eyes that this would be an uphill battle. Graciously she acquiesced. "A hundred and thirty pounds."

"Not a problem. Grab your brace." As she spoke, Reese slipped one arm behind Tory's shoulders and the other under her knees. "Hold on."

As Reese lifted her, cradling Tory securely against her chest, Tory's arms came around her neck. Reese tightened her hold. "Okay?"

For the first time all day, Tory wasn't aware of the pain in her leg. What she *was* aware of was even more disconcerting. A cascade of sensations assaulted her—hard muscles; a slow, steady heartbeat; the light, sweet smell of perspiration. Reese was an intoxicating combination of tenderness and strength, and Tory's response was automatic. She flushed at the surge of arousal and drew a shaky breath, hoping that the woman who held her could not feel her tremble. "Yes, I'm fine," she murmured, allowing herself the luxury of resting her head against Reese's shoulder.

Reese made her way easily to her patrol car and settled Tory into the front seat. As she started the engine, she asked, "Where to?"

"Straight out 6A toward Truro. I'm just a mile outside town."

Within minutes, Reese pulled into the drive of a two-story weathered cedar-shingle home that overlooked the expanse of Provincetown harbor. As she stepped from the car, a dark form came hurtling through the night toward her.

"Whoa!" she cried as a huge dog planted its front feet on her chest, nearly knocking her over.

"Jed! Get down," Tory yelled as she tried to extricate herself from the car. At the sound of his owner's voice, the dog immediately dropped to the ground and raced to her.

"Is it safe to come around?" Reese called, laughing, as she eased toward the passenger side of her vehicle.

"He's perfectly safe," Tory called as she thumped the dog's massive chest in greeting. "He's just excitable."

"What is he?" Reese asked as she leaned down and lifted Tory from the seat.

"Mastiff. That's Jedi, Jed for short."

"That must make you Princess Leia then," Reese remarked as she walked up the gravel path toward the wide deck that encompassed the rear of the house.

"Hmph. What makes you think I'm not Luke Skywalker?"

"Just a hunch."

Tory laughed and settled herself more comfortably within the circle of Reese's arms. When they reached the rear door, Reese held her close while Tory slipped her key into the lock. Out of nowhere, Reese was suddenly conscious of the soft swell of Tory's breasts pressed against her chest and the subtle fragrance of her perfume. In the dim light of the moon, Tory's face in profile was timelessly beautiful. Catching her breath, Reese trembled as unfamiliar warmth suffused her.

"Let me down," Tory said firmly. "You're shaking."

"Sorry," Reese said a little uncertainly. She lowered the doctor gently but kept one supporting arm around her waist, trying to figure out what had just happened. She couldn't remember being this light-headed after a twenty-mile forced march in full pack. She wasn't sure what was wrong with her, but she was acutely embarrassed. "I guess I'm not in as good shape as I thought."

"Nonsense," Tory replied as she pushed the door open. "You're in superb shape, but enough is enough." She reached for the light switch by the door, illuminating the living room and kitchen/dining area beyond. "Just steer me over there," she said, indicating a large sectional sofa fronting the wall of windows and sliding glass doors that opened onto the large deck. The house was designed to take full advantage of the unimpeded view of the harbor beyond the low dunes outside. "Half the time, I fall asleep down here anyway. One more night on the couch won't kill me."

"More ice?" Reese asked as Tory propped her leg up on several pillows.

"Not just yet. But I'd love a drink, and you've certainly earned one. If you wouldn't mind pouring me a Scotch, I'd be grateful forever." She pointed to a cabinet tucked into the corner of the eating area. "In there. There's plenty of other stuff in the fridge if you want something else."

"Gratitude is not necessary. You more than deserve this after the day you've had." Reese found glasses, poured the drink, and grabbed a light beer for herself. Returning, she handed the Scotch to Tory, then sat on the sofa opposite her. She stretched her legs out to accommodate Jed, who had pushed himself against the entire length of the front of the couch. When he raised his massive head and rested it on her thigh, she stroked him absently. The unusual episode at the door had left her agitated and uneasy. Even now, her stomach thudded with a peculiar aching sensation. *Must just be tired.*

"Brianna Parker came by the clinic today," Tory remarked. "She said that you insisted I clear her before she could start training with you."

"Is she okay?" Reese asked, grateful for something to take her mind off her own sense of disquiet.

"She's fine. The young heal quickly, but I still wouldn't advise anything too strenuous for a while." She paused, watching Reese closely. The sheriff seemed distracted and even more remote than usual. "It's a good thing you're doing for that girl."

"How so?" Reese was surprised by Tory's oddly gentle tone.

"You probably don't know that Bri's mother died rather suddenly three years ago. Acute leukemia." Tory sighed. "That's awful enough at any age, but it's especially hard for a teenager. I gather from what Nelson's said that Bri has been getting a little wild. It sounds like training with you may be just what she needs."

"I hope it helps," Reese said at length. "I know what it's like when your whole world seems to change overnight. It can be a dangerous time."

"Was it for you?" Tory asked softly, wanting a glimpse of what lay beneath this formidable woman's steely exterior.

"For a while." Reese gazed out over the moonlit water, thinking of herself at that age. She remembered how she felt when her mother left—the unsettledness and the anger. Her father loved her, she knew that, and he taught her the things he knew. He taught her about responsibility, and discipline, and honor. He taught her the way he had been taught, the Marine way. He expected the best from her, and he got it. In return, he provided her with a life that was orderly, dependable, and predictable. It had seemed enough, for most of her life.

"It might have turned out differently for me," she mused half to herself, "if I hadn't had the service to look forward to. My parents divorced when I was fourteen. My father is career Marine, and he raised me to follow in his footsteps. I've spent my entire life in the Marines, one way or the other. It's true what they say—it has made me what I am. But those first few years until I was old enough for ROTC and college were hard."

"I imagine all of it was hard," Tory ventured, beginning to understand why Reese seemed so controlled. The Marine Corps undoubtedly produced fine warriors, but at what cost?

"Don't misunderstand. I loved the Marines; I still do. In fact, I'm still in the Reserves. But when I was Bri's age, it wasn't easy. Sometimes it got pretty lonely." Reese stopped, suddenly self-conscious. She never talked about herself, and she had no idea why she was now.

"What about your mother?" Tory probed gently.

Reese unconsciously squared her shoulders in that military gesture that was becoming familiar to Tory as she replied flatly, "She wasn't in the picture."

"I'm sorry," Tory said, retreating. "I'm prying."

"I didn't notice." Reese smiled that fleeting, breathtaking smile.

"I doubt there's anything that escapes your notice," Tory said with a laugh. Then, suddenly serious, she added, "You've been more help than I can say today, Reese. I'm not sure how I would have managed without you, this morning on the jetty or tonight."

Even though she meant every word, she didn't want to think too hard about why she was admitting her need now, when she had refused to for so long. She didn't want to think too hard about how different Reese seemed than anyone she had ever met or about how easy it had been to accept her help. She especially didn't want to think about how deeply she had been touched by Reese's calm, unwavering presence. "I...I just wanted to thank you—"

Reese shook her head, halting Tory's words. "Doctor King—"

"Oh, please. It's Tory."

"All right...Tory," Reese amended almost shyly. "It was an honor and my pleasure. So please, don't thank me for something I was glad to do."

Tory caught her breath, moved by the simple honesty apparent in Reese's words. When she looked into Reese's intense, penetrating eyes something visceral stirred in her, and her voice was thick with emotion when she said, "It's more than a job to you, isn't it?"

Reese flushed, but she held Tory's gaze. "You may not believe this, but I took an oath to serve and protect, and every day I'm glad I did."

"I do believe you. I've seen you in action," Tory said quietly, thinking that Reese undoubtedly was the most forthright person she had ever met and, at the same time, the most complicated.

"Good," Reese said as she stood. "Then you won't object to me coming by to take you to the clinic tomorrow. Remember, you don't have a car."

"You don't leave much room for argument, do you?" Tory remarked ruefully, realizing that Reese had once again made help impossible to refuse.

"That *is* a skill I learned in officer's training school," Reese rejoined, her eyes laughing. "Besides, I *still* need my sutures removed."

"Then I accept, Sheriff," Tory teased lightly, watching as Reese strode gracefully to the door and smiling at the quick salute the sheriff tossed on her exit. Then she settled back against the couch, blaming the Scotch for the sudden rush of heat that stole through her.

CHAPTER EIGHT

"It's open," Tory called from the kitchen when she saw the woman outside on the deck. She glanced at the clock, noting it was exactly six a.m. *Always so dependable, Sheriff?*

"Morning," Reese said as she entered, carrying two paper cups of espresso. "Thought you might need this."

She deposited the carry-out containers from Espresso Joe's onto the breakfast counter and slid onto one of the black-and-chrome stools. "It's a double."

"It's a start," Tory groaned, leaning on her cane as she reached with her free hand for the coffee.

"I could make some more," Reese suggested, pointing to an elaborate espresso machine nearby and starting to rise.

"Sit," Tory commanded. "I'm up already, and I'll be functional in just a minute." She sipped the rich brew, noting that Reese looked fresh in her crisply pressed uniform shirt and pants. "I suppose *you've* already run ten miles or something else equally obnoxious."

"Haven't you noticed it's raining outside?" Reese asked mildly. "I only ran five."

Tory stared at her, smiling when she caught the barest flicker of a grin on Reese's handsome face. "I could learn to hate you."

"God, I hope not." Reese laughed, then asked, "How's the leg?"

Caught off guard, Tory looked away for a second, then met Reese's questioning gaze. "Hurts like hell, but it's been worse."

"I guess staying home is not an option?"

"You *do* like to live dangerously, don't you?" Tory asked softly, amazed that Reese's concern did not rankle her the way it did coming from others. For some reason, Reese's attention did not make her feel less than whole.

"Well, it wouldn't do for you to be out of commission," Reese said seriously. "The town needs you too much. So, if it's a question of one day off to prevent a bigger problem, I'll risk suggesting it."

"Thanks," Tory said, "but I'm used to these episodes, and I can tell if there's a real problem."

"Good enough." Reese sipped her espresso and regarded Tory steadily. "What's the problem, exactly?"

"It's really just my ankle," Tory replied, watching Reese's face carefully for her reaction. Concerned interest. Not a hint of discomfort or pity. She took a deep breath and crossed a barrier she had erected years before. "There's irreparable nerve damage, so I can't flex it. It's either the brace or an ankle fusion."

"Wouldn't the fusion be less painful?" Reese ventured carefully, appreciating that this was a sensitive issue for the independent physician.

"Probably," Tory admitted, "but I'd also be less mobile. I'm still good on the water without the brace, and I can work out with an air cast if I'm careful. Besides, I've always hoped..." Her voice trailed off as she looked away.

"Hoped what?" Reese urged gently.

"That I'd row again. I'd never be able to get into the cleats if my ankle was fused."

"How long has it been since you've rowed?" Reese asked quietly.

"Since the day of the accident. Almost ten years. I guess it's pretty ridiculous to keep hoping, isn't it?"

"No," Reese said quickly. "If it's something you want that much, it makes sense not to close any doors. You know how much pain you can take, and if it's worth it."

"Thanks." Tory looked at her gratefully. "My friends and family might not agree with you, though. They think I should have let the surgeons do it when I was in the hospital the first time."

"The first time?"

Again Tory dropped her gaze. "There were problems— infection, some muscle necrosis. It took them a few tries in the OR to get it cleared up."

Reese regarded her steadily, revealing none of her churning disquiet. Her training had taught her neither to personalize pain nor to be distracted by another Marine's injury, because even a split second's loss of focus could mean the loss of more lives. But the knowledge of Tory's suffering penetrated that shield, and Reese had to consciously dispel the vision of Tory in a hospital bed, fighting to keep her leg. Tory would not have wanted her pity then or her sympathy now. "Does the kayaking help?"

"Some. I'm on the water and the rhythm is good. The damn shell is heavy, though."

"I wondered how you got that thing from your Jeep to the water."

Tory smiled. "It's awkward but not that difficult to handle, once it's off the roof. There's always someone around to help with that. Still, it's nothing like the freedom of being in a scull."

Her frustration was evident, and Reese recalled the photographs in Tory's office of the needle-thin sculls, no more than a sliver separating the rowers and the water. She also remembered the long, clean line of Tory's legs pulling through her stroke. "I'm sorry," she said softly on an expelled breath.

"Hey, it's okay. Really." Tory laid her hand on Reese's forearm, squeezing gently. "I only get morose when the damn thing's acting up. Believe me, most days I'm just glad it's still there. But thanks for not saying I'm being a fool."

"You said you still work out?" Reese asked.

"Yes, *Hapkido*, remember?"

"I don't usually forget when someone humiliates me."

"I can't imagine anyone getting the best of you," Tory laughed. "As you saw, I do mostly weapons work with the cane, which fortunately for me is a traditional Asian weapon." At Reese's nod of understanding, she continued, "With a light air cast, I can stand long enough for self-defense drills, and mat work is not a problem. The only things I really can't do anymore are forms. The *katas* are too much of a strain on my leg."

"So, would you be willing to teach me the cane?"

"If you'd be willing to work on the mat with me," Tory countered immediately.

"Absolutely." Reese smiled happily. "I haven't had a training partner in a long time. Just let me know when your leg is better."

"Give me a week," Tory replied just as enthusiastically. "Now, we'd better get out of here before we're both late for work."

Reese looked at the clock over the stove, amazed to find it was close to seven. She couldn't remember the last time she had lost track of the time.

❖

Randy was just unlocking the clinic's front door when Reese pulled the cruiser into the lot. He watched with raised eyebrows as Reese accompanied Tory up the walk.

"Well. Good morning," he crowed with exaggerated emphasis, looking pointedly from Tory to Reese.

"Sheriff Conlon needs her stitches out, Randy, if you could manage to let us in?" Tory said, frowning at his innuendo.

"Oh, *of course,* Doctor. Right away, Doctor," he continued with a grin, his tone lightly mocking.

"Cut it out, Randy," Tory muttered as she passed him.

He managed to follow them down the hall on the pretense of opening the exam room doors. He leaned against the door of the treatment room while Tory removed the sutures from Reese's brow.

"Just keep it clean. It should be fine," she said as Reese stood to leave.

"Sure thing. Thanks, Doctor," Reese said. She nodded to Randy as she brushed past him into the hall.

Randy craned his neck to follow her progress toward the door.

"Oh my, what a butch thing she is," he announced once she had gone. "Does she make your little heart tingle?"

"Randy!" Tory said in exasperation.

"Oh, come on now, *Doctor* King, what would you call her?"

Tory grinned at him. "An incredibly stunning butch thing."

Randy's eyes widened in surprise. He couldn't ever remember his solitary employer commenting on a woman before. He had given up nagging her to get a date on seeing the pain in her eyes whenever he teased her about it.

"And just what was Sheriff Heartthrob doing driving you to work?" he persisted, curious and hopeful that someone had finally managed to capture Tory's attention.

"She drove me home last night." At his questioning look, she added hesitantly, "I simply couldn't."

"Damn it, Tory. I would have stayed. Why didn't you ask me?"

"I'm just not used to asking."

"Then how come you asked her?" Randy was slightly hurt and more than a little exasperated.

"I *didn't*. She didn't give me any choice."

Good for her. It's about time someone refuses to be intimidated by the walls you put up. Then again, I don't suppose anyone intimidates the new sheriff. He raised both eyebrows suggestively. "Sooo...?"

"So nothing," she replied curtly. "She would have done the same for anyone. That's just the way she is."

"Right," Randy muttered under his breath as he watched Tory move stiffly away down the hall. *Just keep telling yourself that.*

❖

Reese entered the office whistling, much to Nelson Parker's amazement.

"Do you mind telling me what's so wonderful when tomorrow is the first day of Memorial Day weekend?" he asked grumpily.

"Excuse me?" Reese asked, perplexed.

"Never mind," he snapped. "You're on twelve-hour shifts for the next couple of days, okay?"

"Sure," Reese responded. "No problem."

"And you've got traffic detail at MacMillan Pier from one to five."

"Yep."

He looked at her closely. She seemed relaxed, smiling faintly, and, if he didn't know better, not totally present. In the one month he had known her, he had never seen her the slightest bit distracted. His curiosity was more than piqued.

"So what gives, Conlon?"

"What do you mean?" she asked, genuinely confused. She glanced at him as if *he* were acting strangely. "Not a thing."

"Never mind," he muttered. "Anything new on the clinic break-in?"

"No. The things that were missing are impossible to trace. Unless we're lucky, we'll never know. There's too much traffic in and out of that place to make any fingerprints useful. Not much to do but keep an eye on it."

"Well, you'd better swing by there a couple of times a shift for the next few weeks. Hopefully that will discourage any repeat break-ins. By the way, nice job out on the jetty yesterday. I heard the guy was a mess."

"I didn't do much. If Dr. King hadn't been there, I think the guy would have bled to death before the EMTs got him out. She deserves the credit."

"Chances are you'll have plenty of work for the doc before this summer's over. We spend half our time dealing with accidents, overdoses, and minor brawls. And all of them end up at her place."

"That's a heavy load for one doctor," Reese commented, remembering how exhausted Tory had seemed the night before.

"Don't remember her ever taking a vacation in the three years she's been here," Parker noted.

Something about discussing Tory made Reese uncomfortable; she had no idea why. She shook off the sudden urge to drive by the clinic. Impatiently, she grabbed her keys.

"I'm going out for a tour before I start the traffic detail," she announced. Maybe that would dispel the odd anxiety.

"Sure," the sheriff called to her departing back.

Reese traveled out Route 6 to Truro, then circled back to town along 6A. It had stopped raining, but the earlier inclement weather had delayed the daily tourist influx. She purposefully avoided the turn onto the street that would take her past the clinic and stopped instead across from her mother's gallery. Sitting with the engine idling for a few moments, she wondered why she had come. For the first time in her life, she didn't feel entirely sure of herself.

Spontaneous impulses were not something to which she had ever fallen prey, and yet, here she was. She cut the engine and climbed from the car before she had any more time to think.

"Reese!" Kate exclaimed, opening the door.

"Bad time?" Reese asked hesitantly.

"Not at all. It's wonderful to see you. Come on back and have some coffee."

"Sure," Reese replied, following her mother through the house to the kitchen.

"How are you?" Kate inquired as she poured coffee.

"I'm fine. I was just passing by, and..." Reese faltered, not able to explain.

"Reese," Kate said softly, "you don't need a reason to come by. Just being able to see you again is a miracle. I'll never get enough."

Reese looked away, then met her mother's eyes directly. She asked the question she had wanted answered for a very long time. "It was part of the agreement, wasn't it? That you not see me?"

"Yes." Her mother's distress was palpable. "Today I would never agree to that, but more than twenty years ago, a lesbian mother had no rights at all. And I couldn't fight it. Your father had pictures."

Reese grew very still, her blue eyes darkening dangerously. "He had the two of you followed?"

"Yes." Kate sighed and placed the cups on the small window-side table. "Sit down. I'll try to explain."

Kate watched Reese take the seat, still astonished at her presence, then began quietly to tell the story.

"We weren't very discreet. Didn't know we needed to be. We met when you were small, and Jean and I were young and terribly innocent ourselves at the time. For a while, we were just friends, and then..." She stopped, a sad smile of remembrance on her face. She looked into Reese's eyes, regret mixed with dignity in her gaze. "It didn't occur to either of us that loving each other could be wrong. Eventually, we became lovers, and when he confronted me, I had to make a choice."

"I remember Jean coming to the house," Reese remarked quietly. "I always liked her."

"I'm so sorry, Reese. I was selfish, I know, but I was so unhappy for so long. Oh, not with you. You were the best part of my life. And then I met Jean, and I felt completely alive for the first time." Her eyes were wet with tears as she looked at the woman her daughter had become. "I am so terribly sorry."

"Don't say that," Reese said gently. "I always knew, somehow, that there was a reason you stayed away. I was old enough when you left to understand that marriages don't always last, and after a while, I thought I understood what had happened between you and Jean. I just needed to know his part." She smiled at her mother, her blue eyes clear and calm. "You chose life. If you had stayed, given her up, I can only imagine it would have been worse for all of us ultimately. I don't blame you." She hesitated the length of a heartbeat. "If I ever felt what you felt for Jean, I think I'd do the same."

Kate studied her daughter's tightly controlled, perfectly contained features and asked boldly, "And have you ever? Felt that way for someone?"

"No." Reese looked past her mother to the smooth water of the harbor, looking inward to a life she had never before examined. "I'm like him, you know. I was happy in the military, and I'm happy now. I love the order, and the duty, and the responsibility. I guess I don't need anything else."

"You have your father's best qualities, Reese. I can see that. You remind me of why I married him, seeing you in that uniform with not a wrinkle, not a fold out of place. It reminds me that he represented something decent, honest, and admirable. Or so I thought. But your father never made room in his life for love, Reese. I hope that won't be true for you. If it finds you, don't turn your back."

Reese smiled ruefully. "I'm not sure I would recognize it."

Her mother laughed lightly, squeezing Reese's hand gently. "Trust me. You'll know."

❖

Reese was too busy the rest of the day to think much about the conversation with her mother. Nevertheless, she had left the small cottage with the sense that one unfinished chapter in her life had been closed. As she set about her comfortable routines, she felt much more peaceful and settled.

When Memorial Day weekend arrived, Reese spent most of that Friday directing slowly moving cars and hordes of pedestrians through the congested, narrow streets in the center of town. Tour buses crowded the pier area, disgorging packs of mostly elderly people who milled about uncertainly, seemingly oblivious to the cars passing within inches of them. Lesbian and gays poured into town for the first gathering of the summer season. Commercial Street was wall-to-wall pedestrians, interspersed with vehicles attempting to navigate around them. Late in the day, Reese greeted Paul Smith, her relief, with a grin.

"Welcome to bedlam, but I guess you expected it."

"Yep, looks about like I thought." Paul looked up and down the street, shaking his head. "Once the sun goes down, most of the out-of-towners will leave. Then all we'll have are the gays, until two or so."

He looked harried, and Reese remembered that his young wife was pregnant. "When's your baby due?"

"Any second. Cheryl's so big now she can hardly sleep, and she's getting really spooked about being home alone at night," he said worriedly.

Reese looked at her watch, then said, "Listen, how about I relieve you at midnight? I can duck home now and sleep for a while."

He looked at her hopefully. "You'd do that?"

"Sure. It's only for a few days. Just let the sheriff know, okay? I'll be home if you need me before then." She waved away his attempts to thank her and walked off to retrieve her cruiser. The enthusiasm and holiday spirit of the people surrounding her were contagious, and she doubted that she'd be able to sleep much. She might as well work. Besides, she was anxious to see the Provincetown that only came to life at night.

At ten minutes to midnight, Reese pulled her squad car into the small lot behind City Hall, across the street from the Pilgrim's Monument and one short block from the center of town. She found

Paul still directing traffic at the intersection on Commercial and sent him home.

Standing with her back to the pier, she looked up and down the main thoroughfare. It was nearly as crowded as it had been at noon, but the entire atmosphere had changed. There was a Mardi Gras energy in the air as same-sex couples of all ages, styles, and garb strolled the sidewalks and spilled out into the street. Men in impossibly revealing shorts, leathers, and spandex passed singly or in groups, openly appraising each other. Women, mostly in couples, and occasional knots of youths were very much a presence as well. They held hands or draped their arms about each other, delighting in their visibility. Reese had never before seen so many gay people in one place. It was clear that Provincetown was every inch the Mecca it claimed to be.

She started west along Commercial, heading toward the Coast Guard station that marked the end of the most populated walk in Provincetown. For the most part, the crowds were congenial and controlled, parting like the Red Sea for the bicyclists and rollerbladers who dared navigate the packed one-way street. She took her time, glancing in the shops she passed, most of which were still open and would remain open eighteen hours a day until after Labor Day. The merchants of Provincetown had a very short season and worked nonstop during the three months of summer. The restaurants and many bed-and-breakfasts were also dependent on a heavy tourist trade during the summer migration of gays and lesbians in order to survive the near desolation of the empty winter months.

Reese walked down to the entrance to the Provincetown Gym and stuck her head inside. Marge was behind the counter, piling T-shirts and sweats onto the shelves behind her.

"Hey, handsome." Marge smiled a greeting. "I thought this was Paulie's shift."

"It is, but he's home with his wife, waiting on the baby. I'm filling in for a few days."

"Ain't it beautiful out there?" Marge remarked with a grin.

"Everything I've been told is true. It's changed overnight," Reese agreed.

"And it isn't even busy yet."

It was hard not to catch the enthusiasm that pervaded the small fishing village. Reese knew that the hardest four months of her year were in front of her and did not mind a bit. This was the job she chose without reservation, and she wanted to ensure that the town and its people were safe and prosperous through another cycle. "I've got to get going. I just wanted to say hi."

"Thanks for stopping by." Marge started to wave her on, then quickly added as an afterthought, "Hey, how about dinner again soon?"

"Sure. How does September sound?"

"Oh, come now, Sheriff," Marge teased. "You've got to find some time to enjoy the goings-on around here. How about this? I'll take you to the tea dance."

"Deal," Reese acquiesced. "As soon as I get a day off."

"It's a date."

"Oh, really?" Reese raised one eyebrow. "What changed your mind?"

Marge laughed. "Get out of here. Go make our streets safe for the young'uns."

❖

Reese rejoined the throngs in front of Spiritus Pizza, the central gathering place for the dozens of men and women who sat on the curb, occupied the benches, or leaned against the light poles eating huge slices of pizza and watching the spectacle of life passing by. Amazingly, there wasn't much in the way of public drunkenness. Generally, someone in the gathering managed to keep the heavy partiers under control or at least off the streets. Reese was glad of that. She didn't want to spend her shift hassling people over fairly harmless substance use, but she'd have to if it became too publicly blatant. She was paid to enforce the law, and she would, but she reserved the right to use her own judgment as to what constituted a real violation.

Glancing down the alley next to Spiritus, she noticed movement in the shadows at the far end. It was dark enough that she pulled out her flashlight, playing the beam over the ground ahead. Two people leaned against the wall of the building, wrapped in an embrace.

Hastily, they pulled apart as she approached. Her light flickered over the face of a pretty blond teenager. The girl looked like any of the leather-clad youths who crowded the streets. She had the requisite multiple piercings along the edge of one ear, a small silver ring through the rim of her left nostril, and a tattoo showing along the inner curve of one breast. The body art was visible because the lace-up vest she wore with nothing under it was open to the waist from what, no doubt, had been an interrupted caress. The top button of her tight black jeans was open as well.

A typical teenage rendezvous, except this girl was holding tight to Brianna Parker's hand and trying to look defiant. Bri stepped quickly forward, her shoulders braced, obscuring the girl from Reese's view.

Reese spoke before Bri could. "It's not safe down these alleys. You two head on back to the street."

Neither of the young girls said a word as they sidled past her, fixing their clothes while simultaneously hurrying toward the end of the alley. Reese took her time, giving them the opportunity to disappear into the crowd. She glanced at her watch. It was 1:20 in the morning. She was willing to bet that Nelson Parker did not know his seventeen-year-old daughter was out on the streets or what she was doing there.

In that moment, Reese was glad Bri wasn't her daughter. She was positive she would make a mess of handling what didn't have to be a problem. As she walked east back to City Hall, she thought about herself at seventeen. She had never had the desire to sneak out to be with anyone, male or female, and for the first time in her life, she wondered why not.

CHAPTER NINE

After the bars closed at one a.m., the street in front of Spiritus Pizza was a mob scene for another hour. Predominantly male, the numbers swelled as those who had yet to find partners for the night cruised each other hoping for a last-minute connection. There were also a fair number of onlookers of both sexes who just wanted to partake vicariously of the sexual energy that literally permeated the air. The party-like atmosphere would be sustained for the next twelve weeks as new vacationers and weekend visitors flooded into town, bringing with them the excitement of being openly gay and unafraid, perhaps for the only time all year.

Still, by 2:30 in the morning, the streets of Provincetown were deserted. Periodically, Reese walked down each of the narrow alleys between the crowded establishments to the harbor beach, checking that no one had decided to sleep off too much alcohol on the sand. High tide was at 5:40 a.m., and by then the waves, still vigorous even in the secluded harbor, would be up to the pilings of many of the buildings. Already, the decks behind the Pied and the Boatslip, two of the most popular lesbian and gay bars, were surrounded by water. Reese didn't intend to have any drownings on her watch.

She knew that the shadowed areas under the piers were favorite spots for quick sexual encounters, but she wasn't interested in busting two adults for a fast grope in the dark. She *was* on the lookout, however, for groups of teenagers hanging out on the beach. Nelson had warned her that drug use and distribution were becoming more of a problem with the youth of the small community. Many of the suppliers seemed to be teenagers from neighboring townships on the Cape.

Reese hated the drug scene and especially those individuals who prospered by drug dealing. Too often, the kids who tried drugs were persuaded by peers and motivated by the normal rebellious, unfocused discontent that seemed inherent in the nebulous world between childhood and adulthood. The suppliers were the real criminals, she had no doubt, and she was determined that Provincetown would become a very unpopular place to commit that particular crime.

The rest of the night progressed uneventfully, and, at six-fifteen a.m., Reese pulled up the short driveway to the rear of her house. She came to a stop, cut the engine, and sat for a moment looking at the person huddled on her back steps. Brianna Parker stared back at her with a steady and defiant gaze.

"You're early," Reese commented as she approached. "Class doesn't start for forty-five minutes."

Reese could tell by the look of surprise on Bri's face, a flicker of expression quickly masked, that Bri had not been thinking of their seven a.m. appointment for her first *jujitsu* class.

"Come in the kitchen and wait while I shower and change," Reese said as she passed the teenager, then fit her key into the back door. She didn't look back as she walked inside, but she heard Bri follow.

"If you haven't eaten, there's bread for toast and juice in the fridge," Reese commented, tossing her keys on the table. She continued through to her bedroom, leaving the youth to sort things out for herself.

When she returned a quarter of an hour later in a clean white T-shirt and crisply ironed *gi* pants, she was pleased to smell coffee brewing. There was also a plate of toast sitting in the middle of the breakfast bar. Grabbing a piece to munch on, she poured a cup of the welcome coffee. "Thanks."

"No problem," Bri mumbled, not looking at her.

"So?" Reese leaned against the counter facing Bri, who was perched on one of the high stools flanking the center island that divided the cooking area from an eating area, which was large enough to accommodate eight at the modern glass-and-chrome table. "What's up?"

Bri stared at the woman facing her, impressed despite her discomfort by the taut muscles outlined under the tight T-shirt and the piercingly direct gaze. The sheriff presented an awesome figure, and thinking about her coming upon Carre and her in the alley the night before made Bri's stomach hurt just a little. She took a deep breath and plunged ahead. "I came to talk to you about last night," she managed to say without a hint of the unsteadiness she felt.

"I thought you came to train," Reese responded evenly.

"Maybe you won't want me to now," Bri said, a slight quiver in her voice.

Reese raised an eyebrow, her eyes never leaving the troubled teen's face. "How so?"

Bri shrugged. "I...I came to ask you not to tell my dad."

"I wasn't planning to. But you should."

"Yeah, right," Bri snorted. "Like he wouldn't kill me."

"He's got to know sometime. Maybe you should give him a chance," Reese suggested mildly as she refilled her coffee cup. "I don't know him real well, but he seems to be okay about the gay thing."

"Oh, sure. It's okay with him, *maybe,* for some other kids... but not for me."

"You're right." Reese studied Bri seriously. "There's no way to tell how he's going to react. But, for sure, he is going to be a lot better about it if he hears it first from you. I could have been anybody, Bri."

"I *will* tell him. Just not now." Her fear broke through, and her eyes filled with tears. "We're only seventeen. He can keep me from seeing Caroline if he wants to. And if *her* father finds out, he'll kill her."

The girl's anguish was evident, and Reese suddenly realized how many additional terrors being gay added to the already tumultuous world of adolescence. It was something she didn't know much about, and in a town like Provincetown, she truly needed to. She did know that an informed decision couldn't be formulated in a void. So, for the moment at least, she didn't know enough to make a reasonable decision or to offer meaningful advice.

"I'm not going to say anything to your father, and if I decide it's necessary at some point, I'll tell you first. You can decide then from whom he hears it, if you haven't already told him. In the meantime, I want your word that you and your girlfriend will stop meeting in dark alleys or under the pier."

Bri tried to cover her surprise. *How does she know about the pier?*

"It's dangerous, Bri, especially for two women." Reese raised her hand against Bri's protest. "There's no point in pretending that you and Caroline could stand up to a bunch of guys. That's not sexist. That's reality. One way a woman defeats a man is to use her brains—first to avoid the fight and then, if she must fight, to win the fight. Don't stack the odds against yourself."

"There's nowhere for us to go," Bri muttered, knowing the truth of Reese's words. "That's why I need to learn to fight."

"Self-defense is one of the many reasons to train." Reese crossed the kitchen into the hallway beyond and returned with a folded bundle, which she handed to Bri. "This is your uniform, your *gi*. It is only to be worn in the *dojo*, when we train. It will take time and patience and a lot of work on your part, but I *will* teach you to defend yourself. Is that still what you want?"

Bri reached for the uniform. For her, it represented her first steps toward self-determination. "Yes."

"Then let's get started. Dr. King told me your leg was better, but today is just an introduction. You can get dressed in the bathroom down the hall."

After Bri changed into the uniform Reese had provided her, she followed Reese through the breezeway to the garage. She copied Reese's actions, bowing at the threshold before entering the thirty-by-forty-foot space. After removing her shoes, she placed them beside the expanse of mat-covered floor. She waited uncertainly as Reese crossed to the center of the mat, knelt, and rested her hands gently on her thighs.

"Kneel and face me," Reese said. When Bri complied, Reese continued, "It is customary for the student to bow to the teacher, or *sensei,* at the beginning and end of each class. This is not to show obeisance but to convey respect and to offer thanks for the opportunity to train. I will also bow to you, to honor your commitment to learn."

After the initial ceremony was completed, Reese stood and motioned Bri to her feet. "Basics first. You need to learn how to fall before I can teach you to throw. You need to learn how to block before I can teach you to punch and kick. *And* you need to learn to move out of the line of attack before I can teach you how to counter an attack. These are the foundations for all that you will learn in the months, and hopefully the years, to come."

Bri nodded her understanding, eager to begin and anxious to prove her serious desire to learn. In the hour that followed, Reese introduced her to the fundamentals of *jujitsu*, demonstrating forward and backward rolls, proper fighting stances, blocking drills, and the first joint locking technique.

Bri was young, supple, and athletic. She made good progress. She concentrated on Reese's every move, trying to imitate the way her teacher stood, turned, and rolled. It seemed impossible to her that she would ever be able to attain the grace and power that Reese manifested with every move, but she was determined to try.

"Grab my lapel," Reese instructed. As Bri complied, Reese said, "*Kata dori,*" the Japanese term for the attack. Reaching up, she trapped Bri's hand against her shoulder, turned her wrist, and with both hands applied a wristlock. "Go with it. Don't resist. We're training, not fighting here."

Bri gasped sharply at the pain in her stretched wrist but held on wordlessly. As Reese leaned slowly toward her, the escalating pressure in her wrist forced Bri to her knees.

"*Kata dori—nikkyo.*" Reese named the defensive maneuver.

When Bri stood, Reese grasped her lapel. "Now you."

Bri repeated the movements, exactly as she remembered Reese had done, and was awestruck as Reese went to her knees before her.

"Very nice," Reese commented. Bri flushed with pride. "These techniques are powerful and potentially devastating. They are only to be used here in the *dojo* or on the street when you have no other choice but to use them."

"Yes, *sensei,*" Bri answered quietly.

Reese turned away with a smile. She sensed that Bri would be a good student, and she had enjoyed the chance to teach her. At the end of the session, Reese showed Bri where to store her *gi* and explained how to clean the training space so it would be ready for their next meeting.

They then bowed to each other, and Reese knelt to carefully fold her *hakama,* the black skirt-like garment worn by experienced practitioners. Bri lingered tentatively at the door and Reese looked over to her, a question in her eyes.

"Can I come tomorrow?" Bri asked softly.

"If you come, we will train."

Bri smiled and bowed slightly, naturally. "Thank you."

Reese bowed back, watching as Bri walked away down the drive. She remembered the feeling of excitement when she had first begun training more than twenty years ago and reflected upon how her training had enriched her life. She hoped this experience would allow Bri to find that balance, too. At the moment, however, there were more pressing things to consider. And much more that she herself needed to learn.

CHAPTER TEN

"Morning, Chief," Reese said when she entered the station an hour later.

"What are you doing here?" Parker asked abruptly.

"Sir?" Reese halted halfway to her desk and regarded him in surprise.

"Didn't you just finish the night shift a couple of hours ago?"

"Yes, sir, but I'm scheduled to work today."

"Conlon," the sheriff said with a sigh, "you're a civilian now. I know I told you that you needed to be available twenty-four hours a day if I needed you, but I didn't mean that you actually had to *work* twenty-four hours a day."

"I know that, Chief, but I offered to take Smith's shift without clearing it with you, and I fully expected to work today. Really, I'm fine. I slept last night between shifts." She made a detour toward coffee, adding over her shoulder, "Grabbing sleep at odd hours is not a problem. When I was on active duty, it was necessary for some of the night ops, and there'll be more of the same on my Reserve drill weekends."

He looked at her in exasperation, but he wasn't angry. She just didn't have any idea how unusual she was. Any other officer, no matter how good he or she might be, would have jumped at the chance to be relieved of a shift. She seemed to actually want to take hers. Being single and new in town, she probably hadn't had much of an opportunity to make friends, but at the rate she was going, she never would. That she seemed perfectly content with her solitary life perplexed him. Such single focus dedication was rare in a man, but in a young woman like her—he was at a loss to figure it.

"Okay, okay. But no more doubles unless I approve it." He caught the flicker of unease in her usually impenetrable gaze. "What?"

She faced him, squaring her shoulders, unconsciously coming to attention. "I told Smith I would take the last half of his shift until his baby is born. It shouldn't be more than a few days. I didn't clear it with you because you told me that as deputy sheriff I had authority to reorganize the shifts as needed."

"Well, I *was* thinking more along the lines of an emergency when I told you that, Conlon, although having a baby certainly feels like an emergency at the time. With any luck his won't be two weeks late like mine was." He shrugged in defeat, leaning back in his swivel chair to gaze up at his tall second in command. "Go ahead, Reese, but take time off during the day if you need it. I'm depending on you to keep things organized around here this summer. We've got a small force, compared to the size of the crowds we'll have to deal with, and Smith probably won't be worth a fart in a windstorm once his kid is born."

"Yes, sir. Thank you."

"Speaking of kids—did mine show up at your place for her class this morning?"

"Yes, she did."

"On time?"

"She was early."

"Good. I thought she must either have been up and out early or that she slept through it. She didn't answer when I knocked on her door this morning."

Reese said nothing. She was pretty sure that Bri hadn't been home at all the night before, and she was uncomfortable keeping that from her boss, a man she was coming to like. On the other hand, Bri wasn't exactly a child, and Reese felt she owed her the chance to work things out with her father in her own way. At least for the time being, she had given her word to keep silent. Besides, she was fairly certain she could keep an eye on Bri's nighttime excursions, now that she was aware of them.

"She do okay?" he asked gruffly. He felt as if he knew less and less about his daughter with each passing day. They didn't talk as they used to when she was small, when he seemed to have all the answers to her endless questions. Now he didn't have a clue as to what motivated his only child or what might make her happy. He couldn't help but think that if his wife were still alive, she would know what to do with their headstrong offspring.

"She did very well."

"Yeah?" he said with a smile of pride. "Good."

"Who's out on traffic?" Reese asked, not wanting to linger on the topic of Bri. "Jeff?"

"Yeah. Things won't get busy until eleven or so when the tour buses start arriving."

"I'm going to catch up on some paperwork, then, and go out around noon. That okay?"

"Sure. I have to be at the town meeting at ten. There's likely to be some heat over the application to build that condo unit out at the end of Route 6. The mayor wants me to talk about the manpower shortage and more tourist influx. Same old story."

"Gladys coming in for the phones?"

"You bet. Eleven till seven."

"Right," Reese said, pulling a stack of evaluation forms, payroll vouchers, and other employee paperwork in front of her. "I'll catch up with you at Town Hall then."

Nelson Parker nodded and tossed a wave as he headed out the door.

Reese left several hours later, leaving her patrol car at City Hall and walking west along Commercial to get lunch at the Cheese Shop. She carried her sandwich to a small sitting area behind the Galleria, a collection of shops catering to the tastes of quick-stop tourists who wanted a piece of "authentic" Cape Cod memorabilia. The deck in the rear was equipped with picnic tables and offered a great view of the harbor. Reese sat on the bench with her back to the table so she could watch the tide on its way out. The sight and smell of the water settled her in some deep way for which there were no words. She only knew she would never live far from the ocean again.

She glanced east along the shore, trying to pick out her mother's studio. An image of her mother, father and her on one of their rare family outings to the beach materialized in her mind. It hadn't been too long before her mother left. She had never asked him about her mother, had never tried to find her—before now. She wondered why that had been. Her father and she were as close as a stern, reserved man and a solitary, private daughter could be. She respected him, even if she did not always agree with him, and he was proud of her accomplishments.

The general was deeply disappointed, however, when she left active duty, even though she remained in the Reserves. They had not spoken since her move to Provincetown. He did not know she had contacted her mother; she wasn't even sure he knew that his ex-wife lived here. She had no doubt, though, that her father knew exactly where *she* was and what she was doing. She hadn't kept it a secret from him, and he had friends and contacts all over the world. If he wanted information, he would have no trouble getting it. Reese knew she needed to call him soon, but she wasn't sure quite what to say.

That thought brought Brianna Parker to mind and the rift that seemed to be growing between her and Nelson. Maybe part of it was the inherent differences between fathers and daughters, like men and women, but Reese knew that for Bri it was much more than that; there was also the complication of her sexuality. If she were to help Bri in any real way, she needed to know more about that.

She stood, adjusted her cap against the sun's glare, and moved quickly through the crowded aisle back to the street. A few minutes later, she was at the gym.

Marge greeted her with a grin. "Hey you, anything new?"

"Nope," Reese replied, grinning back. "But I would like to talk to you. Can you get away sometime this afternoon?"

"How about now? Annie's here. She can watch the place. Is this business or pleasure?"

"Let's say it's personal."

"Damn! You're a tough woman to get information out of."

Reese nodded toward the door. "Come on. Let's take a walk."

They joined the crowds and started toward the far west end of Commercial Street. There, the narrow one-way road joined the confluence of 6A and Route 6 at the jetty that led to Long Point. They didn't say much until they had settled on the same bench where Reese and Victoria King had sat a few days before. Reese scanned the narrow, treacherous walkway, amazed once again that Tory had braved it.

"So, what's up?" Marge asked, startling Reese for a second.

Reese pushed the image of Victoria King's face from her mind. "Did you know that you were a lesbian when you were a teenager?"

"I had a pretty good idea."

"How did you handle it?"

"I tried to kill myself," Marge said after a moment's consideration.

Reese stared at her intently, her chest tight, sorrow for Marge's pain mixed with rage at a world that would drive a young person to such desperation. Her jaw clenched while she searched for words. At last, she asked, "Can you tell me about it?"

Marge gazed out to the ocean, lost in memory. "It wasn't quite as dramatic as you might think. I grew up in a little town in the middle of nowhere. My parents were good, hardworking people without much imagination. I was a surprise, you might say. From the time I was small, I preferred boys' clothes, boys' games, boys' toys. All I wanted for my birthday was a six-shooter and a pair of jeans. My parents thought if they bought me dolls, I would forget about the guns. It didn't work."

"I'll bet." Reese laughed softly, remembering how special she'd felt the first time her father had given her a pistol. Only hers had never been toys.

"By the time I was ten," Marge continued, "I was in love with the rec director at the playground down the street. She was tough and taught the girls to play baseball. If I got there before everyone else, she would play catch with me. Ha! I got there early every day for an entire summer."

Marge reached down for a pebble and began to roll it between her fingers. "By twelve, I had a special girlfriend I would gladly have died for. We went everywhere together, spent every evening in one another's houses, and slept over with each other frequently. We never touched—not in a sexual way—but there was no doubt that I loved her in the way boys and girls do. Our friendship lasted into high school. One day, when we were sixteen, she told me she had been to bed with her boyfriend. Up until then, we had both dated, but no one had ever come between us. Not like that."

Marge drew a quick deep breath, and Reese could see the pain of memory etched in the lines around her mouth. "At that moment, my life changed forever. I knew then that she didn't feel what I felt and never would. She was no longer mine, in the deepest part of herself, the way she had been. It broke my heart, and there was no one to tell."

"I'm sorry," Reese murmured, knowing there were no words to heal this particular sorrow.

"It was a long time ago, but it was probably the greatest pain of my life." Marge tossed the pebble into the marsh opposite where they sat. "I had no idea what was to become of me. It felt like everything beautiful in my life just...disappeared. My innocence certainly died. I couldn't stand the pain, and I knew I felt the way I did because I was somehow very different from my girlfriends. I had no name for it, except 'queer,' and I knew that was not a good thing to be. So, I started to drink and managed to stay drunk through my last year in high school. That's what I meant when I said I tried to kill myself. It wasn't pretty, but it was very nearly effective."

She took another deep breath and let it out slowly, shaking off the vestiges of the past. Turning questioning eyes to Reese, she asked, "What made you ask?"

"A girl," Reese said. "A girl who can't tell her father she's in love with another girl. She acts pretty tough, but I get the feeling she's scared. Mostly scared that someone will keep them apart, I think. I'm trying to understand what that's like."

"Why?" Marge asked, not with censure, but with true curiosity. "What makes you care?"

Reese shrugged. "I have a feeling she's not the only kid in town in this situation, Provincetown being what it is. She says she has nowhere to go to be with her girlfriend. I need to understand what life is like for these kids, if I'm going to interact with them fairly."

"They're not like other kids, Reese. They have to fight hard to survive. Most of the time the whole world tells them they shouldn't be the way they are—they shouldn't dress the way they do; they shouldn't enjoy the things they do; and God knows, they shouldn't love the way they do. The boys get beat up, or they act out sexually all over the place in unsafe ways. More often than not, the girls who admit to themselves what they feel end up leaving school or underachieving. If they're not being self-destructive with drugs or alcohol, they're getting into trouble some other way. You'll do them more harm than good if you try to prevent them from being who they are. That's about all they have."

"I can't let them have sex in dark alleys or under the pier."

"Why not?"

"Because it's not safe," she stated adamantly. "If I can't see them, I can't protect them. If a group of redneck toughs stumbles across two boys, or two girls for that matter, making out in some dark corner, they could do them real damage."

"You've got a point, but there isn't much you can do about it," Marge acknowledged reluctantly. "They have to be together somewhere, and most likely, it won't be at parties, or dances, or at each other's homes, the way it is for straight kids. These kids feel like outcasts, and just about everything they see and hear reinforces that. They don't have much alternative to the dunes or the piers if they want privacy."

"A coffee house?"

"Good idea, but you have to remember that, although Provincetown looks like the center of the gay world, most of these lesbians and gay boys don't live here. After the season ends, this town is about as prejudiced as any other. And the few gay kids aren't going to want to make any public announcements, I wouldn't imagine."

"But at least for the three or four months of the season, they can blend in a little," Reese observed, seeing the dilemma Bri and her girlfriend faced. "Isn't there some place these kids can go?"

Marge nodded. "There's a little hole in the wall out on Shank Painter Road that caters to the kids. The music is god-awful, and the food's even worse, but at least they're welcome there. A couple of old queens own the place. They don't sell alcohol until ten p.m., which is how they get around having underage kids in the bar."

"That's got to be just up the road from the station," Reese remarked, wondering if Nelson Parker gave the place any thought.

He certainly hadn't mentioned it to her as a place she ought to keep an eye on.

"Yeah. I think they're calling it the Lavender Lounge this year."

"Thanks, Marge. All the information helps. I didn't know about this place. I'll have to drop by."

"Reese," Marge warned, "if you go in there looking like a cop, you're going to scare some kids away. They don't have much as it is."

"Point taken," Reese remarked. "I'll go in disguise."

Yeah, right. With that build and that walk, she just about screams "cop." Marge chuckled. "Try not to be too conspicuous. Better yet, take a date."

"Are you volunteering?"

"Hell no. Then you'd just be more obvious." She laughed, then thought for a moment. "Why don't you ask the doc? She can interpret for you."

"I hardly think I need a guide," Reese said, suddenly uncomfortable with the conversation.

"I just meant that she's a lesbian, and she's good with the kids," Marge said, not missing her friend's discomfort. "Hey, Reese. Did you ever have a crush on one of your girlfriends?"

Reese stood abruptly, her face expressionless. "I didn't have any girlfriends. All my friends were Marines."

As Marge joined her for the walk back to town, she wondered about the strange life her new friend had lived.

CHAPTER ELEVEN

"Reese—you there?"

Reese fingered the button on the microphone clipped to her shirt.

"I copy, Gladys."

"See the couple at the Lobster Pot. There's a child missing."

"Ten-four," Reese said curtly. On foot, she hurried the few blocks to the restaurant. It was not unusual for children to wander away from their parents, but it was always cause for concern. Traffic was heavy and unpredictable, and with the miles of beachfront, the water posed a very real danger as well. She found anxious parents and a boy who looked to be about ten waiting for her just outside the restaurant.

"I'm Deputy Sheriff Conlon," she said. "What happened?"

"It's our daughter," the father, a youngish fair-haired man in polo shirt and shorts, said anxiously. "She's lost. We were just walking along, looking in the windows. When we stopped for ice cream for the kids, Sandy was gone. We thought Greg—"

"Bill," his wife interrupted in a cautionary tone.

"It's my fault," the young boy, a near carbon copy of his father in appearance and dress, said tremulously. "I was supposed to be holding her hand. But then a couple of guys on rollerblades came between us, and we got separated. She was still right beside me..."

When he broke into sobs and hung his head, his mother pulled him close. "It's all right, Greg, we'll find her. It's not your fault."

"How long ago did you last see her?" Reese asked gently, trying to keep them calm.

The husband and wife looked at each other in confusion.

"Maybe a half-hour?" the father said tentatively.

"And her full name?"

"Sandra Lynn James. She's six."

"What is she wearing?" Reese continued, jotting notes on her small pad.

"Blue jeans, a yellow T-shirt, and red sneakers," her mother informed Reese.

"Sheriff," the father said softly, "our daughter is handicapped."

Reese looked up quickly. "How?"

"She can't communicate very well. She's not very verbal and is easily distracted. She won't react the way a child usually does if they're lost."

"What will she do?"

He shrugged. "It's hard to say. She might sit for hours watching something that catches her attention, or she may just wander."

"Can she swim?"

The mother stifled a cry and grasped her husband's hand.

"No," he said desperately.

"Tell me what she likes. What does she like to do?"

For a moment, both parents appeared confused.

"She likes the color red," her brother said into the silence.

"Good man," Reese said. "What else?"

"And she loves birds, any kind of birds." He took a step toward Reese, his face determined. "I want to go with you—to look for her."

Reese knelt down until her face was level with his. "Your parents are pretty upset. I need you to stay with them, to make sure they're okay. And I need you to think of anything else about your sister that will help us find her. I'm going to give you a special number that you can call to reach me anytime. Okay?"

He searched her face, then nodded. "Okay."

"Good," she said as she straightened. She stepped away out of the family's hearing range and keyed her mike. "Gladys?"

"Go ahead, Reese," a static-laden voice replied.

"Wake up Smith and have both him and Jeff Lyons call me. Inform the chief and Dr. King of what we have. If someone finds a little girl, they may take her to the clinic. I'll get you a full description in a minute."

"I'll make the calls right away."

Reese turned to the family. "I want you to wait at the police station. I'll have an officer take you there in a minute. I'm going to start a store-by-store search back along the way you came. Do you have a picture I can take?"

"Yes," the child's mother replied, fumbling through her handbag for her wallet. "Here's her school picture." She smoothed the picture tenderly with the tips of her fingers before handing it to Reese. "Please find her, Sheriff."

Reese tucked the photo into her front shirt pocket. "Yes, ma'am, I will."

She radioed headquarters as she walked to the nearest shop. "Gladys, have Smith pick up this family and transport them to the station, and tell Lyons to start a car check at the town line." She gave Gladys a detailed description to relay to everyone involved. "I'll have copies of a photograph brought around to you as soon as I can, too."

"You don't think someone took her?" Gladys gasped in alarm.

"It's routine, Gladys," Reese replied grimly. "And call me with any information you get, okay?"

"Absolutely."

Reese spent the next two hours personally talking to every shopkeeper west of the last place where the Jameses were sure their daughter had been with them. She scanned the crowds constantly, checking the benches and doorways along the route where the child might have stopped. There was no sign of Sandra James. Finally, she phoned the station to speak with Nelson Parker.

"It's no good, Chief. We need more help. It's going to be dark in an hour and a half, and it will be twice as hard to sort through the crowds. She's either injured somewhere, someone has her, or she's hiding somehow. Can you get volunteers to start a street-by-street search with a copy of her picture?"

"Yeah. There's a women's health group that's pretty organized. They can pull people together faster than I can at random. Where do you want them?"

"Have them meet me at Town Hall in half an hour."

On her way there, Reese stopped to have more photocopies made of Sandy's picture. She was gratified to find fifteen people waiting for instructions when she arrived. As she handed out the child's picture and organized the volunteers into pairs with specific assignments, she saw Victoria King and her office staff arrive. She motioned for the doctor to join her.

"Did you speak with her parents?" Reese asked.

"Yes."

"Is there anything special I should tell the volunteers about the child?"

"Aside from what sounds like some form of autism, she's perfectly healthy. My biggest concern is that it's getting colder, and if she's out all night, hypothermia is a real threat, especially if she's gotten into the water."

"I know. I want her found before dark." Reese turned back to the searchers, repeating her instructions. When all the teams had been dispersed, she walked back to where Tory waited. "I've got the Coast Guard out scanning the shore and the water. Where will you be if I need you?"

"Randy and Sally are both out looking, so I closed the office. I might as well wait there. You can page me. I've got the Jeep, so I'm mobile. Here's my card," she said, scribbling her beeper number on the back. "Will you call me when you have something?"

She searched Reese's face, knowing that the sheriff must be feeling the stress. The dark blue eyes were more intense than usual, if that was possible, and her voice was a little brusque, but her face betrayed nothing of her emotions. Tory couldn't help but wonder at what cost the stoic sheriff maintained her calm. As a physician, she knew how high that price could be. *God, is she always this controlled?*

"Reese?"

Reese was staring out over the harbor, her concentration barely penetrated by Tory's voice. Softly she asked, "Do you see that?"

"What?" Tory followed her line of sight, perplexed. "The kites?"

"She likes birds, her brother said...and the color red." Her gaze followed a particularly decorative red wide-winged kite. "Red birds."

Tory stared at her, and then up at the sky. "Where would she go to get closer to them?"

"Toward the water. Maybe out onto one of the piers," Reese said grimly. "Will you call the chief and have him send one of the men out to check the piers at the west end? I'll start closer to where she was last seen."

"Yes, of course."

Reese gazed at Tory as she gently took her hand, then pressed her fingers lightly. "Thanks."

Tory felt the brief touch all the way to the bone. The sounds of the crowd receded as her eyes locked with Reese's. She was riveted in place, scarcely drawing a breath. In that moment, she realized that Reese Conlon was the most intriguing woman she had ever met. And she was beautiful. *And I'm in big trouble.*

Tory swallowed, wondering if she would ever be able to look away. Wondering if she even *wanted* to. Thankfully, someone demanded Reese's attention at that moment, and Reese released her hand, turning aside. Tory took a shaky breath. *Right, find a phone, Tory girl. You can do that. Just walk away from her. She has no idea what she's doing—she hasn't a clue to the effect she has on any lesbian with a heartbeat.*

And in the next instant, Tory realized with a start that that was probably true. Reese didn't know. And if she didn't know, what did that say about her? Tory considered what little she knew of Reese's past, and remembered the night they'd talked on her sofa. Reese had never mentioned a lover or a relationship. Only the Marines. Tory always assumed that Reese was a lesbian, because she seemed like one, and because Tory found her attractive. But perhaps she wasn't. Or perhaps she didn't *know* that she was.

Tory shook her head. *Either way, it lets me out. There's no way I'm getting involved with someone who's just coming out, or God forbid, straight.*

She watched Reese stride down the sidewalk toward the center of town and willed her heart to stop pounding. It didn't work, but she tried to tell herself it was only her worry over the little girl.

❖

It was close to eight o'clock when Tory tossed the last chart onto the cart beside her desk. It had been dark for two hours. She couldn't imagine how the parents must feel or how frightened the child must be. She hated it when children were sick. It was often impossible to explain to them what was happening or why she had to do things that hurt them. Too often, she simply had to do what needed to be done, accepting that sometimes she caused pain in the name of healing. But it never got easier.

She thought about K.T., the woman she had loved throughout college, med school, and residency—until it had ended four years ago. K.T. had a surgeon's wonderful, and often irritating, ability to detach herself at will from emotions that threatened her equilibrium. Indeed, it was a necessary skill for the operating room, but a deadly one for a relationship. K.T. had been so damn hard to resist, though, that Tory had forgiven her for every hurt but the last. Even her disarming grin and her pledge of undying love could not sway Tory then. That was part of the reason Tory needed to avoid any fantasies about the enigmatic deputy sheriff; Reese Conlon had that same irresistible quality of bravado and dashing appeal that K.T. had had. The sheriff might be charming, gallant, and brave, but she was dangerous, too. *Once was more than enough.*

Tory jerked in her seat when the phone rang.

"Yes?" she said abruptly.

"I have her, Doctor. We'll be there in five minutes. The parents are on their way," Reese stated over the cellular phone in her cruiser.

"What's her status?" Tory asked as she rose from behind her desk.

"She's not talking. She's not even crying. But I don't see any obvious injuries. We're just up the street—"

"Bring her back to the procedure room."

"Roger that."

Tory looked up a few moments later to find Reese standing in the door of her examining room with a bundle in her arms. A tousled blond head poked out of a green flak jacket emblazoned with the Marine Corps insignia.

"Put her up on the table," Tory indicated brusquely as she reached for a stethoscope. Reese settled the child carefully on the paper-covered surface as Tory turned to the little girl with a smile on her face.

"Hi, sweetie," she said. "I'm Dr. King. Can you tell me your name?"

She laid her hand gently on the child's knee as she spoke. The little girl's skin was cool to her touch. "Reese, there's a blanket in the warmer behind you. Get it for me, will you?"

"Sure." Reese wrapped the soft flannel around the young patient's shoulders as Tory placed a plastic thermometer sleeve against the child's earlobe. The little girl watched her in silence, but she didn't seem to be afraid.

"Her temperature is a little low, but not dangerously so," Tory commented as she placed the bell of her stethoscope against the small chest. She noted the strong, steady beat with satisfaction. Looking down, she realized the girl's shoes and socks were missing. "What happened to her shoes?" she asked as she slipped the stethoscope into her pocket.

"I took them off," Reese replied. "They were wet."

Now that she was satisfied that the child was in no danger, Tory really looked at Reese for the first time.

"You're soaked, Reese. What happened?"

Reese shrugged. "She climbed out to the edge of a tide pool, following the kites I think. The tide had come in quite a ways before I found her."

Tory shuddered inwardly at the image of a small child trapped by the swirling waters, unable to climb out and unlikely to be able to swim. She knew that rescue had come barely in time and only then because of the intelligence and tireless dedication of the woman beside her. A woman, she noted now, who was shivering slightly while she waited to help further. Gently she said, "You need to get out of those clothes, Reese."

"I'll stay if you need me," Reese responded quietly.

"No. Go on. She's fine. Her parents should be here soon."

"I've got clothes in the squad car. I'll just be a minute," Reese said, reluctant to leave. She had known instinctively that the little girl was in no danger before she brought her to the clinic, but now she was captivated watching Tory King work. Tory took charge with a degree of command that Reese was used to from years in the military, but with a gentleness and empathy that had been absent in the world of men that Reese had inhabited. Reese was moved in a way she didn't understand, stirred by the interplay of fierce concentration and compassionate warmth that suffused Tory's elegant features.

"*Go.*" Tory gave her a stern but fond look.

Reese smiled, snapping a crisp salute. "Yes, ma'am."

She slipped out as Sheriff Parker entered with the little girl's parents rushing before him. The satisfying sounds of relieved cries and a happy reunion followed her retreat.

It took a few moments for Tory to convince the child's parents that Sandra was absolutely fine, but finally, they relaxed after the hours of frantic worry. At length, she glanced toward the hall, stunned to silence by what she saw.

Reese stood quietly at the door, watching. She had pulled on a pair of faded gray sweat pants and a T-shirt, well-worn clothes that accentuated the sheer physicality of her form, stretching tight across her broad shoulders, exposing the highly defined muscles in her arms, clinging to her narrow hips and strong thighs. Tory's throat tightened as her heart raced. She wanted to look away; she wanted to deny the unmistakable wave of desire; she wanted not to find this unusual woman more beautiful than anything she had ever seen.

Mercifully, the parents spied Reese standing there and descended upon her, releasing Tory from the gaze that unwittingly held her captive. Reese was clearly uncomfortable with the attention as Mr. James gripped her hand, shaking it furiously as he exclaimed, "Thank you so much, Sheriff. I can't tell you how much we appreciate what you've done."

"You're welcome. Really," Reese responded, while trying to extricate her hand from his vise-like grasp. At last, he stepped aside, only to be replaced in an instant by his wife. She gazed up at Reese for a moment, her tear-reddened eyes fixed on Reese's. Then, unexpectedly, she laid her palm against Reese's cheek in a gentle caress.

"I don't know what I would have done if you hadn't found her," she whispered softly.

Tory watched, transfixed, as Reese tenderly placed her hand over the woman's trembling fingers and clasped them softly. "I would never let you lose your daughter," she murmured.

Reese's blue eyes lifted above the woman's head and found Tory's. The depth of her unguarded compassion was so clear that Tory was chagrined that she had ever questioned Reese's feelings. Her caring, exposed for an instant, had the intensity of a mortal wound.

Tory comprehended in that moment that what Reese hid so well, with her strict professionalism and rigid discipline, was a degree of empathy that clearly verged on painful. That she hid it unconsciously, probably even from herself, almost certainly came from years of habit. Tory had no doubt of that. She wondered what hurt had necessitated those barricades and found herself even more intrigued by the impossibly handsome, impossibly compelling sheriff.

Reese blushed under Tory's intense scrutiny, finally looking away. The parents continued their thanks as they gathered their children and followed Sheriff Parker out, leaving Tory and Reese alone in the sudden silence.

"Well, I—" Reese began.

"Have you—" Tory said simultaneously.

They laughed, both relaxing as the hours of tension finally dissipated. Reese leaned against the doorjamb and regarded Tory with a smile. "You were saying?"

"I'm starving. How about you?"

"I didn't have dinner, and I don't remember lunch." Reese glanced at her watch, frowning. "Unfortunately, it's eight-thirty on a Saturday night. We'll never get in anywhere."

Tory held up one finger, motioning her to silence as she lifted the phone from the wall behind her. She dialed a number from memory. "Colleen? Tory King. Can you fit me in? Yes, right away would be great."

Pausing for a second, she glanced up at Reese. "No...for two." She laughed at the ensuing remarks, coloring slightly. "Don't jump to conclusions. We'll be right over.

"The Flagship," she said as she replaced the receiver. "Let's go."

"Wait a second," Reese protested, gesturing to her attire. "Look at me. I can't go like this."

Any further looking at Reese Conlon was exactly what Tory did *not* want to do. "You look great," she said, meaning it. "Besides, this is Provincetown. There *is* no dress code. No arguing."

For once, Reese accepted the order, sensing there was no room for negotiation. In truth, the crowd was casual as the hostess led them to a corner table with a beautiful view of the harbor. When chilled champagne in a bucket appeared at their side, she raised an eyebrow in question.

Tory shrugged, embarrassed. "Old friends. I know both the owners from Boston years ago." *And now they're trying to match- make.*

She busied herself pouring the champagne, disconcerted by Reese's silence. She looked across the table into Reese's searching eyes. "What?"

"Tell me about Boston," Reese replied. The look on Tory's face when she mentioned it told Reese that whatever had happened there haunted Tory still. She wanted very much to know what caused that fleeting glimmer of pain.

Tory could pretend she didn't understand but, in an unguarded moment, decided not to evade. She rarely spoke of her personal life, but she wanted to now. Reese was looking at her as if her next words were the only things that mattered, and Tory wanted her to know. She wasn't ready to ask herself why.

"I lived there for almost ten years, during my residency and a few years after. My lover trained there also, and we both went into practice at Boston General when we finished. Colleen and Sheila, the women who own this place, were good friends of ours. They moved here to follow their dream of owning a restaurant, and when K.T. left me, they convinced me to move here. At first, I thought it would just be temporary, until I got my life in order. But now I know that this *is* my life."

"Had you been together long, you and K.T.?" Reese was surprised at her own question, but this felt important, like something she needed to understand in order to know this woman better. And she wanted to know her better. Her eyes never left Tory's face.

"Since college. Almost twelve years." Without being asked, Tory continued. "I was an ER attending. She was a trauma surgeon and attractive as hell. All the women were after her, and finally, she strayed. I found her with one of the nurses in an on call room in the middle of the day. She said it was the first time, but I'll never know, will I? We separated a short time after that."

Tory couldn't keep the pain from her voice, and she was shocked to find tears in her eyes. Tears that she knew were not so much for K.T. but for her own disappointment in love.

"I'm sorry," Reese murmured, hearing the anguish in Tory's voice. "That was stupid of me. I didn't mean to open old wounds."

"Don't be sorry. It's not your fault." Tory's smile was bitter. "I thought what we had was forever. I was mistaken." She reached for her champagne and said softly, "I won't make that mistake again."

Reese understood the subject was closed. Searching for safer ground, she said, "My *dojo* is finished for all practical purposes. There are final touches that I saved for Bri to do. Still interested in training?"

"Absolutely," Tory responded enthusiastically, grateful to turn the conversation away from herself and genuinely eager to discuss their mutual interest in the martial arts. "When?"

"I thought your leg needed a week?"

"I estimated on the safe side. It's had some time. I'm fine."

Reese laughed. "You remind me of Bri. Always ready to go."

"Thanks, I think. How's she doing?"

"Really well, for her first time. She's got natural ability, and if she stays with it, she'll be good."

"I'm glad to hear it. She's needed some direction."

Reese debated discussing her concerns about Bri with Tory but decided she shouldn't betray the girl's confidence. She sensed Tory would know what to do if things got out of hand and resolved to talk to her if and when the need arose. "So how about a workout tomorrow morning? Seven-thirty?"

"I'll be there." Tory laughed ruefully, realizing that Sunday was no different than any other day of the week for Reese. She obviously had no concept of sleeping in. "Now let's order. I have to go home and go to bed."

Reese cocked an eyebrow in surprise before Tory's gentle laughter informed her of the joke.

The meal passed quickly as they spoke of the tourist season and exchanged light gossip about the small town's inhabitants. The food was excellent and the effect of the shared champagne relaxing. They had just ordered coffee when Tory realized that Reese's eyes were riveted on someone across the room.

"Something wrong?" Tory asked quietly.

"No. Excuse me a moment. I'll be right back." Reese rose and quickly moved away.

Tory glanced after her as Reese approached two women seated across the room. The pang of loneliness she felt at Reese's sudden absence surprised her. For a time, she had forgotten where she was or what she needed to do the next day. She had been totally immersed in the moment and enjoying Reese's company tremendously. The sheriff was unexpectedly insightful, humorous, and attentive. When they had talked, she had been entirely focused on Tory. She was a heady mixture of compelling characteristics and, considering how physically attractive she was, a dangerous combination as well. In that way, she reminded Tory of K.T., and for the briefest of instants, Tory panicked. Then she took a breath and reminded herself that they were just having dinner, not getting engaged.

Still, she was irrationally happy to see Reese threading her way back to their table. When Reese sat down, however, she seemed oddly subdued.

"Are you all right?" Tory asked at length.

"Yes, of course." Reese shrugged apologetically. "I'm sorry. I'm afraid I got distracted there. Where were we?"

"Do you know them well? Jean and Kate?" Tory asked.

"No, not really," Reese responded quietly. "Kate is my mother."

Tory was momentarily at a loss. *God, this woman is full of surprises. Her mother's a lesbian.* She remembered what Reese had said of her parents' divorce and her mother's subsequent absence, surmising that it must be a painful subject. Carefully, she asked, "Did you know that she was here in Provincetown?"

"I knew," Reese said as she slowly stirred her coffee.

"And...?"

"And—I'm not sure what, really," Reese admitted with a sigh. "I know she was part of the reason I came here, but I'm not sure what I hope to accomplish. I haven't told my father she's here, and that must mean something."

"Will he be angry?"

"I'm not sure. I think so. He still hasn't accepted my leaving active duty, and I'm certain he would think she was part of the reason."

"Was she?"

Reese was silent for a moment, staring across the moonlit harbor, trying to find the words to explain what she had felt six months ago when her life changed so drastically. She had given herself many reasons why the Marine Corps, the only family she had ever known, no longer suited her. She had given herself just as many reasons why Provincetown was the place she should be, but she had never admitted what part her mother's presence played in those decisions. She turned her gaze to Tory, hoping her confusion didn't show in her face. "I'm not sure."

Tory regarded her calmly, seemingly content to wait. There was no hint of judgment in her eyes, only kind acceptance. The tension ebbed from Reese's body, and she stretched her long frame before giving Tory a wan smile.

"Yes, I suppose she was," Reese said slowly. "I've known for a while she was here, but it's been years since we had any contact. I grew up trying not to think about her. Most of the time I succeeded. My father made it impossible for us to see one another when I was young, and we never spoke of her."

"That must have been very hard for you," Tory observed gently.

"Don't misunderstand," Reese said quickly. "I love my father, even though he was wrong. He probably acted out of wounded pride, but I never doubted that he loved *me*. Two things I always knew for sure—he loved me, and he loved the Marines. For most of my life, I loved the Marines, too."

"Oh, I don't doubt that." Tory laughed. "In uniform or out, you will always be a Marine." Suddenly serious, wanting very much to know, Tory asked, "So why *did* you leave? And why come here?"

It finally felt like time. Reese chose her words carefully, because it seemed important for Tory to understand. "I was born and raised a Marine. I had never questioned or thought of leaving that environment until a short while ago. Then I got restless, felt unsettled, and I just knew. I'd been living my father's dreams, my father's *life*. It was time to leave, time to build my own life. I think I wanted my mother to be part of it."

"I hope it works out," Tory said softly.

"Thanks." Reese nodded, pushing her empty cup to the side. She glanced at her watch and said apologetically, "I'm afraid I have to go. I have to get back to work. I'm still working splits."

"Of course," Tory replied, rising to walk out with her. She was growing accustomed to Reese's devotion to her job and also coming to recognize that working was what made her comfortable. She wished their evening wasn't at an end. And she wished even more that she hadn't enjoyed it quite so much.

Chapter Twelve

As Tory walked up the driveway of Reese's house at 7:20 the next morning, Brianna Parker, in a body-hugging black T-shirt, low-riding leather pants, and motorcycle boots, appeared from around the rear and started toward her. The split-level wood dwelling stood on a hill overlooking the wetlands at the end of Bradford Street, and when Tory stopped to appreciate the view, Bri halted silently by her side. Tory looked out over the marshes and dunes. They were alive with the flutter of gulls and other birds searching for breakfast.

"Hi, Bri," Tory said. "Pretty spectacular morning."

"Yeah, I guess," the teen responded unenthusiastically.

"Tough class?"

"No, it was great." Bri's face brightened. "*Sensei's* teaching me to breakfall."

"Already? Hey, that's terrific."

"Yeah." Bri looked away, her smile fading.

Tory had the feeling the youth was about to say more when she abruptly mumbled a goodbye, strode to a red motorbike, and retreated hastily. Watching her disappear in a torrent of dust and gravel, Tory wished she knew how to make a connection with the teenager. Each time she saw Bri, the girl seemed a little more withdrawn and a little more unhappy.

Realizing the time, Tory turned and hastened up the drive. The side door to the attached garage was open, and she stepped over the sill into a large square space that was almost completely covered with *tatami* mats, a traditional shock-absorbent material found on the floors of most *dojos* in Japan. Along the near wall were a bench and a rack for shoes. On the wall opposite the bench were a small hand-carved shelf with a vase of flowers, several ornamental statues, and a picture of a formidable-appearing Japanese man. Tory bowed in the direction of the *kamiza,* the traditional altar, to show her respect for the training hall and Reese's former teacher, then slipped her shoes onto the rack.

Reese had been kneeling on the mat with her eyes closed when Tory entered, and she looked up now with a smile. "Welcome. I'm glad you could make it."

"Thanks. I've been looking forward to it."

As she spoke, Tory sat down and leaned over to remove the metal brace from her right leg. She replaced it with a much lighter short plastic air cast that prevented her ankle from dropping into its paralyzed position.

"Tell me about that," Reese said, indicating the support.

Tory's hands tightened and her shoulders grew tense with the automatic resistance to any inquiry about her condition. Invariably, such an inquiry was accompanied by thinly disguised pity, discomfort, or misconception of her abilities. It didn't matter that Reese had never seemed the least bit judgmental or dismissive. Tory's response was fostered by years of anger and disappointment. She couldn't find the words to answer and didn't look up.

After a moment, Reese asked, "How long has it been since you've trained with anyone?"

"Since before my accident." Tory met her eyes defiantly.

"Well, then, I guess we'll just have to find out together what you can handle. Can you stand with that?"

Reese was so direct, and so matter of fact, that Tory relaxed.

"Yes, but I can't really walk well with it. My balance is affected."

"So we start from stationary positions. Can you take a fall?"

"No problem."

"Leg sweep? Shoulder throw?"

"Either," Tory stated with assurance, "as long as you don't sweep the bad leg." She decided not to add that no one had thrown her since her injury, but she had practiced her drills and cane defenses diligently since her rehab was finished. *I will be fine.* She hoped.

"I thought we might alternate," Reese continued. "We can work on grappling one day, and you can teach me the cane the next. Sound okay?"

"Yes, fine."

They bowed to one another, and for the next hour, Reese reviewed with Tory the fundamentals of *jujitsu* grappling techniques. Since Tory already held an advanced belt in a style that employed joint locks and takedowns, much of what they practiced was familiar to her with only slight variations. They were evenly matched in terms of stamina, thanks to Tory's rigorous conditioning from kayaking. Her mobility was hindered, but most of the techniques were designed for performance in very close quarters, and she was able to adjust.

When they bowed to one another at the end of their session, Tory felt invigorated in a way she hadn't for years. She felt strong and capable. She didn't want to stop, even though she knew she would be sore the next day.

"Thanks. That was excellent," Tory enthused as she folded her *gi* jacket.

"Yes," Reese agreed. "So, same time tomorrow?"

Tory hesitated, momentarily caught off guard. It hadn't occurred to her that Reese would want to train quite so seriously. *God, she's intense. Just the look in her eyes makes me want to say yes.*

"Absolutely," Tory replied, feeling pleasantly challenged by the offer. Reese rewarded her with a dazzling smile that burst from nowhere and seemed to flicker away all too quickly.

"If I have an emergency, I'll call—" Tory qualified.

"No need," Reese interrupted. "If you aren't here, I'm sure it will be for some very good reason. I know you'll make it when you're able."

"Are you always so centered? So unflappable?" Tory asked unexpectedly. "You never seem the least bit uncertain."

"Is that what you think?" Reese regarded her seriously. "I'm uncertain sometimes, just not about what I believe." She looked at Tory pointedly. "Or about whom I trust."

Tory blushed, pleased. Reese had a way of making things seem simple, and Tory suddenly felt as if she never wanted to disappoint her. That thought was enough to disturb her for the rest of the day.

❖

Tory managed to get to the *dojo* five or six mornings a week for the next two weeks, especially after discovering that if she rose an hour earlier every day, she still had time to kayak. She knew absolutely that Reese was up even earlier, because sometimes on her way to Herring Cove, she passed Reese out for a run. Tory wondered when the sheriff slept.

Most mornings, Bri was just leaving as Tory arrived at the *dojo*. Bri's determination and Reese's tirelessness were impressive. Happily, Tory found that her own endurance was increasing and noted with cautious optimism that her ankle and leg seemed a little stronger. She was moving better with the lighter air cast, and although she wasn't deluding herself with the hope that her leg would ever be normal, each small improvement cheered her.

In addition to the physical benefits of her new training regimen, she had to admit that Reese's company was the most enjoyable part of the whole experience. Reese was so single-minded, so focused, that it was exciting just to be around her. Tory tried not to think about just how much she looked forward to her time with Reese, or how much she liked Reese's slow, easy smile and her deep, resonant voice.

On the last Saturday in June, Reese was in her customary position, kneeling in the *dojo* with her eyes closed, meditating, when Tory arrived.

"Good morning, *sensei*," Tory murmured quietly as she entered, not wishing to disturb Reese's concentration.

Reese opened her eyes, smiled a greeting, and then bowed off the mat. She sat beside Tory on the bench while Tory got ready for their class.

"Was that Bri's girlfriend with her this morning?" Tory asked as she switched to the light splint. "I saw them out front as I was leaving."

"How did you know?" Reese asked in surprise. "Caroline came to watch a class."

Tory laughed. "I think it was the way she was hanging onto Bri, or maybe that she looked like she wanted to lick the sweat off Bri's neck."

"Not too subtle, are they?" Reese remarked almost grimly. When they had arrived, Bri had one arm flung possessively around the young blond's shoulders, and Caroline had her hand tucked into Bri's back pocket. It hadn't escaped Reese's notice that Caroline's eyes never left Bri the entire time they were in the *dojo*, and the look in them was positively hungry. She had hoped they would be a little more restrained on the street.

"Why should you expect them to be any different?" Tory frowned slightly. "It's young love. They don't have any awareness of anything but each other. They probably wouldn't notice a ten-car pile-up right in front of them most of the time." She smiled to herself as she stood and tied her *gi* top. "Does Nelson know about this?"

"No," Reese said with some concern. "Bri is afraid to tell him. She's afraid he'll try to keep them apart."

"She might be right," Tory acknowledged with a sigh, "but there's no way they'll be able to keep it quiet for much longer. Especially not if they go anywhere together in the light of day. Anyone who's ever been in love, or lust for that matter, could tell with just one glance."

Reese wondered briefly if *she* would have known if she hadn't found them locked in one another's arms that night. Would she recognize what she'd never experienced? Was there really something so consuming that she could lose herself, and her eternal vigilance, even for a minute?

"Maybe I should say something to her," she mused aloud.

Tory answered carefully, fighting her own defensiveness. "Reese, those girls are acting like any two teenagers in love. They're high school seniors, nearly adults. If you ask them to hide what they feel, you're telling them there's something wrong with what they're doing. It would be devastating for them if someone they obviously trust took that stance. You must realize Bri trusts you, or she never would have brought her girlfriend here. She's asking you for your acceptance."

"I'm worried about them," Reese countered. "A young gay boy was beaten up outside a bar in Truro two weeks ago, and I saw a report from Easton yesterday about a suspicious robbery of two gay men that looked like gay-bashing. We haven't had any problems here, yet."

Tory frowned at the news. "I'll certainly keep an eye out at the clinic for anything that looks like it was gay-motivated. But the best thing you can do for those two girls is exactly what you are doing. Keep the streets safe and offer them a supportive adult presence."

"I'm not too comfortable in that role," Reese admitted. "No firsthand experience."

"It's no different from what straight teenagers experience, Reese." Tory regarded her with more than a tinge of disappointment. It was pretty clear from that admission that Reese wasn't gay. She hated to admit she had been hoping otherwise. "It's just more difficult for some of them who are afraid or, sadly, ashamed. Just remember your first time."

"That's my point, Tory," Reese said quietly, her expression almost rueful. "I never had a first time, so I'm afraid I can't be much of an advisor or support to anyone else."

The statement was delivered so matter-of-factly that Tory wasn't sure how to respond. Was it possible that a thirty-something woman, especially such an interesting, attractive one, had never been in love? Or was she simply saying she had never been a crazy teenager in the throes of hormonal insanity?

Thankfully, Reese saved her from further confusion by saying, "A few weeks ago, Marge said that there's a bar where a lot of the gay kids go. I've been meaning to check it out, but Marge keeps insisting that I look too much like a cop. Would you consider going undercover with me to take a look?"

"Reese," Tory said, trying to keep a straight face, "there is nothing on this earth that could make you look like anything *but* a cop. But sure, I'll go with you. When?"

"How about tonight? After dinner? Dinner is my treat."

"Tonight is fine, and it's your treat only if it's on me next time."

Reese smiled. "Deal."

As Tory knelt to bow in for the start of their workout, she wondered just what she had let herself in for. After a moment, however, she didn't have time to think about anything at all. By their very nature, their workouts were intimate in the sense that, of all the styles of martial arts, *jujitsu* was the one that required the most physical contact. Usually, such contact was automatic and completely devoid of any sensual connotation, as the mind and body engaged in the priority of self-defense.

As they worked on a finishing pin, Reese literally lay across Tory's body, applying pressure to her elbow and wrist. Tory's only goal was to dislodge her. Being held flat on her back with her arm locked out and a forearm pressed against her trachea was not a position Tory relished. She responded instinctually, thrashing and twisting to free herself.

Reese felt Tory struggling as she attempted to reverse the pin. Immediately, Reese let up on the pressure against Tory's wrist joint. "Tory, wait," she said firmly.

Tory immediately relaxed. This was not a contest; it was a training session. And as the most experienced stylist, Reese was in charge.

Reese pushed herself up on her arms, looking down at Tory with a smile. The weight of her body rested lightly along the length of Tory's body. "You'll wear yourself out if you thrash like that, especially if your opponent is much heavier."

"I..." Tory looked up into the blue eyes just inches above her own, and suddenly, the *dojo* receded. Instantly, she felt the pressure of Reese's thigh between her legs. She was aware of the firmness of Reese's body, the subtle swell of her breasts beneath the cotton *gi,* and the faint blush of perspiration on her tanned chest. Tory's heart beat a little faster, and her skin tingled where Reese's fingers held her. She had the insane desire to press her lips against the moist skin of Reese's neck. Shocked at the sudden wetness between her thighs, she gasped at the onslaught of sensations.

"What is it?" Reese exclaimed, immediately rolling off her. "Did I hurt you?"

"No," Tory replied, acutely embarrassed. In all the years she had been training, nothing like this had ever happened. She had to drag her senses away from the impact of the woman beside her. *Trouble, trouble, trouble.* Her body trembled. *Fool, fool, fool.*

"Tory?" Reese continued, worried. Tory was shaking; she could see it. The very thought that Tory was hurt made her stomach clench. They were lying side by side, inches apart. Reese reached out instinctively, brushing her fingers against Tory's cheek. "Is it your leg?"

"No, Reese, it's not my leg." Tory sat up, struggling to keep her voice calm. "Just a cramp. It's gone now."

Tory looked into the troubled face, knowing Reese didn't have a clue about what had just happened. She fought to ignore the persistent throbbing between her thighs. *God. Does she have to be so damned attractive?*

"Really, I'm okay." Tory moved a few inches away. "Let's just switch techniques for a while."

"You're sure?"

"Absolutely."

They finished their workout, both unusually subdued. Tory was trying to keep her mind off what had been an unmistakable rush of potent physical desire. Reese was trying to understand why the mere thought of Tory in pain moved her in a way nothing ever had.

"Do you want to take a day or two off?" Reese asked after they finished.

Tory glanced at her, seeing the concern in her face. *It's not fair to make her worry just because you can't control yourself.*

"What's the matter, Sheriff?" she teased lightly. "Are you tired?"

"No, I just thought..." Reese stopped, blushing slightly. "I guess you'll tell me if you need a break, huh?"

"You can trust me to take care of myself." Tory smiled gently, finding Reese even more attractive in her slight embarrassment. "But thanks for asking."

Reese grinned. "Marge would say I'm doing my butch thing. Right?"

It was Tory's turn to blush. *And exactly how would Marge know?* She busied herself with her gear, rejoining, "Actually, yes. But on you it just seems natural. Don't worry about it."

"So, I'll see you tonight?"

"Yes, of course."

❖

They met outside Front Street, a restaurant in the center of town favored by locals and tourists alike. Reese wore a white open-collared shirt, crisp blue jeans, and highly polished black boots. Tory was equally casual in black jeans and a scoop-neck black singlet that highlighted her well-developed shoulders and arms.

Reese had called ahead for reservations, and they were seated immediately. The waitress, who knew Tory by name and Reese by the usual town gossip network, was attentive in an unobtrusive way. Tory was aware that they turned more than a few heads as the restaurant filled up. Reese seemed totally unaware of the attention, sipping a glass of red wine as she leaned back in her chair, recounting for Tory the four years she had been stationed in Japan.

"The part I loved best, of course, was the opportunity to train with the Japanese at one of their own schools. My teacher in the States had written ahead with an introduction, which helped pave the way. The Japanese are much more receptive to American students than they used to be, including women, but it certainly helped to have a personal connection. I had been training for over ten years by the time I got there, which didn't hurt either." Reese grinned a little ruefully as she emptied her glass. "I'm boring you, aren't I?"

"On the contrary," Tory remarked, reaching to fill both their glasses. "I was just thinking how I envied you. My own training took a back seat to my rowing for many years. About the time you were in Japan, I was getting ready for Seoul."

Reese caught the flicker of pain that clouded Tory's expressive features for an instant before the other woman visibly drew herself out of the past. Reese reached spontaneously for her hand and held it gently. "I'm sorry for the pain, Tory. You don't have to talk about it—"

Tory shook her head. "I'm pretty well over it. It's just so damn frustrating. I had come close to winning the gold in the previous Olympics, and I was in the best shape of my life. It was just a warm-up run, not even the preliminary heats. One minute I was flying. The sun was on my back, the surface was perfect, like glass, and I knew it was my time. The *next* thing I knew, they were fishing me off the bottom with my leg in pieces. I looked down at my foot hanging there..." Distant anguish flickered across her face. "I couldn't feel it, and I knew my Olympic moment was all over."

"Tory," Reese breathed softly, wishing desperately that she could turn back time, erase the past. She'd give anything to return Tory to that golden moment just before the accident and make it as if it had never happened.

Tory took a deep breath, dispelling the memory. "Then I spent the next year just hoping I would walk again." She looked at Reese apologetically. "Now, *this* is really awful dinner conversation."

As Tory talked, she had unconsciously entwined her fingers with Reese's. She studied their interlaced fingers now as they lay against the white tablecloth. Reese's compassion and unspoken sympathy seemed to flow into her through those long, strong fingers. It was comforting and not the least bit pitying.

"Reese," she said quietly, her throat suddenly dry. "If people see us like this, they're going to assume this is a date." She kept her voice light, but she couldn't control the slight quiver in it. She felt raw and uncomfortably vulnerable.

"Are you telling me it isn't?" Reese asked gently, no hint of banter in her voice.

Tory jerked in surprise, her pulse racing. She searched Reese's face for the suggestion of a joke and found only Reese's serious blue eyes gazing back. "Reese, I am a thirty-six-year-old woman. I have finally recovered from losing a lover with whom I thought I would grow old. I'm not sure 'date' is a word in my current vocabulary. Most importantly, I have no idea what the word means to you."

"I'm afraid my answer may not make sense," Reese began. "I've never actually *been* on a date. I think what it means to me is spending time with someone I find interesting, someone I want to know better. Someone...special."

"And eventually?" Tory asked gently. "What then?"

Reese flushed, but she didn't look away. "Uncharted territory."

"Oh, Reese," Tory sighed, giving the sheriff's hand a little shake. "You're putting me in an impossible position. For me, dates are not about friendship, not in the ordinary sense. Dates are about the possibility of something more, something deeper." She hesitated briefly. "And dates usually occur when two people are sexually attracted to one another."

"Is that the case with us?" Reese asked slowly, her eyes holding Tory's. *Do you feel that way about me?*

"I can't afford any more heartbreak, Reese," Tory rejoined, avoiding the answer. "And you, my beautiful friend, are heartbreak material."

"Are you trying to let me down gently?" Reese asked with a hint of levity. She could tell that Tory was uneasy, and after hearing the still-raw hurt in Tory's voice when she had spoken of K.T., Reese thought that she understood Tory's reluctance to become involved again. More importantly, she couldn't clearly describe what she felt. It was too new. She only knew that sitting there with Tory's hand in hers felt completely natural and completely right. And she also knew she didn't want to let go. "Marines are tough, you know."

"I don't doubt that for a minute," Tory said with a small laugh, appreciating Reese's attempt to lessen the pressure on her. But for her own preservation, and in fairness to Reese, she needed to be clear. "I'm not ready to take a chance on someone who may not even be a lesbian. I'm not sure I want to risk that much anymore. I'm sorry."

As she spoke, she gently disengaged her hand from Reese's.

"Don't be sorry." Reese shook her head, smiling softly. "Until now, the only words that ever applied to me for certain were 'officer' and 'Marine.' I never gave anything else a thought."

"Let me know if something else comes to mind," Tory replied teasingly.

"I'll be sure to do that."

Tory laughed again, inwardly congratulating herself for steering their relationship onto safer ground. And she steadfastly ignored the way her pulse raced every time she looked up to find Reese's disconcertingly appraising eyes upon her.

CHAPTER THIRTEEN

"So, tell me what's going on with you and our good doctor," Marge said as she lined up her shot. She stroked lightly through the cue ball and eased the nine ball into the side pocket.

"Nice shot," Reese commented as she balanced two fresh beers on the thin shelf that ran along the wall. "What do you mean by 'what's going on?'"

Marge glanced up briefly as she slowly circled the table, planning her next salvo. The slightly perplexed look on her young friend's face told her the deputy sheriff really didn't know what the rumor mill had been churning out. "Word has it that the two of you are an item."

"Because we had dinner together?" Reese inquired as she carefully chalked the end of her custom cue.

"*Romantic* dinners. More than once, I'm told," Marge added, banking in her next shot. "And because she seems to spend a lot of time at your place. *And* because the two of you have been seen together at the Lavender Lounge the last two Saturday nights."

"Sounds like you're information central," Reese commented dryly, impressed with the accuracy of the local reporting.

"It's the tea dance. Everybody trades news there. I keep trying to tell you what you're missing. And don't avoid the issue."

Reese approached the table as Marge narrowly missed a tricky combination. Stretching her long form low to get the proper sight along her stick, she neatly deposited the three ball in the corner pocket. "We're not an item. We're friends."

Marge waited. When nothing further seemed to be forthcoming, she sighed with exaggerated impatience. "And? Do you have any intentions?" she asked, watching Reese move gracefully around the table. It was looking like they'd need to go four out of seven for a fair match.

"She isn't interested," Reese said flatly. She gently tapped the cue ball the length of the table, angling the seven into the corner.

Marge raised a questioning eyebrow at the vague answer. "I was asking after *your* plans."

Reese leaned her stick against the edge of the pool table, regarding her companion seriously as she reached for her beer. "I can't answer that."

"Well, if you don't want to tell me—" Marge looked peeved.

"That's not what I meant. I don't know *how* to answer your question."

"Well, you like her, right?"

"Of course. She's terrific."

"And she's great looking, right?"

"She's beautiful."

"So, at the risk of sounding like the crude old dyke that I am, have you given any thought to taking her to bed?"

"Aren't there a few steps you left out?" Reese studied the foam on her beer.

"Such as?"

"Like, well, like courting?"

Marge coughed on the mouthful of beer she was swallowing. "God, you are priceless. *Courting.* If the women in this town only knew what you were really like, you'd have to beat them off with a stick."

Reese asked cautiously, "What do they *think* I'm like?"

"Hmph. I think Carol from the Cheese Shop put it best. She said you were an impossibly good-looking, unapproachable butch, who probably does the asking. And, my friend, there're a fair number of women waiting in line, hoping that you'll ask." Marge nudged her playfully with a shoulder. "Only *I* know that you're an old-fashioned romantic."

"No, Marge, I'm not that either. What I *am* is someone who's always been happy with my life just the way it is. I never thought to look for anything more. It never occurred to me there *was* anything more." Reese smiled ruefully. "Then, these last few weeks, watching those kids in that tiny little bar, just so happy to *be* together, I'm starting to see what I've missed." She didn't add that every time she saw Tory, the realization that there was more she wanted from life grew stronger.

Marge started to protest, then grew quiet. At length, she voiced what she initially had found inconceivable. "You've never been with a woman, have you?"

"No."

"Oh, boy," Marge whistled. She looked at Reese suspiciously. "You're not straight, are you? There'll be hearts breaking all over town."

Reese looked away with a shrug.

"Don't tell me you don't know," Marge said in disbelief.

"It's not that simple," Reese stated. "I've spent my life with mostly men, many of whom I commanded. The rules were very clear and very strict. I never had that kind of relationship with anyone. It never seemed to matter to me."

"What about, you know...sex?" Marge persisted.

"I've had feelings," Reese said, remembering with absolute clarity the way Tory had felt in her arms when she had innocently carried the doctor into her house. She remembered the warmth of Tory's fingers in hers at dinner and the rightness of it. "The opportunity just never arose."

"Unbelievable." Marge simply shook her head. "But you still haven't answered my question about the doc. Do you have *feelings,* as you so delicately put it, for her?"

"It doesn't matter." Reese picked up her stick and focused her attention back on her game. "She's been hurt. She shouldn't be hurt again. I'm the last thing she needs."

"Why?"

"Because she doesn't trust me not to hurt her."

Marge kept silent, considering the new information. She was well aware that Reese had avoided discussing her own feelings for Tory. Despite her respect for the unspoken barrier, Marge still wasn't ready to let her friend completely off the hook. Left to her own devices, Reese would never figure out what she was about or realize that, sometimes, women just needed you to keep trying. Marge had no doubt that Tory King was cautious. She hadn't known the doctor to date anyone the entire three years she'd lived in town.

But she also knew that occasionally rumors started because those on the outside looking in saw more than the people who were in the thick of it. Reese might not know what was happening between her and Tory King, but that didn't mean there wasn't something there.

"So, how about coming to the tea dance tomorrow? It's the Fourth of July weekend. You've never seen anything like it," Marge pressed.

Reese sighed. "You know I'm working."

"Right. And I know damn well you're still working splits with Smith until his new baby is bigger. You can come to the tea dance and have plenty of time to sleep before the late shift."

Thus far, Reese had refused to accompany Marge to the popular afternoon event, somehow worried that it would conflict with her official position. To go dancing amidst the people she was supposed to be protecting seemed a little like the taboo of an officer fraternizing with the enlisted troops. She had to admit, though, *that* excuse was getting a little thin. She lived in Provincetown; attending the dance wasn't likely to cause any greater stir than simply going out to dinner seemed to. And she did want to be personally familiar with as much of the unique community's life as possible.

"Okay," Reese finally relented, "for a little while."

"Excellent," Marge enthused. "And Reese? Lose the uniform, or you'll have every woman in the place hanging on you."

❖

At four-thirty the next afternoon, Reese met Marge at the gym. Marge looked her over and found the results quite satisfactory. The white tank top displayed Reese's impressive shoulders nicely; the tight faded jeans hung low on her slim hips. Not for the first time, Marge felt the stirring of desire aroused by her new friend. She was certain that Reese never noticed the open stares she received whether in uniform or not. Being obviously unaware of her effect on others made her all the more attractive. For her part, Marge simply enjoyed looking at her, knowing she would never act on these feelings.

"What?" Reese regarded her quizzically. "Am I late?"

"You're never late," Marge asserted dryly. "Come on, Sheriff. Let's go to the dance."

They heard the music from two blocks away, and once inside, found the small dance floor already crowded. For two hours at the end of the day, after the beach and before the night's activities began, most of the gay tourists made the pilgrimage to the Boatslip for the tea dance. The huge rear outdoor deck that overlooked the harbor had tables and a pool, several bars, and a dance floor that never seemed big enough but somehow always managed to accommodate the crowds. The ratio was probably four men to one woman, and everyone got along. The atmosphere was usually one of unrestrained enthusiasm and abandon.

"What're you drinking?" Marge asked as they threaded their way through the throngs.

"Just a Diet Coke," Reese said.

"I'll get this round," Marge offered.

"Thanks."

While Marge joined the long line at the bar, Reese headed toward the end of the deck that overlooked the beach. Once there, she leaned against the rail, one booted foot up on the lower rung, and watched the couples strolling along the water's edge, some of whom were running playfully in and out of the froth. Two women stopped to share a kiss, then walked on, arms around one another. The sight stirred her unexpectedly, and she had to look away. She was unsettled enough that she wasn't aware of the woman beside her until she spoke.

"I thought I saw you come in," Tory said, one hand shielding her eyes in the sun. Reese had a strangely distant look in her eyes. "You all right?"

Reese shook her head, smiling. "Just daydreaming."

Tory smiled back. "Glad to hear it. Listen, there's someone here I want you to meet. Have you got a second?"

Reese looked around and saw Marge deep in conversation with someone in the bar line. "Sure."

"Great. Cath just got here and—"

Cath? Who is...oh, Christ...K.T.? Reese recoiled with an involuntary gasp, stepping back a pace in surprise. "No, I...I don't want to intrude," she managed to say as an unfamiliar tightening in her throat threatened her voice. Whatever was causing the icy ache in her chest was enough to force her to turn away, searching frantically for Marge's familiar form and the offer of escape.

"Reese?" Tory reached for the tanned forearm, shocked at the reaction. She had never before seen Reese lose her composure, and now, her entire body was stiff with tension.

"Reese," Tory cried again in alarm. "What's the matter?"

"It's late." Reese struggled for an excuse. She couldn't explain to Tory what she didn't have words for herself. She only knew that if Tory was here with her former lover, she didn't want to see them together. "I...I should go."

"Damn it, Reese. I *know* there's something." Tory continued to study her intently. There was no mistaking the turmoil in those deep blue eyes. What she didn't understand was the fleeting look of pain that had marred Reese's usually imperturbable features. "I'm not going to let you go until you tell me what's wrong."

"Nothing. Really," Reese responded evenly, her feelings now firmly in hand. "I'm sorry. It isn't you. I really can't stay."

Tory didn't believe her, but she knew by now how stubborn Reese was. She wouldn't talk until she was ready. "At least stop and meet my sister?"

"Your sister?" Reese couldn't keep the confusion from her voice. "But I thought—"

"Yes," Tory replied, just as surprised. "Who did you thi—" She stopped in mid sentence, staring, trying not to blush. "You thought I meant *K.T.,* didn't you?"

It was Reese's turn to blush. "Yes," she eventually managed to whisper.

Inches apart, they stared at each other, the air thick with feelings to which neither of them dared put words. Tory finally broke the silence, her hand still grasping Reese's arm.

"It wouldn't be her," she said softly, "for a number of reasons. We haven't kept in touch, and I don't want to see her. There is nothing between us now." As she spoke, her fingers slid slowly down to lightly clasp Reese's. It was important that Reese understand that K.T. held no claim on her.

"You don't need to explain," Reese responded quietly.

"No?" Tory queried just as gently, feeling Reese's fingers intertwine with hers, trying to ignore the quick thrill of excitement that the small closeness produced. "Perhaps not, but I wanted to."

"Still, I'm glad that you did." Reese smiled slowly, giving Tory's hand a tug, breaking the tension. "Come on, then. Introduce me to your sister."

Eventually, Marge joined them at the small table they had commandeered. Tory's younger sister Cath, a fair-haired, blue-eyed version of Tory, was as extroverted and gregarious as Tory was solitary. In no time, she had talked Marge into taking her off to the dance floor.

"That's the last we'll see of them for a while," Tory remarked as she glanced after her sister fondly. "Cath loves to party."

"At least she's in good company." Reese stretched her long legs out to the side of the table and settled back with a sigh. "Marge has enough energy for two or three people."

"Besides that, Marge is a great dancer, and Cath could dance all night," Tory added. "It's so great to have her here. She's got two kids and a demanding job."

"What does she do?"

"She's a freelance graphic artist. Even with a husband who's willing to help, it's hard for her to take time away. She's between jobs now, so I've finally got her to myself." Tory laughed, craning her neck to catch a glimpse of Cath and Marge on the dance floor. "I was worried about showing her a good time."

Reese saw Tory glance down at the brace protruding below the cuff of her white cotton slacks. In some part of her mind, Reese was always aware of Tory's injury, too. When she and Tory worked out, she was careful to temper the force of her throws and takedowns. She would never risk the possibility of Tory being re-injured. Not when Tory had suffered so much all ready.

Even when they walked through town in the evenings after a dinner out, Reese was aware of their pace, the surface of the pavement, the unpredictable surge of the crowds around them. Although she never thought of Tory as disabled or less than totally capable in any way, she nevertheless felt an instinctive desire to protect her. Just knowing that Tory felt inhibited by her injury made Reese long to change it.

"You know something," Reese said abruptly. "I've never learned to dance. I always managed to avoid the obligatory military balls by volunteering to take the duty."

Tory stared at her. How could it be that someone so accomplished could have missed so many of the simple pleasures of life? And why didn't it seem to bother her? Could she really be so self-sufficient that she didn't need what most people spent their lives seeking—some connection with another human being?

The thought that Reese might be happy living such a solitary life saddened Tory unaccountably.

"Waltz? Two-step?" Tory asked with an arched brow.

"Nope." Reese grinned.

"Well, that has to change," Tory stated emphatically. "As soon as Cath gets back, I'm assigning her the task of teaching you."

"If I have to learn, I'd rather it be with you."

Reese's tone was so gentle that Tory found herself struggling with tears. "I'd love to," she managed finally, "but I don't think I can."

Reese pushed back her chair and held out her hand. "Let's find out."

There was something about the compassionate insistence in Reese's voice, and the steady comfort of that outstretched hand, that Tory couldn't resist. Without wanting to think what it might mean, she stood, grasping the strong fingers. "All right, but we have to at least wait for a slow song."

Reese nodded and led the way through the crowd to the edge of the dance floor. When the pulsing music slowed, they stepped to a corner of the small space and faced one another.

Tory leaned her cane against the railing that encircled the area, looked up into Reese's smile, and stepped into her arms. Quietly, she said, "You lead."

"As long as you keep me on track," Reese replied as she slipped one arm around Tory's waist. Tory fit effortlessly against her, and despite the frequent physical contact they had on nearly a daily basis in the *dojo*, this felt vastly different. Reese was aware of the press of Tory's breasts against her chest and the length of firm thigh just touching her own. Tory's head rested lightly on her shoulder, her hair rich with the scent of sunshine and sea. For a second, Reese was breathless from the sudden assault of unexpected sensation.

"You're shaking," Tory whispered, hoping that Reese couldn't feel the trembling in her own body.

"Nervous," Reese murmured, closing her eyes, unconsciously tightening her hold as they moved together, tentatively at first, then with a growing confidence as each sensed the other's rhythm.

Tory couldn't remember the last time anyone had held her, and she could no more control her response than she could stop her heartbeat. It was as if her skin were opening, allowing the heat from Reese's body to penetrate to her core. And the fire that flared within had a life all its own. Unconsciously, she pressed closer, cleaving to the strong frame, her fingers on Reese's back tightening as waves of heat eclipsed all other sensation. When Reese's hips shifted naturally forward into her, she couldn't prevent a soft moan.

"Okay?" Reese questioned softly, her breath warm against Tory's cheek.

Tory tried to steady her voice as she replied, "Just out of practice. Don't let go. I may topple over." She fervently hoped Reese couldn't feel just how true her words were.

"Don't worry about *that,*" Reese answered. She scarcely recognized her own body, which seemed to have developed new senses in just a few scant moments. Her skin tingled, her pulse pounded in her ears, and she swore she could feel Tory's heart beat in time with her own. Whatever was happening, she had no desire for it to stop. In fact, when the music changed to a faster beat, she didn't even notice. The heady mixture of physical stimulation and emotional mystification muted her awareness of anything beyond Tory and herself.

"I have to sit this one out, Reese. It's going to get very fast in a minute," Tory said as she leaned back to look up into her taller partner's face.

"Okay."

Aware that Reese was staring at her in the strangest way and feeling the grip on her waist tighten, Tory tilted her head questioningly. Relaxing once more in Reese's embrace, she raised her voice as the music pounded and more people crowded onto the floor. "What is it?"

Reese looked around, fully cognizant of her surroundings for what seemed like the first time in hours. Her loss of connection with external events was enough to frighten her; that coupled with the apparent mutiny of her senses left her totally baffled. She leaned close, her lips against Tory's ear. "I'm ready to sit down, too, but my legs seem to have acquired a mind of their own. And they're saying stay."

"Come on," Tory said with a laugh. Slipping her fingers down Reese's arm, she grasped her hand. Like the night at dinner, their fingers automatically entwined. It felt so natural and so right, Tory's heart swelled with quick joy. When she spoke, her voice was husky. "I'll lead the way."

Reclaiming her cane, Tory turned to guide them through the crowd and was acutely aware of Reese pressed against her. She told herself it was because of the throng of people close around them and not due to any intent on Reese's part. Regardless of the reason, she couldn't deny the surge of pleasure the contact incited.

Marge and Cath, sandwiched against the narrow rail enclosing the dance floor, watched them go. Marge had just replenished their drinks, and the two of them were catching their breath before the next round on the dance floor.

"I can't believe my eyes," Cath muttered. "I haven't seen Tory on a dance floor in ten years. That friend of yours must be a magician."

Marge grunted. "The likes of her I've not seen before."

Cath looked alarmed. "Don't tell me she's some kind of playboy—*playgirl*, rather—or something worse. My sister has already had her heart broken once by someone like that."

"That's not what I meant," Marge soothed. "Hell, Reese is about as honorable as they come. Maybe *too* honorable. She'll protect your sister to the point of holding back what the doc might like offered."

"She's not straight, is she?"

"Haven't seen any signs of it," Marge said with a grin. "But then, *you* don't exactly shriek married mother of two."

"Well, thanks, but I don't look like a combination of k.d. lang and Jude Law either." Cath followed Reese and Tory with her eyes as they slowly maneuvered through the crowd. Her sister was holding tight to the sheriff's hand. They looked good together. "That woman is gorgeous."

"True enough," Marge conceded as she sipped her beer. "But I don't think it's just her looks that caught the doc's attention."

"I just hope Tory's careful," Cath said almost to herself. She hadn't forgotten how devastated her sister had been after the breakup of her relationship with K.T. She never wanted Tory to be hurt like that again. *Still, you don't want her to spend her life alone, do you?*

"I've known Tory for three years, and I know damn well she can take care of herself. Reese Conlon is a tough one to figure, but I get nothing but good feelings from her. And I can tell she thinks a lot of your sister. Besides, I'd bet my last dime that she's gay. Now, I suspect you're still going to worry, but it won't change anything."

"I know. It's just that Tory's had so many lousy breaks. She deserves so much more."

Marge nodded. "Whatever happens between them, you don't have to worry about Reese Conlon. She believes that Marine Corps stuff, including the *semper fi.*"

God, I hope so. Cause I saw the way Tory looked at her.

"You ready?" Marge asked, nodding toward the dance floor as an old disco song came on and people surged onto the floor.

"Yeah," Cath replied, grabbing Marge's hand. "Let's dance."

❖

"I can't believe how crowded this place has gotten," Reese exclaimed as she maneuvered the Cape Codder in its tall frosted glass onto the small table in front of Tory. She slid into the seat beside her, nearly draining her own seltzer and lime in one deep draft. "Dancing is quite the experience. Thank you for the lesson."

Tory searched for a hint of sarcasm but found none. "My pleasure," she said, knowing only too well how dangerously true those words were. "You're a natural. I didn't do anything except follow your lead. You'll have to ask my sister to fast dance with you. She's great."

"No thanks," Reese said emphatically. "Let her wear Marge out if she can. You're more than enough for me."

Tory couldn't help but blush, even though she knew perfectly well that Reese wasn't flirting. *She wouldn't know how to flirt if she wanted to. You have got to get over yourself with this woman.*

"How would you like to have an early dinner?" Reese asked. "I have to work tonight, but I thought..."

"Oh." Tory hesitated. If she didn't know better, she'd swear the woman was asking her out. And here *she* was, still searching for calm after the way she had felt while dancing. She'd been inexplicably happy in Reese's arms, and, she had to admit, aroused as well. Reese looked so damn handsome with the sun highlighting her blue-black hair and her tanned, golden skin. Tory's body refused to behave, another shiver of pleasure streaking down into the pit of her stomach. The fact that Reese was watching her intently didn't help.

Her pulse skipped, her stomach fluttered, and there was no denying the heat that pounded insistently between her thighs. Reese excited her, and that was impossible. That way lay disaster. With relief, she saw Marge and her sister finally returning.

"I can't," Tory said quickly, beckoning her head toward the approaching women. "I need to spend some time with my sister."

"Of course," Reese replied swiftly, ignoring the sharp stab of rejection. The hurt made no sense at all. It was quite reasonable that Tory needed to see her sister. Her acute disappointment was embarrassing. Abruptly, she stood, suddenly needing the comfortable familiarity of her work. "I should be going anyway."

"I..." Nonplussed, Tory stared. Reese looked about to say more, but then she simply turned and disappeared into the crowd.

Marge looked after her retreating back in surprise. "Where's she off to?"

"To work would be my guess." Tory sighed. "Where else?"

Now Marge stared at Tory in astonishment. *What is it with these two? They both look as if they just lost their last friend.*

"Marge and I were just discussing dinner," Cath announced. "You ready for that?"

Tory pushed herself up, reaching for her cane from the back of the chair. "I'm not really hungry. Why don't you two go? I'll be at the clinic. You can pick me up later."

She didn't wait for their reply. She was too preoccupied with the memory of Reese Conlon's face when she had walked away. Despite an attempt to hide it, Reese had looked hurt, and that upset Tory more than she wanted to admit.

CHAPTER FOURTEEN

It was close to two a.m., and Reese was sitting in her cruiser on MacMillan Pier, facing Commercial Street, watching the last of the visitors straggle out of town. She was looking for anyone who wasn't fit to drive after the long day of celebration, which had culminated in a fireworks display at the Pilgrim's Monument.

"Reese? You copy?" the disembodied voice of the night dispatcher called over the car radio.

"Roger," Reese responded. "Go ahead."

"We just got a request for you to call the East End Health Clinic."

"What's the situation?" she questioned, her voice tight as she simultaneously gunned the engine, flipped on her lights with one hand, and wheeled out into the street. "Another break-in?"

She was two minutes away, and every second felt like an eternity.

"Unknown. Handle as routine."

A call from the clinic at this hour could hardly be routine, and Reese knew it. No one should even have been there. It had to be Tory. Tory was in trouble.

Reese slammed into the lot and was halfway out the door before she even had the car in park. Tory's Jeep was the only vehicle in sight. Scanning the entire area, looking for signs of an intruder, she raced up the steps to the small porch. The front door swung open just as she reached for the doorknob.

Suddenly, Tory was there.

"Reese."

"Are you all right?" Reese asked hoarsely, grasping Tory's shoulders, searching her face intently. In the next instant, she pulled Tory out of the backlit doorway and peered into the interior of the building, automatically shielding the other woman with her own body.

"Hey!" Tory was momentarily off balance and pressed both palms against Reese's chest to steady herself. The body beneath her hands was tightly coiled, shimmering with tension. Reese's heart pounded violently.

"Whoa! Slow down," Tory gasped. "I'm fine."

There was a fierceness in Reese's eyes she had never seen before—a feral intensity that should have been frightening, it looked so dangerous. What Tory felt instead was closer to excitement. The power of Reese's emotions stirred her, in more ways than one. "Reese, I'm fine."

As she spoke, Tory grasped Reese's arms, shaking her lightly to get her attention. "I called you about a patient. Everything is all right."

Reese looked at her then, not yet accepting that she was safe. What she had felt in those few minutes when she thought Tory was in danger was completely foreign to her. Her entire life had been spent preparing for defense—in the military, in the police force, in the *dojo*. She was trained to confront any threat with the cold calm of a warrior. The gut-wrenching near panic she had just experienced rocked her to the core. For the first time in her life, she had felt the iron grip of fear. Without conscious thought, she pulled Tory to her. "Jesus," she whispered, her cheek against Tory's temple. "I thought something had happened to you."

The suddenness and intensity of the embrace was more than Tory could resist, and she yielded to it. She pressed into Reese, her arms slipping around Reese's waist. "I'm sorry," Tory murmured, holding on tightly. "I only asked that they have you call me."

"What happened?" Reese asked softly, her lips close to Tory's ear. She shifted, pulling Tory closer still, unintentionally sliding her leg between Tory's.

Tory couldn't seem to manage any further explanation—it was all she could do to control the trembling. And she wasn't shaking from fear, but from sheer overwhelming desire. With a soft moan, she brought her lips to Reese's neck, needing to feel her skin. Desperately, she clung to Reese's solid presence while her senses raged, reason rapidly surrendering to the escalating arousal she couldn't contain. Her nipples stiffened, screaming to be touched. The press of Reese's hard thigh brought the blood surging into her clitoris. She gasped as the unexpected pressure made her ache for release. *Oh, God, I want you so much.*

"Hey, hey," Reese soothed, stroking her back gently. "I didn't mean to scare you." Her own sense of relief, now that she finally accepted Tory was safe, was so powerful that she, too, was shaking.

Tory struggled for composure. She was on fire, and she was seconds away from touching Reese in a way that could leave no doubt about her desire. She was going to make a fool of herself. *God almighty, Tory. You can't do this now. She doesn't even know what's happening to you.*

"Let me catch my breath," Tory said as lightly as she could manage. With more restraint than she thought possible, she pushed away from Reese, breaking the agonizingly exquisite contact.

"Tory?" Reese questioned, confused by Tory's abrupt withdrawal. She stared as Tory moved resolutely inside and started down the hall, putting even more distance between them. The abrupt separation seemed far more than physical.

As close as they had been an instant before, a chasm stretched between them now. The pain of a deeply buried wound, the agony of abandonment and loss, seared through her. Automatically, as she had done for two decades, Reese pushed it away. That stoicism had protected her since childhood, and it was second nature to her now. Whatever vulnerable place Tory had unwittingly touched was safely defended once again. By the time Reese followed Tory into her office, she felt nothing.

"What happened?" Reese asked again, her voice neutral. Her professional voice.

Tory sat behind her desk, needing to get as far away as possible. She prayed she would be able to look at Reese without revealing her turmoil. Even now, she was trembling with the urge to touch her. She took a deep, slightly shaky breath and pulled forth her own defenses. She had called Reese as a doctor, and that's how she would deal with her. On that level, she was safe.

"I just finished suturing a teenager's forehead," she began, her voice sounding flat to her own ears. "He and his boyfriend were walking back to town along Route 6, out near Herring Cove. Apparently, they had been up in the dunes."

"Damn," Reese muttered, intent on Tory's story. She gave no sign of her own lingering agitation.

"They said a group of men in a truck tried to run them off the road, and apparently, one threw a beer bottle. It struck one of the boys in the head. He had a nasty scalp laceration. I didn't think I should wait until morning to tell you, in case the men in the truck are still cruising around, looking for trouble."

Finally calm enough to look at Reese, Tory caught her breath at the undisguised fury in Reese's face.

"Where are the boys now?" Reese questioned in a voice taut with anger.

"I couldn't get them to wait, Reese." Tory shook her head apologetically. "I tried. They're local kids, and they're scared. They don't want their parents to know about them."

"God damn it! How am I supposed to protect these kids? They won't let me."

Tory had a feeling that some of Reese's frustration was motivated by her increasing concern for Brianna Parker. She knew that Reese was fond of her and that their bond was growing as a result of their nearly daily contact in the *dojo*. And she also had a feeling that the outwardly tough, inwardly sensitive young woman reminded Reese of herself at that age. "Reese, I know how hard it is for you. I'm sorry. It's not that they don't trust you."

"I know you tried, Tory. You did exactly right in calling me now. Did they give you any other details?" She knew better than to ask for their names. She knew Tory couldn't breach her bond of confidentiality, and she wouldn't put her in that position. But she felt so powerless.

"It was a pickup truck, dark blue or black. They didn't get the make. There were at least a couple of men inside. One boy thought the truck had Massachusetts plates. It's not much to go on."

Reese smiled thinly. "It's a start. At least I can keep an eye out for similar vehicles. I'll drive through that area a little more often. Maybe my presence will be a deterrent." She sighed. "It's more than I knew an hour ago. I just hope this isn't related to the other incidents up the Cape."

"There's something else," Tory said tiredly, rubbing her face with both hands. "The other boy had a nasty infection in his eyebrow from a piercing. I couldn't help but notice it, and when I asked him about it he got very vague. Almost defensive."

Reese looked at her with interest. "And?"

"I think that he probably had it done in someone's basement or garage. It occurred to me that the items stolen from my clinic would be just what someone would need to set themselves up in the body-piercing business."

"Nice detecting. You might be right." Reese grinned faintly. "I'll ask around town if there are any rumors of an underground piercing parlor. It would help if you'd let me know if anyone else turns up with problems from piercings."

"I'll do what I can, Reese, but I have to respect patient confidentiality, too."

"Fair enough." Reese studied Tory's face in the dim glow of the desktop reading light. The doctor looked drawn in a way that seemed more than simple fatigue. There were stress lines etched into the fine skin around her mouth and eyes. Her hands were shaking. She knew Tory had been keeping long clinic hours since the summer began, but she had never seen her look quite so strained. "What were you doing here at two o'clock in the morning?"

"I wasn't here. The boys called the number I leave posted on the door for emergencies."

"You look worn out." Reese stood. "Let me drive you home."

"I've got my Jeep. I'm fine."

"I'd feel better if you'd let me drive you," Reese said softly. She couldn't explain it any better to herself. She simply wanted the peace of mind of knowing that Tory was safe at home. "Please, Tory."

Tory inclined her head in agreement, too exhausted emotionally and physically to argue. And she wanted just a few more minutes with Reese. "Cath can drive me to work in the morning."

❖

They were silent on the short ride to Tory's home. Reese pulled up the drive beside the darkened house, flicking off her lights and killing the engine. Jed's deep woofing inquiry came from somewhere in the back. Turning to face Tory, who sat silently framed in moonlight, Reese was amazed by both her beauty and an unusual aura of vulnerability. An instinctual response, at once protective and possessive, awakened in her. Softly, she murmured, "Tory."

The eyes that Tory turned to her were liquid in the moonlight. Questioning and raw and unguarded.

"Something happened to me tonight when I thought you were in danger. I was—afraid," Reese confessed quietly. "All I could think was that I had to get to you. Nothing ever mattered so much."

When Reese tentatively reached out a hand to touch Tory's hair, Tory flinched.

"Don't, Reese," she choked. "Don't touch me right now."

"Why not?" Reese slid closer, her voice husky with concern. "What is it?"

"Because I want you so much it hurts," Tory said in a strangled whisper. "I won't be able to stand it if you touch me."

Tory tried unsuccessfully to contain a sob, her need so overpowering that her defenses shattered. She tried to focus out the window into the darkness, searching for the familiar, *anything* to keep her from coming apart.

"And you think I don't want *you?*" Reese said hoarsely, her breath constricting in her chest.

She had leaned so close that her words ruffled Tory's hair. Tory's stomach churned with emotions so powerful she ached. Turning to face Reese at last, Tory cried, "God, Reese, don't play games with me."

"I'm not." Reese's eyes were deep with longing as she cupped Tory's face gently with both hands. "I have never been more serious in my life," she breathed softly as her lips found Tory's.

It was a kiss like none Tory had ever experienced. Questioning at first, just a gentle brush of flesh, tentatively seeking. Then bolder, as Reese drew her closer with a hand spread wide across her back, pulling her deep into a swirling vortex of sensation. Finally ending, with a last soft stroke, in something as tender as a prayer.

Tory didn't feel as if she had been simply kissed; she felt as if she had been worshipped. When Reese lifted her lips away, Tory cried out at the loss. With her hands twisted in Reese's shirtfront, Tory clung to her, gasping.

"Where'd you learn to kiss like that?" Tory asked unevenly when she could draw breath again.

Reese laughed shakily, pulling Tory against her chest, burying her face in silken hair. "I have no idea where that came from. But I can tell you this. I want to do it again, and I don't ever want to stop."

"God, you're beautiful," Tory whispered. "And you're scaring me to death."

"Why?" Reese questioned gently, pressing her lips to Tory's forehead before wrapping her in an embrace, wanting to feel all of her near. Groaning softly, Reese closed her eyes. Everywhere their bodies touched, she burned, and inside, a pressure so agonizing, and so sweet, rose to consume her. In a ragged voice, she gasped, "You feel so good."

"I want you to make love to me, Reese." Tory trembled. "So much, I feel as if I'll come apart if you don't. And I'm terrified of wanting you this badly. You don't know how you make me feel—"

"I know how you make *me* feel," Reese said hoarsely, her hands stroking Tory's neck, her collarbones, moving closer to the full curve of her breasts with each caress. "And I know, beyond a doubt, that I want you."

"No." Gently, Tory pushed away from her, although it took every ounce of her willpower to do it. She shook with the effort of not touching Reese. Her lips felt bruised, and she was swollen with desire to the point of pain. But for the sake of what little sanity she had left, she needed time. She knew with absolute certainty that if this woman made love to her, her life would never be the same.

"Reese Conlon," she whispered softly, "I do not intend to sleep with you in your patrol car."

Reese laughed unsteadily, grasping Tory's hands to keep her near but accepting her unspoken request for time. Every instinct in her body demanded that she kiss Tory again, every cell cried out to touch her, but she would not unless welcomed. She brushed a kiss against Tory's palm, the taste of her skin sending a surge of electricity down her spine. Almost frantically, she said, "Then tell me when I can see you again."

Tenderly, Tory brushed the dark locks off Reese's brow, loath to let her go. "I'll see you in the *dojo*, just like always," she said softly as she slipped from the car. "Now, go back to work."

She watched until the red taillights disappeared around the bend toward town, fearing that Reese had just left with a piece of her heart.

❖

"Are you just getting up, or haven't you been to bed yet?" Cath asked as she walked out onto the rear deck.

Tory was hunched over in a canvas deck chair, her feet curled up under her. Jed lay beside her, asleep. The dawn was moments old; the tentative shafts of sunlight had yet to dispel the clouds that hung over the harbor. Cath placed a cup of coffee in her sister's hand and pulled a chair up beside her. She propped her sneaker-clad feet up on the rail and waited.

Tory sipped the hot brew gratefully, shifting from her cramped position. She must have been there for hours, but she couldn't recall now what she had been thinking.

"What time is it?" she asked at length.

"A little after five."

"So soon?" Tory groaned.

"I take it you've been out here all night?"

"Not all of it. I had an emergency call about one."

Cath studied her in silence. The dark circles under her eyes weren't just from a few hours' lost sleep. She had sensed something amiss with her sister from the moment she arrived. Gently, she asked, "What's going on, Tor?"

"Nothing," Tory replied automatically. To her horror, her eyes unexpectedly brimmed with tears. But she was just so damn tired—of sleeping alone, of waking alone, of *being* alone. She passed a trembling hand across her face, desperately searching for composure.

"Talk to me, Tory. Please," Cath implored.

"I don't know where to start," Tory managed.

"Is it work? You know you could use some help here."

"No. I wish it were." Tory turned the cup in her hands, reluctant to face the tumult of emotions that threatened to crack her control. "That I know how to handle."

"You're starting to scare me, sis," Cath said softly. "You're not sick, are you?"

"No! No, I'm fine." She laughed a little shakily. "Actually, I'm a mess, but I'm not sick. It's...oh God, how can I explain this? It's a woman. I mean, I've met this woman, and...and I have absolutely no idea what I'm going to do."

Cath regarded her intently. "How long has it been, Tor? Since there's been someone?"

Tory fought back tears again. She fixed her gaze on the harbor, willing away the memories. "Four years. Since K.T. left me."

"Not even a night here or there?"

"No. For so long I couldn't get her out of my mind. Couldn't imagine touching anyone else." Tory's voice faltered, then she laughed hollowly. "And then it was so much easier just not to want at all."

"I'd still love to kill her," Cath muttered. She reached for Tory's hand. "Something's changed, I guess, huh?"

"Yes. And God, I positively *don't* want to do this again."

"How serious is it?"

"I don't know. I don't know anything. I'm not even positive she's gay."

"Aha." Cath blew out a breath. "That tall, gorgeous cop."

Tory looked at her in surprise. "How did you know?"

"Because for a minute there, she almost made me wish *I* was gay. She's charming and sexy as hell." Cath shrugged and smiled. "And because I saw the two of you dancing. She held you like you meant something to her. She held you like she cared."

"Oh, Jesus." Tory caught back a sob. "Now you *have* made me cry."

Cath got up to search for tissues and returned with the entire pot of coffee.

"Here," she said, handing Tory the box of Kleenex. She poured them both more coffee, waiting silently while Tory shed the tears she needed.

"Have you slept with her?" Cath asked when Tory regained her composure.

"No," Tory admitted softly.

"Want to?"

"Oh, yeah. I don't trust myself around her anymore." Tory shrugged ruefully. "I hurt, I want her so badly."

"Jesus. God, Tor, does she know?"

"Not exactly. I didn't want to admit it to myself, and then last night..." Her voice trailed off as the memory of Reese's touch enveloped her like a caress.

"What? Last night *what?*"

"She kissed me. I mean...we kissed."

Cath expelled another long sigh. "That ought to be some indication's she's gay, don't you think?" she queried with just a hint of laughter in her voice. Her laughter died as a haunted look flickered across her sister's face. Gently, she said, "Tory, tell me what's really happening here."

Tory's hands clenched the clay mug while she struggled for words. Haltingly, she gave voice to her fears.

"I haven't wanted anyone in so long. And...I don't mean sex." She looked away, blushing. "Although come to think of it, I haven't wanted that either. I've made a good life for myself here. I've been happy."

She met her sister's eyes directly. "Now, all I can think about is Reese. I can't look at her without wanting to touch her. I can't be near her without wanting her hands on *me*. I don't even recognize myself—it's like I'm another person. A stranger."

Involuntarily, Tory's hand rose and her fingers lightly touched her own lips. "Then, when she kissed me, every sensation I thought I'd lost forever came roaring back. All I've been able to think about all night was how she made me feel, how her breath brushed against my neck, how her hands seemed to reach inside of me. I'm losing my mind." Tory's expression was agonized. "What if it doesn't mean anything to her, Cath? What if it's all a mistake? How will I bury all these feelings again?"

Cath slid her chair closer and removed the cup from her sister's unconscious grasp. She took both Tory's hands in hers.

"Tory, honey, you've been sleepwalking the last four years. You think you've been happy, but it's more like you've been numb. Those of us who love you know that. I don't know a thing about this woman, but for her to move you like this, there has *got* to be something there. I don't know if she deserves someone as wonderful as you, or even if she has the good sense to know how lucky she is that you want her. But I could kiss her myself for making you feel this way." Cath gave Tory a quick kiss on the cheek, then looked into her eyes. "God knows, I never want to see you hurt like you were before, but Tory, you're *alive* again."

"I don't know if I want these feelings, Cath," Tory whispered. "I'm afraid to trust her, afraid that I'll be wrong again. I trusted K.T. completely, and I was so wrong."

Cath smiled sadly. "Some things we can't chose, Tory. Sometimes our life just finds us."

Tory was silent a long time. At last, she gave her sister a tremulous smile. "I sound like a lunatic, don't I?"

"You sound like a woman mad with lust," Cath laughed. "What are you going to do?"

"I wish I knew. I'm almost afraid to see her again." Tory looked fretful. "I'm afraid I might have imagined last night. And I'm just as terrified that I didn't."

Cath chose her next words carefully. "Are you in love with her?"

"I can't think about that, Cath. I really can't." Tory stood and walked to the rail, leaning out with both hands braced on the top. Without turning around, she said quietly, "I never want anyone to be able to hurt me the way K.T. did ever again. I'm not sure I can ever really love anyone after her."

"You might want to think about that before you sleep with Reese, then."

"I know," Tory whispered softly. *It might be better for her, and me, if I stop this before it gets started.*

CHAPTER FIFTEEN

"Bri. Wait a minute after class, will you?" Reese asked when she and the teenager finished their training.

Bri looked uneasy but nodded her assent. She followed Reese through the breezeway to the house, then stood inside the kitchen door, her eyes wary.

"Sit down," Reese said, gesturing to the stool by the counter. She poured them both orange juice and took a seat next to her student.

"Bri," she began, "has anyone been hassling you or any of your friends?"

"What do you mean?" Bri mumbled, uncertain of the conversation, still suspicious of any adult. As fair as Reese had been, she still worked with her father.

"Is anybody giving you a hard time about being gay?"

Bri snorted in disgust. "Shouldn't you be asking who *hasn't* hassled us?"

"How? What are they doing?"

"Nothing I can't handle." That wasn't exactly true, but Bri wasn't yet ready to believe that Reese was really on her side, as much as she wanted her to be. Every day was a battle, and she tried so hard to be strong, especially when Carre was with her. She had to be able to stand up for them, didn't she? Deep inside, she feared that if Carre saw her uncertainty and her vulnerability, she would realize that Bri didn't really deserve her. And then, Carre would leave her.

"You don't have to handle it alone, Bri," Reese said quietly.

For the first time, Bri looked at Reese directly and found eyes filled only with concern looking back. She took a deep breath and took a chance. Sometimes, it was just too hard to be alone.

"Most of the kids at school who know about Carre and me just avoid us. All of a sudden, we don't get invited to anything anymore." She turned her attention to her orange juice glass and stared at it as she spoke. "Some of them make noises when we walk by or call us names under their breath. Nothing you can really call them on. They just make it real clear that we don't belong. There're not that many of us gay kids, at least not that I know about. Some of the guys are pretty obvious. You know, kind of campy. A couple of them have been beat up."

"Who beat them up?" Reese asked, her voice like flint.

"Some of the jocks." Bri shrugged. "They were mostly showing off, I think."

"Has anyone bothered you?"

Bri looked away, shaking her head noncommittally.

"Bri?" Reese persisted gently.

"Not exactly. There's a guy who had the hots for my girlfriend. He tried to...push me around once."

Reese forced down the surge of anger. "What happened?"

"I kicked him in the balls."

"And that was that?" Reese would have smiled if the situation weren't so serious and so intolerable. "Nothing lately?"

Bri shrugged again, her expression nonchalant. "Not that I'm aware of."

"Have you heard of anyone being followed or threatened by a bunch of guys in a truck?"

"No." Bri stared at her suspiciously. "What's going on?"

"I'm not sure *anything* is going on," Reese admitted. "Two boys were bothered last night by some men in a drive-by thing. I'm not sure it was because the kids were gay. But it worries me. Ask around among your friends. If there's gay-bashing going on, I want to know."

"Why?" Bri asked bitterly. The teachers knew. They *had* to know. But no one did anything about it. "What difference would it make?"

"Because I won't have it in my town," Reese said darkly.

"Yeah, well, you're the only one, then."

"I don't think so, Bri. There are plenty of people who wouldn't tolerate it, your father included."

"He's said the only reason the gays and lesbians are welcome here is because it's so good for business," Bri exclaimed.

"Maybe he did say that, Bri, but that doesn't mean he feels that way himself." Reese could tell the young woman remained unconvinced, but she needed to get her message across. "Bri, I want you and your friends to be careful. And I need you all to help me out. If you see or hear of anything happening, please tell me."

"Okay," Bri agreed grudgingly.

"And you've all got to stay out of the dunes at night."

Bri's face set in defiance. "Right."

"Bri—"

"You don't get it, do you? You act like you do, but you don't." The teenager stood, her dark eyes flashing. "I want to be able to kiss my girlfriend, okay? That's what it's about—out there in the dunes—it's about making love with the person you love. Do you think my *father* would understand that? What I want to do with my *girlfriend?* Do you understand?"

"Getting beat up won't solve anything."

"I'll take care of her!" Bri turned away, a cry of frustration and desperation escaping. "If I can't make a place for us, I don't deserve to have her."

Reese laid a hand on her shoulder, meaning only to offer some comfort. She was shocked when Bri turned suddenly and buried her face against Reese's chest. Bri sobbed like a child, but Reese knew she wasn't. She didn't need to have experienced it herself to believe that Bri and Caroline were in love. And she had an idea what that meant for a girl like Bri. She would need to feel that she deserved Caroline's devotion, and she would need to feel that she could protect her.

Reese hesitated for only a second, then she gently folded the trembling youth in her arms.

"I do understand, Bri," she whispered, rocking her softly. "I understand exactly how you feel. I know that the two of you need to be together."

She had only to think of Tory to know how true her words were. Would she do anything differently were she in Bri's place? "Just give me a chance to keep you safe. Please. Just give me a little time."

"Yeah, sure, all right," Bri whispered, still shaking but calmer. It felt good not to be alone with her fears. Swiping an arm quickly across her face, Bri drew a shaky breath, then stepped away self-consciously. "I'll talk to my friends. Tell them what you said. Okay?"

"It's a start." Reese nodded. "I appreciate it, Bri. Thanks."

Bri studied her shyly. "I guess you won't tell me if you're gay, huh? Some kind of teacher thing."

Recalling Marge asking her the same thing and her inability to give an honest answer, Reese thought she had a clearer answer now. "Think of it as a cop thing," she responded lightly. "But you can believe me when I tell you I know what you're feeling about Caroline, okay?"

Bri grinned. "I guess that's answer enough."

"Get out of here." Reese grinned back. "I've got to go to work."

Glancing at the clock, Bri headed for the door. "I guess Tory's not coming today, huh?"

"No, I guess not." Reese knew without looking that it was well past the time for Tory to have arrived. She had known for some time now; she just didn't know what it meant.

❖

Tory came fully awake at the first ring of her bedside phone.

"Tory King," she said tersely, her pulse racing. No matter how many hundreds of times she had received these emergency calls, she never became immune to the sudden surge of adrenaline, wondering what challenge awaited her.

"Tory, it's Nelson Parker. I've got a situation out here at Race Point, and I need you."

She was already sitting on the edge of the bed with the phone tucked between her shoulder and ear while she strapped the velcro binders on her leg brace. Reaching for the pair of sweats she had dropped near the bed earlier, she asked, "What is it?"

"Can't say on this line," he replied in a voice taut with strain. "Just get here fast."

The line went dead as Tory tossed the receiver down.

In the middle of the night, it took her less than five minutes to reach the barricade of emergency vehicles crowding the parking lot below the ranger's station at Race Point. It took her a few minutes longer to convince an unfamiliar police officer that she belonged there. Officers, many of them from neighboring townships, were milling about, walkie-talkies blaring. There was also an impressive array of weapons on display. The air crackled with tension. Someone finally directed her toward a clump of people crouched behind the crest of a large dune. The roar of the Atlantic just beyond was unmuted by the noises of the crowd.

She found Nelson peering down toward the beach below with night binoculars. "Nelson!" she called, shouldering her way toward him. "What's going on?"

He turned at the sound of her voice, handing the glasses to the man next to him. His face was grim. "A Coast Guard cutter tried to board a suspicious craft running without lights a mile off shore. The cutter was fired upon and ended up in pursuit. That's when they radioed us for backup on the beach. Before we knew what was happening, the suspect ship ran aground and fired on my people. I've got an officer down out there on the beach."

Officer down! Tory fought to draw a breath against the crushing fear that gripped her. In a voice that sounded foreign to her own ears, she asked, "Is it Reese?"

The shouts, the crowds, the occasional crack of what must be gunfire receded from her consciousness. All of her awareness was fixed on his face, awaiting the words that would change her life.

"It's Smith. First night he's worked since his kid was born," he answered tightly. "Conlon's right over there."

She looked where he pointed, almost afraid to believe him. When she recognized Reese's unmistakable form, the rush of relief was so intense that her legs threatened to desert her. *Thank you, God.*

As Tory struggled for calm in the midst of chaos, Reese turned abruptly from the men with whom she had been talking and crossed the sand toward them with powerful strides.

"Nelson," Reese snapped, her face rigid with anger, "you're going to have to back me on this. You have jurisdiction here, not the Coast Guard. We're wasting time Smith may not have."

As she spoke, Reese pulled off her jacket and unbuckled her gun belt. Tory looked from one sheriff to the other in confusion. Nelson's face was set as he watched Reese, clearly unhappy.

As if she sensed his vacillation, Reese locked eyes with him. In a surprisingly gentle voice, she said, "You know it's the right thing to do. Even by helicopter, the SWAT team is twenty minutes away. I am a lieutenant colonel in the United States Marine Corps. I have been trained for this type of situation. There's no one here more fit than me for this maneuver."

He stared at her then, nodded his assent. "At least get a vest," he rasped.

"Right," she said as she stripped off her uniform shirt. The dark T-shirt she wore underneath was stretched taut across her chest as she restrapped her automatic into a shoulder holster.

"What the hell is going on?" Tory demanded. She stared at Reese with the sinking feeling that she wasn't going to like the answer.

Nelson looked at her as if he had forgotten he had requested her.

"We need to get Smith off the beach," Reese answered in his stead.

"And you're going to go?" Tory asked, the fear back, growing now, pulsating with every heartbeat. "Out there?"

"Yes."

"Is there no one else?" Tory asked almost desperately.

"This is for me to do, Tory." Reese's voice was strong and sure.

Tory searched her face and discovered a part of Reese she'd never seen before. What she saw there was something ferocious, something dangerous—an invincible conviction that she knew men would follow into battle. Everything about Reese, from the set of her shoulders to the piercing focus in her eyes, telegraphed certainty and purpose. Tory's words of protest died on her lips. As much as her mind recoiled from the specter of seeing Reese lying bloodied on that beach, she could not deny the rightness of her going.

"Do not die out there, Conlon," she whispered fiercely, stepping close enough that she could have touched her. She didn't;

she was too afraid she might not let go. "Don't you dare let that happen."

Reese's face softened for the briefest moment. "I won't."

Looking to Nelson then, Reese's eyes were like ice, her tone unrelenting. "Give me five minutes to circle around behind that line of scrub, then have the Coast Guard lay down a steady barrage of fire on that boat, and don't quit till I have him under cover of the dunes."

"Got it." As Nelson brought the radio to his lips, Reese melted into the night.

Even as Tory watched her shape fade into shadow, a part of her prepared for the pain she feared was coming. The simple fact that life as she knew it hung in the balance was as clear to her as any truth she had ever known.

"Give me those glasses, Nelson," she demanded.

Wordlessly, he handed them to her, motioning to a man next to him to relinquish his. Together, they cautiously crept to the top of the last dune and looked down into a nightmare.

A large vessel wallowed in the shallow waves just off shore, illuminated by the lights of half a dozen Coast Guard ships ringing the grounded craft. A body lay in the sand twenty yards from the board stairs that led up from the beach. With the night glasses, Tory could make out Smith's features, but she couldn't tell if he was alive. She could barely make out the shadows of other officers crouched in the scant shelter of the stairs.

Suddenly, the night was ablaze with flashes of light as gunfire erupted across the water. Tory flinched involuntarily, but her eyes never stopped scanning the eerie tableau below. From out of the darkness a shadow raced along the sand, crouched low but clearly visible, and vulnerable, in the merciless light of the moon. Reese dove and rolled, coming to rest beside the body in the sand. In the next instant, she was up, with Smith balanced across her shoulders as she sprinted toward the protection of the dunes. Tory saw the flickers of fire from the guns on the outlaw ship; she saw Reese falling; she heard Nelson's groan beside her.

A scream of protest at the unthinkable exploded from Tory. Something deep inside of her shattered, bleeding her soul into the darkness. She hadn't realized she had started to rise until a firm hand pulled her down.

"Stay down, for Christ's sake, or you'll get hit, too!"

"Let me go!" she raged, blindly clawing at his arm. "God damn it, let me go."

"Tory!" Nelson shouted, shaking her hard. "Tory. She's *up*."

She stared back down the slope, unbelieving. Reese crawled toward the cover of the scrubs, dragging Smith with an arm around his waist. What seemed an interminable time later, as gunfire continued bursting above the beach, shapes emerged from the night and surrounded Reese and the wounded officer, shepherding them to safety.

Tory sank to her knees, stunned, choking back the sobs that tore at her throat. The hand on her shoulder shook her again, softly this time.

"It's up to you now, Dr. King."

"Yes," Tory gasped, struggling to stand. "Yes."

Squaring her shoulders, she pointed to the emergency vehicles pulled up beside the patrol cars. "Have them brought to me there. I'll need their equipment."

Smith was the first to arrive, carried on a stretcher by three men and a woman, all in body armor, bristling with weapons Tory scarcely recognized.

"Put him down gently," she cautioned. Looking past them for the other stretcher, she saw no one. "Where's Conlon?" she asked, her throat painfully tight, her stomach still rebelling.

"Debriefing the chief," one of the men grunted.

"Get her over here. No excuses," Tory ordered as she knelt by Smith's side. She didn't look up again until she had two IVs inserted in the large veins just under his collarbones, saline running through both of them, and a compression bandage on the sucking wound in his chest.

"Somebody hand me a number thirty chest tube, on the double," she called. An EMT opened a sterile cut down tray so that Tory could make a one-inch incision between Smith's ribs, then pass the firm plastic tube into the space around his deflated lung.

"Hook this up to a suction pump, now," she instructed the woman assisting her. As soon as the negative pressure was applied, dark blood poured from the tube. Tory continued to monitor his pulse and blood pressure as the lung reinflated. Finally, she was satisfied that he was as stable as she could get him. "Okay, let's transport. Advise them that they have a GSW to the chest, hemopneumothorax, probable lung injury. He'll need an open thoracotomy ASAP."

"Right, Doc," the male EMT replied. "We're rolling. You want us to send a second squad back for the other one?"

"What's her condition?"

"Looks like just a flesh wound. She was walking and talking."

"Have her transported to my clinic. I'll handle her there."

"I'm not sure she'll leave," he called as he climbed into his vehicle. "It was a struggle just to get a look at her."

"Get going," Tory shouted, fire in her eyes. "I'll deal with her."

She found Reese and Nelson hunkered down behind the dune where she had left Nelson what seemed like another lifetime ago. They were sketching out some kind of map in the sand. The left side of Reese's T-shirt was stained dark with what had to be blood. Her face in the bright glare from the emergency halogen lights was white and beaded with sweat.

Tory forced herself between them, taking them both by surprise. "You're done here, Reese. You need medical attention, and you need it right now."

As Reese started to protest, Tory calmly turned her back. "Nelson, I'll have your job for reckless endangerment if you don't order her to come with me."

Nelson's eyes widened in shock, then he nodded. "Of course, you're right. Conlon, get your butt out of here."

"Yes, sir," Reese conceded. She rose to accompany Tory, wincing involuntarily as she became aware of the pain in her side for the first time. She found she couldn't straighten up, and her legs were a little rubbery.

"Easy, Sheriff." Tory steadied her with an arm around her waist, carefully avoiding the wounded area.

"Thanks," Reese managed through gritted teeth as another wave of pain shot through her.

"Don't thank me," Tory informed her remotely. She steeled herself against the awareness of Reese's pain. For now, she was only a doctor, and Reese just a patient in need. "Just lean on me. I'll take you to the clinic in my Jeep."

It took them longer to get Reese into and out of the Jeep than it did to make the short trip, but twenty minutes later they were in the procedure room.

"This place is getting to be too familiar," Reese grunted. She wasn't quite as dizzy as she had been.

"Can you get up on the examining table?" Tory asked neutrally as she led Reese slowly to a padded surgical table under the round overhead operating light.

"Yes."

"Get your shirt off, then. I need to get the instruments out of the sterilizer."

When Tory returned, Reese was trying hard to sit up straight, but she was obviously in pain. An eight-inch gash just below her ribs leaked a steady ribbon of blood down her left side. Tory had never seen her without clothes before and noted with clinical detachment the prominent pectoral muscles and etched abdominals of a superbly developed body. Despite her tone and muscle mass, Reese's breasts retained a soft fullness. She embodied the image of a female warrior. Unfortunately, at the moment, she was a wounded warrior.

"Lie down, Reese," Tory murmured as she set up the instrument tray and pulled on sterile gloves. At a glance, she could tell the bullet track was tangential to the abdominal cavity, and she automatically relaxed. Although the wound was deep, Reese was not in any serious danger, as long as the wound was treated properly and didn't get infected.

"How did the bullet get through that vest?" Tory questioned as she injected the area around the wound with lidocaine.

"I wasn't wearing it," Reese replied, breathing deeply as the burning pain subsided.

"You took it off?" Tory asked, trying to keep the anger from her voice.

"It was slowing me down."

"And the bullet didn't?" Tory responded acerbically.

"It was a judgment call," Reese answered calmly.

"I see," Tory said, not wanting to admit to herself just how frightened she was by Reese's willingness to risk her life. "Tell me if this hurts."

She irrigated the wound with Betadine and saline, cleansing it of clots and debris from Reese's shirt. The tissues had been separated down into the muscles of her flank, but thankfully, there was no deeper penetration. After gently probing the bullet track to be certain there were no fragments left behind, she closed the wound in layers with absorbable sutures. She concentrated on her work to keep the terrible knowledge of how close Reese had come to death from her mind. If she let that realization sink in, it would incapacitate her.

"Are you angry?" Reese asked quietly into the expressionless green eyes that stared down at her.

"I can't talk about that now, Reese. Just let me do this."

"Tory," Reese began, disturbed by Tory's distant tone and the detachment in her expression. The last time they were together, they had been breathless in one another's arms. Now, Tory wouldn't even meet her eyes. Reese felt the loss of that connection and was afraid for the first time that evening. "Tory, what's wrong?"

Silently, ignoring the urgency in Reese's voice, Tory started on the skin sutures, placing them far enough apart so that the inevitable swelling would not tear them through.

"Please, tell me why you're angry," Reese implored again.

"Don't talk."

Reese lifted a hand to touch Tory's arm, but she stepped away. A minute later, Tory gently taped a compression bandage in place and stripped off her gloves. "There. That should do it."

Tory took a deep breath and threw her gloves at the wastebasket, not caring that she missed. Then she spun back toward Reese so quickly that Reese jumped. Leaning down, Tory grasped Reese's shoulders, just managing not to shake her. Her eyes burned into Reese's, inches away.

"Now I'll tell you why I'm angry. I am angry because you nearly got yourself killed—and *willingly* at that. I'm angry because it doesn't seem to occur to you that your demise would have ruined my life. I'm angry, Reese, because...because..." Her fury evaporated as she saw the confusion in Reese's face. *You are so damn beautiful.*

"Oh, hell," Tory muttered, doing what she had wanted to do forever. She kissed her, hard, not caring what it meant, because she had to. Because she wanted to, more than anything else in the world.

For a millisecond, Reese stiffened in shock. Then she was lost. Tory's mouth was warm, the hands on her shoulders holding her down gentle but firm, the tongue that skimmed across her lips a teasing promise. Reese yielded to the pressure of Tory's mouth against hers, opening, breathing her in. She closed her eyes and surrendered to the waves of heat that coursed through her. There was no pain, only an ache more devastating than any bullet could ever inflict. Grasping Tory's arms, she tried to pull Tory closer, knowing that only her touch could satisfy a longing beyond any need she had ever known.

"Ah, Jesus," Reese gasped as Tory wrenched away. "Tory, please don't stop. I need...I need you to—"

Tory pressed trembling fingers to Reese's lips while drawing an unsteady breath. "This is insane. God, I want you so much."

"Christ, I'm on fire." Chest heaving, Reese struggled for air. "Please."

"You can't feel your wound because it's numb now. But you will later." Tory took a step back, groping for Reese's shirt. Reese's nipples were hard, her breasts flushed with arousal. "God. Put this on before I totally forget myself."

"This is killing me." Reese groaned in frustration. "I'd rather be shot."

"Don't tempt me, Conlon." Tory laughed wistfully. "I swear to God I'm not responsible for my actions. Now get dressed. We're going to my place. You need to rest."

Rising slowly to a sitting position, Reese fixed Tory with an icy glare. "What I *need,* Dr. King, is for you not to run from me every time we kiss."

"I don't want to." Tory slumped against the wall, struggling for words as she watched Reese fumble into her bloody shirt. "It's just...I've never felt quite like this. And now is certainly not the time for sex. You may not think anything of it, but you've just been shot."

Reese grinned despite herself. "Actually, I think quite a lot about it. It hurts like hell, even with the local. But just now, when you kissed me..." Her eyes found Tory's and everything else disappeared. "All I felt was you."

Reese tried standing, and when successful, she crossed the few feet between them and rested her hands lightly on Tory's waist. "I've missed you. You haven't been to the *dojo* all week. How come?"

I was scared to death of how much I want you. I was afraid if I saw you, I wouldn't be able to not touch you.

When Tory didn't answer, Reese said softly, "I wanted to call, but I didn't know if you wanted me to. Tory...when you touch me... I...it rips holes in my soul."

Tory couldn't look at her any longer. There was too much wanting in Reese's face, and too much desire in her own body. She sidestepped out of Reese's grasp, catching her hand as she did. "Come on, Sheriff. Let me get you out of here. You're going to crash any minute."

Relenting, Reese allowed Tory to lead her to the Jeep. As they drove through the night, exhaustion finally claimed her. She was asleep by the time Tory pulled into her drive.

❖

"Is she asleep?"

"Closer to unconscious." Tory sighed as she leaned against the deck rail. "Let me have one of your cigarettes."

Cath raised an eyebrow but handed the pack to her sister, forgoing the obvious observation that Tory didn't smoke. But then again, neither did she—most of the time. Together, they leaned side by side against the deck rail and waited for yet another imminent sunrise. "Is she going to be all right?"

"Yes," Tory murmured as she blew out a soft stream of smoke. She could still see the flashes of gunfire, and Reese falling, and the torn muscles in her abdomen. "She'll be all right."

"Will *you?*"

"I don't think so." Tory laughed shakily, then took another deep drag on her cigarette, enjoying the acrid bite of the harsh fumes. It suited her disquieting unrest. "I don't know what I'm going to do about her."

"You know, Tor, there's something really spooky about her."

Tory looked at her sister in surprise. "What do you mean?"

Cath stared out over the harbor, her voice pensive. "I had the strangest experience just now, when I was helping you put her to bed. I have never seen anyone quite so beautiful."

"She is, isn't she," Tory mused softly.

"Yes, but that's not what I meant."

Tory regarded her curiously.

"I mean, it was like looking at a painting of some ancient goddess-warrior queen or something. I was standing there, staring at this naked woman like an idiot, when she opens her eyes and looks right at me. 'Thank you' was all she said, and I thought my heart would break. She seemed so innocent—she reminded me of my children. Not their helplessness, but their untarnished goodness. But that can't be, can it? There aren't any adults like that. Tell me, Tor, what do you see?"

Tory smiled softly as she reflected on the woman asleep upstairs in her bed. "She is the most infuriatingly noble person I have ever met. She believes in doing the right thing," her voice caught, and she brushed impatiently at the tears clinging to her lashes, "even if it kills her." She stubbed out the cigarette carefully, continuing in a quiet tone. "And that is as near to innocence as you can get."

"It would be hell to be in love with her," Cath ventured.

"Yes."

"Yet, it's hard *not* to fall in love with her," Cath laughed.

"Impossible."

"This place can't always be so dangerous, can it? I mean, what's the chance she'll ever get shot again?"

Tory shuddered at the thought. "Cath, she is going to ride out on her white charger every day of her life, and if it isn't her body in danger, it will be her heart. She has layers of armor, but one kid in trouble tears her apart."

"Anybody with half a brain would stay away from her," Cath concluded. "Too risky."

"Yes."

"You know what the real problem is with people like her? The heroes, well, heroines, I guess."

"What?" Tory asked.

"They're so single-minded. Everything is either black or white. Nothing halfway. Like with love, it has to be this grand passion, you know? Mate for life, die in the name of it..."

"Don't, Cath," Tory warned. "Don't push me on this."

"Why not, big sister? Are you scared that you might love her?"

"Yes!" Tory snapped, the terror and strain of the last six hours finally erupting. "Yes, I'm scared. Because I've known her just a few months, and I've kissed her exactly twice, and she's already claimed some essential place in me. I want her in my life, for God's sake, and I haven't even slept with her. Already I *cannot* imagine what life would be like without her. The last four years—even the time before that with K.T.—seem like pale imitations compared to what she makes me feel."

She stared at her sister, her eyes dark. "Now, *tell* me I haven't lost my mind."

"You *have* lost your mind." Cath slipped an arm around Tory's shoulders, hugging her in the chill morning air. "That's what happens when you fall in love."

"I've *been* in love. I loved K.T. with all my heart. But this. This is too much. She is too goddamned much. This isn't my heart we're talking about. This is my soul. I could lose myself here, Cath. When I saw her go down tonight, I thought she was dead." She stopped, the horror resurfacing. It took a minute for her heart to stop hammering. When she spoke again, her voice was haunted. "I felt something inside of me begin to die, too. That terrifies me, Cath."

"Yes, I know," Cath rejoined softly, "but what's your alternative?"

"I just don't know, but I can't let this happen."

As a brilliant sun broke through the cloud cover, the two sisters stood in silence, wearily awaiting the new day.

CHAPTER SIXTEEN

Reese lay on her back with her eyes closed, listening to Tory breathe and taking stock of her situation. Except for her briefs, she was naked under a thin sheet that lay tangled across her thighs. Her side throbbed, but when she cautiously stretched, it didn't feel any worse. Experimentally, she shifted her body until she was able to turn onto her side. Still okay. Opening her eyes, she studied the woman beside her.

Tory lay mostly on top of the covers, dressed in a sleeveless ribbed T-shirt and loose green scrub pants. The tanned flesh of her smooth abdomen was exposed where the shirt had rolled up. One hand rested on her thigh, the other on the bed between them. Her breasts stretched the front of the thin cotton, rising gently with each breath. Her wavy hair was spread out over the pillow, a few wisps clinging to her cheek. When Reese caught the loose strands with one finger, lightly brushing the cheek as she did, Tory smiled slightly in her sleep.

Reese couldn't ever remember being this close to another human being. She laid her hand against the bare skin of Tory's abdomen and was rewarded by a flicker of muscle and a soft sigh from the sleeping woman.

Warmth spread up Reese's arm from Tory's skin, and she tightened within, a pulse beating hard between her thighs. Leaning on her uninjured side, she watched Tory's face in wonder as she gently stroked the curve of rib with her fingertips. Tory's lips parted as Reese reached the swell of her breast, and when Reese closed her hand slowly around the sensitive flesh, Tory gasped. Reese was holding her breath without realizing it, mesmerized.

Tory's delicate lids fluttered, then opened as insistent fingers caught her nipple in a teasing caress.

"Oh!" Tory moaned, searching the face so near hers. Hazy blue eyes swallowed her whole.

"Hi." Reese's voice was husky and low.

"Reese," Tory murmured brokenly as the hand slid to her other breast. Her back arched, responding to this new sensation. A pinpoint of pleasure streaked from her nipple straight down her spine. "Oh God, wait—"

"No," Reese asserted, her breath quickening with Tory's. "I won't." She pushed the T-shirt up and exposed the taut nipple, then lowered her lips, catching it lightly in her teeth. Involuntarily, Tory threaded her fingers through Reese's hair, holding Reese's mouth to her breast as the breath fled from her chest.

As Reese worked first one, then the other nipple between her lips, drawing small incoherent cries from Tory, she stroked Tory's quivering abdomen. Blood rushed into Reese's head and rising tension coiled tightly with each groan from Tory's throat. Tory was rigid beneath Reese's hands, pushing into her mouth, twisting fretfully amidst the tangled covers. The fingers in her hair trembled.

"Oh please, Reese, stop," Tory finally begged, knowing she could no more push her away than she could stop breathing. Her control was shattered, and her need was so powerful. Her legs parted involuntarily, wetness soaking through the light cotton of her scrub pants.

"Never," Reese rasped, raising her head, capturing Tory's emerald gaze with her own. "Not this time. Not ever."

Tory stared back into eyes full of fire and promise, unable to look away as her body surrendered to Reese's slightest caress. Her vision grew cloudy as a long-fingered hand stole beneath the ties of her pants. She whimpered, aching, already close to bursting when fingers brushed over the fine hair at the base of her belly. For a second, she couldn't breathe at all. Then she had to clench her jaws to keep from crying out. Her hips rose of their own accord, seeking that elusive stroke.

"Reese, if you touch me, I'll explode." Gasping, she turned her face away. *Oh God, you're going to make me come.*

"Look at me, Tory," Reese demanded softly, her fingers caressing the velvet inner thighs, allowing her fingertips to stray into the heat. She parted soft folds, teased the distended clitoris.

"Oh. Reese. I'm coming." Tory bit her lip, succumbing to those eyes. Her pelvis lifted, the muscles in her thighs tightening. When finally Reese stroked the length of her clitoris, pressing the stiff shaft, Tory came instantly. She could no more stop the scream than she could halt the eruption that rocketed through her. Her last conscious sensation was of Reese's mouth claiming hers.

❖

An insistent tapping at the bedroom door roused Tory. In reflex, she reached for a sheet to cover Reese's nakedness. Her own clothes were still on, though the scrub pants pushed down on her hips accused her of her earlier abandon. Reese slept soundly, possessively encircling her waist with one arm. Tory quickly scanned the gauze taped to Reese's side, noting with relief that there was no sign of fresh bleeding.

"Tory?" Cath called softly.

"Come in, Cath," Tory answered, straightening her clothes hastily.

If Cath was surprised by the sight of her sister in the arms of the woman Tory had only hours before claimed was "too much" for her, she didn't show it. She simply crossed the room to stand by the bed, whispering urgently, "There's a horde of people downstairs threatening to come up here if they don't get a progress report on your, uh, patient." She couldn't hide her grin. "This might strike them as unorthodox treatment."

"It strikes me that way, too," Tory said with real concern. She hadn't intended to fall asleep next to Reese. She hadn't even meant to lie down when she had come to check on her. But the raw fear of nearly losing her just hours earlier was still so fresh, and she couldn't bring herself to leave. For just a moment, she had eased onto the bed to listen to Reese breathe.

"Well, ease your conscience, Doctor," Reese said, opening her eyes. "It wasn't your idea." She flashed a smile to Cath, who grinned back. "Who are they?"

"Your boss, two kids who look like punk rockers, and your family."

"My family?" Reese repeated with a frown.

"Your mother and her lover."

Reese started to rise. "I better get down there."

"Not so fast," Tory ordered, swinging off the bed. "I need to check you over first." She tossed her sister a stern look. "Tell them *I'll* be with them in a minute."

Reese started to protest, then thought better of it when she saw the look on Tory's face. She lay back quietly with a sigh.

"Gotcha." Cath decided her sister was not in the mood for levity and made a hasty retreat.

"This looks fine," Tory said as she inspected the wound. Her eyes flickered over Reese's face neutrally. "How do you feel?"

"Like a million bucks," Reese responded, unable to contain a grin.

Tory glared at her.

"Okay, it stings like hell, but I don't feel too bad." She grasped Tory's hand, suddenly serious. "Tory—"

"You ambushed me this morning, Conlon." Tory extracted her hand to reach for new bandages, determinedly avoiding eye contact. She bent her head to work on the dressings.

Reese slipped a hand into Tory's hair, stroking it back from her face, then running her palm along the edge of her jaw.

"I didn't mean to, not at first," she whispered, tracing one finger down the side of Tory's neck. "You are so beautiful. I had to touch you, and then, nothing could have stopped me."

"You're doing it again," Tory choked, finally looking at Reese, whose blue eyes were hazy, almost wounded with desire.

"Can't help myself," Reese murmured, her hand behind Tory's neck, intent on pulling her near for a kiss. "I can't think when I touch you."

Tory placed both arms straight against the bed on either side of Reese, stopping her descent. "Neither can I, it seems," she groaned, "but one of us has to. Please, stop."

"I can't look at you without wanting you," Reese confessed, not loosening her hold. Every fiber of her body sang with nearly unbearable tension.

"God, I'm glad," Tory muttered before laughing shakily. "But if you don't take your hands off me this minute, I will not be responsible for my actions. Besides, you're in no condition for what I want to do to you. And besides *that*, we're likely to have an audience if one or both of us are not downstairs soon."

"Tory," Reese implored, her breath constricting in her chest, "just kiss me. Just a kiss—please."

Tory couldn't have resisted the plea in those eyes if twenty men had trooped into the room. She took Reese's mouth with bruising authority, shocked by her own possessiveness. Reese opened to her, her whole body pressing urgently upward as the kiss deepened. When Tory's hand claimed Reese's breast, squeezing hard on the erect nipple, Reese groaned and shuddered convulsively. Incredulous, Tory raised her head, stunned to silence, as Reese clung to her, shaking with after-tremors.

"Ah, God," Reese gasped at length, collapsing against the pillows. "Some Marine. One kiss and I'm wasted."

"Did what I think just happened really happen?" Tory asked in wonder. "Just like that?"

Reese smiled shyly. "It seems to be happening every time we touch."

"Every..." Tory's mouth was dry, her head pounding. "*Every* time?"

"This morning, with you—"

"Oh my God," Tory said, shocked. "You're incredible; in fact, you're dangerous. You are definitely not safe on the streets of Provincetown."

"You don't have to worry," Reese said seriously. "It's you that does it to me."

"Sweetheart," Tory said with a soft smile, "I don't think I had all *that* much to do with it."

"No?" Reese asked quietly. "It's never happened before."

"Never...oh my God." Tory brushed her fingertips over Reese's face in awe, amazed by the feelings just looking at her inspired. "I'm getting up, because if I don't, I'm going to make love to you for the rest of the day."

"Hey, don't think I'm going to let you forget that," Reese warned.

❖

Conversation stopped as every eye focused on Reese when she walked out onto the deck. She wore a pair of Tory's jeans and a frayed cotton shirt, both of which were a little snug. She grinned at everyone as if she hadn't almost been killed the night before. "Hey, what's the occasion?"

Tory hoped no one was looking her way; she was afraid what she was feeling might show on her face. Reese had to be the most captivating woman she had ever seen, and the most desirable. They'd only been apart a matter of minutes, but the urge to touch her was nearly painful. To her great consternation, when Reese smiled at her, she blushed.

"Are you all right, darling?" Kate asked anxiously.

"I am, Mom. Just fine."

Kate looked to Tory, uncertain whether to believe her daughter. She was in time to catch the look that passed between the two of them. At first surprised, she was then immensely pleased. She relaxed perceptibly as she added, "Jean and I just had to be sure."

"Dr. King is taking very good care of me."

Tory blushed a deeper crimson as Reese grinned rakishly at her. *I'm going to kill you for this.*

Mercifully, Nelson chose that moment to speak, dispelling the silence and drawing Reese's eyes from Tory. "The doctors say Smith is going to be okay, too. Thanks to the both of you. You sure you're okay?"

"Yes, sir. I'm fine."

"There've been a lot of calls from reporters," Nelson went on. "This is big news. They're camping out over at your place. I'd stay clear of there for a few days, if you want my advice."

"She can stay here," Tory responded.

"Good," Nelson rejoined. "So, I'll see you in five or six days."

"Excuse me?" Reese asked in confusion. "Five or six days?"

"Doc said you'd be okay for desk duty next week."

"Desk duty?" She turned to Tory in astonishment. "*Desk duty?*"

"What I actually said was that you *might* be ready for desk duty next week," Tory replied stonily. Her expression suggested any further discussion from either of them would be extremely unwise.

"Right," Reese conceded, deciding to fight this particular battle another day.

Nelson seemed satisfied that his irreplaceable second in command was in good hands. As he turned to leave, he asked, "You coming, Bri?"

"I want to talk to Reese. I've got my motorbike."

"Well, be careful with that damn thing if you're carrying a passenger," he admonished with a nod toward Caroline.

Bri gave her father a look that said plainly that he had just insulted her. The stiffening of her shoulders and the tilt of her chin reminded Tory of Reese. *Oh Lord, not another bullheaded baby butch. God, they almost look alike. Black hair, wild blue eyes, handsome as the day is long.*

"I'm always careful, *especially* when I'm carrying Carre," Bri replied, as if her father should know better than to suggest otherwise.

It was Nelson's turn to look confused. He was rescued by Tory's suggestion that they all go inside and have some lunch. The sheriff declined, but Reese's mother and Jean offered to lend a hand. They followed Tory and Cath as the two sisters turned to go inside.

"I'll be right there," Reese said, then looked at Bri and Caroline. "What's up?"

The instant her father started down the path to his car, Bri clasped Caroline's hand. Her eyes were smoldering with anger. "Someone's been bothering Carre," she seethed.

"Sit down," Reese said seriously. "And start at the beginning."

"At first, I didn't pay much attention," Caroline informed her shyly. She sat pressed to Bri's side, her hand on Bri's thigh. "There were some notes pushed into my locker a while back—the usual stupid stuff."

"What did they say?" Reese asked.

Caroline glanced uncomfortably at Bri.

Reese waited.

"They just called me names." With a sigh, Caroline recounted, "You know, like dyke and queer. Then once—"

She hesitated again, and Bri stared at her suspiciously.

"What?" Bri asked. "Is there something you didn't tell me?"

Caroline nodded, looking miserable. "Someone wrote that if I knew what was good for me, I'd get rid of Bri and find a man. Otherwise, they'd show me what I was missing." Her face crumpled slightly. "And now, I think someone is following me."

"Mother*fuckers*," Bri swore, pushing Caroline's hand aside as she jumped to her feet and stormed across the deck. She grasped the railing with all her strength to hide the trembling.

"Bri!" Caroline rose too and started to follow, close to tears.

Reese motioned for her to wait, then walked over and stood next to Bri. "Your anger is just, but if you let it, it will make you weak. If you don't control it, it will strike anyone in its path. You will hurt those who love you."

"I want to *kill* them," Bri choked, struggling for air.

"I know," Reese said.

"When I think about someone hurting her," Bri said, the anguish making her voice crack, "I can't stand it. I think I'll go crazy."

"Yes," Reese agreed, "but you can't. You cannot afford to be defeated by words, or threats, or your own undisciplined emotions. You're being tested, Bri. It's not fair, and it's not just, but that is beside the point. I'm going to need your help, but more important, Caroline needs you."

Bri glanced over at her girlfriend, who watched them anxiously. Just the sight of Caroline made her heart catch, the joy almost like pain. She wanted so much to deserve Caroline's love. To be brave and strong and sure, only sometimes she didn't feel that way at all. Bri straightened her shoulders, drew a deep breath, and crossed the deck to her.

"I'm sorry," Bri whispered as she sat back down beside Caroline and slipped an arm about her waist. Caroline kissed her neck, murmuring reassurances against her skin.

"Okay, let's have the rest of it," Reese directed.

As Caroline was finishing her story, Tory reappeared from the house. She eyed the two young women, both of whom looked scared. At first glance, they seemed tough enough in their leather pants, silver arm bracelets, ear cuffs, and punk haircuts. She thought that Bri had a tattoo on her upper arm that hadn't been there before as well. But she could tell from the way Caroline pressed against Bri's side and the rigid set to Reese's features that something was wrong.

"What's going on?" Tory asked.

Reese said a few more words that Tory couldn't hear as Bri and Caroline stood to leave. Tory waited until they were out of earshot before she asked again, "Trouble?"

"Yes, I think so." Reese nodded, turning to enter the house. "I'll tell you when we're alone."

Tory noted Reese's uncharacteristically slow approach. "You're in pain, aren't you?"

"Some," Reese admitted reluctantly. *More than that, actually.* "Is my mother still here?"

"They're in the kitchen. I really think she just wanted to see that you were all right. Come have something to eat; then you're going back to bed."

Reese followed, wondering how she was going to tell Tory that she needed to go to work, not bed. Just as they entered the dining area that adjoined the kitchen, Cath turned to them with the phone in her outstretched hand.

"Somebody wants to talk to Colonel Conlon. Won't take no for an answer," she announced with an edge to her voice.

Reese took the phone. "This is Lieutenant Colonel Conlon." She straightened unconsciously as she listened, her face unreadable. "Yes sir. That's correct, sir...In my opinion it was the best course of action, yes sir...He's going to live, sir...I'm fine, sir. Just a scratch."

She looked over at her mother, who was watching and listening intently. "She's here, yes sir...No sir, I'm staying at the doctor's... Victoria King, yes sir."

Her fingers tightened on the phone, her blue eyes darkening. "Are you sure you want me to answer that, General? I seem to recall it's specifically against regulations to ask questions of that nature."

Her eyes met Tory's and held them fiercely. "I won't deny it. I won't deny *her*. Sir."

After a moment, Reese slowly replaced the receiver. Every face looked questioningly at her. She spoke into the silent room. "That was my father. Apparently, he has very good intelligence sources, and it wasn't just my *career* he was monitoring." She looked at her mother sympathetically. "I appreciate what you must have gone through. He was asking some pretty personal questions about my lifestyle, and he was fairly accurate with his assumptions. He just threatened to have me court-martialed if I admitted to a relationship with a woman. Tory's name came up."

At that, she glanced at Tory with a wry grin.

"Can he do that?" Cath exclaimed, clearly shocked.

"If he wants a very messy, very public trial." Reese shrugged. "I'm an attorney, and he knows me well enough to know I would never give up my commission without a fight. I think he was just testing."

Despite Reese's calm tone, Tory could see the conversation had taken a toll. Reese was pale, and her forehead was dotted with perspiration. There was a fine tremor visible in her hands. Quickly, Tory went to her, taking her hand. "You need to be in bed. I never should have let you up as it is. Come upstairs."

"I'll fix a tray," Cath called after them.

"I'm afraid Tory has her work cut out for her," Kate observed as she watched Tory guide her daughter upstairs with an arm around her waist. "Reese has very few of her father's bad qualities, but she does get her stubbornness from him."

She pointedly ignored the snort of disbelief from her lover.

"My sister can handle her, I'm sure," Cath stated as she accompanied Kate and Jean out to their car. Jed trailed along behind and then tried to climb into the back seat. Cath grabbed his collar and held him back with effort, adding with a grin, "I'm glad I'm going to be here to see it. My kids will be with their grandparents until school starts, and my husband is on retreat at Kripalu."

"It should help that Reese appears to be in love with her. Is Tory aware of that?" Kate asked.

Cath hesitated, not sure just how to discuss this with Reese's mother.

"Oh, I don't want you to betray any confidences," Kate assured her. "I couldn't be happier."

"I think cautious would be the word to describe my sister at the moment," Cath responded, hoping fervently that Kate was right about Reese's feelings. In truth, it was painfully clear that Tory was hopelessly in love with the handsome, hardheaded cop, regardless of how she tried to deny it.

"In time, I have no doubt that Reese will prove herself to Tory."

"Will her father really make trouble for Reese?" Cath asked with concern.

"I doubt it, not after Reese made it clear she would fight it. Roger was always too ready to use his power for personal gain, unlike Reese, who seems to really believe that service is the highest form of honor. Given the publicity involved, he would not want his own reputation tarnished. He could pass off a lesbian wife as some acquired perversion on my part, but a lesbian Marine officer daughter?" She laughed. "How fate has conspired against the man."

"Obviously, Reese got her good parts from you."

For a moment Kate looked pained. "I wish I could take the credit, but I believe Reese has simply taken what was once commendable about the military to heart. She is proud to 'serve and defend.'" She looked away for a moment, then smiled faintly. "And I'm proud of her for that."

"I like her," Cath said with a grin. "And so does my sister."

"Call if you need us for anything," Kate offered as she and Jean pulled away.

Cath waved cheerfully, hoping that they had had all the excitement they were going to see for one summer. But it was only mid-July, and a nagging voice told her that it was going to be a long month.

CHAPTER SEVENTEEN

"Are they all gone?" Tory asked cautiously as she ventured out onto the deck. She found Cath stirring a pitcher of margaritas and nearly wept at the sight. "God, am I ready for one of those."

"We are alone at last," Cath informed her, handing her a drink. "And how is the famous patient?"

Tory blushed. "Out like a light. I can't get her to take any narcotics, and I think the pain is wearing her out." She sank into the canvas deck chair with a sigh. "I'm wondering if I shouldn't send her to Boston for follow-up."

Cath looked at her in surprise. "I thought you said she was going to be fine?"

"She is, but I'm *sleeping* with her, for God's sake."

"I was meaning to ask you about that," Cath said teasingly. "Just how did that come about? I got the sense this morning, or was it last night, that you weren't quite ready for that."

"Who says I'm ready? It just happened. Well, actually, she seduced me. Oh, hell, that's not quite true. I've been wanting her for weeks."

"Is she as good as she looks like she'd be?"

"Jesus, Cath."

"Well, you said she'd never been with a woman. Naturally, I'm curious."

"*Naturally,*" Tory remarked sarcastically. "Well, sis, she is far better than she looks, if you can imagine that. It's got nothing to do with how she makes love—" She stopped, blushing again as she remembered their brief interlude just an hour before. "Well, of course, there *is* that."

"Of course."

"I just meant there's so much more to it than that. Oh, I can't explain it. She just has to look at me, and I'm ready. God. You can obviously see my judgment is impaired. And you can see why I shouldn't be treating her."

"Tor, your brain is still functioning, even if the rest of your circuitry is shorted out." Cath laughed. "Don't worry about it; you're not doing anything wrong. If you two had been together for years and this had happened, you'd feel perfectly comfortable looking after her, wouldn't you?"

"It's not the medical issue I'm worried about," Tory confessed. "I'm afraid to send her back to work. Actually, I'm afraid *of* her work. Last night, I saw her get shot, and I thought she had been killed. I didn't realize until that moment how much she means to me. Now we've made love, Cath. She's opened the door to places I'm not even sure I wanted to know about. God, I don't even know if she loves me, and I'm terrified of losing her."

"Tor," Cath said gently, "I can't even imagine how horrible last night was for you. The woman you're crazy over almost got herself killed. Everything must seem shaky right now. You're exhausted. Go upstairs, lie down beside her, and try to sleep. I just want to remind you of one thing."

She put a comforting hand on Tory's arm. "Ten years ago when you were lying in a hospital bed, none of us ever wanted to see you in a scull again, *because* we had almost lost you. Now every day, I pray that you will someday row again, because you love it and you need it. If Reese weren't the woman she is—the cop, the soldier—you wouldn't love her. I don't imagine loving her will be easy, but I can see that you do. You can't change that, any more than you can change her."

"I'll admit she's captivated my attention, but I'm going to try to look at this as a momentary loss of reason." Tory brushed tears of fatigue and fear from her face, offering her sister a tremulous smile. "I'm not ready for love, especially with someone as dangerous as Reese Conlon. If she doesn't get herself killed, she's bound to have every woman on the Cape chasing her after this."

"Go," Cath ordered, thinking that the woman upstairs was just what her sister needed. She knew instinctively what her sister fought to accept. Tory and Reese were already inextricably involved.

❖

"I'm awake," Reese said as she lay watching Tory undress in the late afternoon sunlight. A cool ocean breeze wafted through the thin blinds on the open window, streaming across her naked body.

"You're not supposed to be," Tory commented as she reached for a T-shirt, her back to the bed.

"You don't need that," Reese called softly. Her voice was husky, and unmistakably seductive.

Tory hesitated for a second as heat rushed into her belly, making her legs weak. Then, resolutely, she pulled the thin cotton over her head as she crossed to the bed. This was ridiculous. Reese needed to rest, not get twenty years of sexual experience in a single day.

"I'm beat, and I have no idea why you're still able to form sentences. So, please, just meditate or something, but for God's sake, get some sleep." She lay down and purposefully faced away from Reese.

"I will," Reese assured her, turning so the length of her body pressed against Tory's back. She slipped her hand under the T-shirt to clasp the soft swell of breast and slowly pressed her lips along the bare skin from Tory's shoulder up the side of her neck. "In just a minute," she whispered into Tory's ear. With the other hand, she raised Tory's head enough to catch the corner of her mouth with an exploring tongue.

Tory hadn't moved, but she couldn't resist opening her lips to admit that teasing tongue. Reese groaned, cleaving harder to Tory as she tried to get even deeper into the woman whose very presence kindled a twisting fire in her.

Tory felt Reese surge against her, even as her own pulse pounded in response. She didn't have the resolve to resist her, but this time, she would set the tempo. Reese was already moving on the razor's edge of excitement. *Oh, no you don't. You're not coming yet. You need to learn a little patience.*

She pushed away, turning until she faced Reese, who stared at her in innocent confusion.

"What's wrong?" Reese managed. She had been soaring, her entire being sensitized by Tory's nearness.

"Don't think you're getting off that easy this time, Conlon," Tory warned. She pushed Reese gently but commandingly onto her back. "Don't move, don't talk, don't do anything. This time I'm in charge."

As she spoke, Tory rose to her knees, pulling the T-shirt over her head and tossing it into the corner. Reese's eyes widened as she surveyed the woman above her, her gaze following the soft curves fusing into firm muscle, the sweeping planes and angles, the interplay of strength and grace that she had sensed these many weeks. Seeing Tory now, Reese could not have imagined the beauty.

"Oh, God, Tory. Let me touch you," she whispered, her throat dry.

"Quiet," Tory said softly, smiling at Reese's response. She had never felt so powerful or quite so sensual. Reese's obvious desire fueled her own. She wanted to take her time; she wanted to explore every fiber of Reese's being. She wanted Reese to feel her in every inch of her body.

Tory leaned forward with her breasts just out of reach of Reese's lips. Her fingers lingered on Reese's full brows, tracing each bold arch. She followed the sharp ridge of cheekbone and strong angle of jaw with her hands. She lowered herself until her hardened nipples, achingly taut, brushed across Reese's lips, then pulled back just as Reese touched them with her tongue. She gasped at the swift shiver of arousal, smiling as Reese groaned in frustration at her withdrawal.

"You're killing me," Reese pleaded.

"You'll live," she answered throatily.

Bending once again, Tory licked the sweet sheen of sweat in the hollow of Reese's throat and tasted the mist of moisture that ran down the center of her elegantly muscled chest. With the flat of her hand, she stroked the hard planes of Reese's abdomen, exulting in the quivering response to her touch. She brought her face close to the damp hair between Reese's thighs, breathing her scent, feeling the heat rising from her.

As Tory indulged her senses, Reese moaned, lifting her pelvis, her leg muscles straining, urging Tory wordlessly to touch her. Tory held her there, feeling her tremble with urgency, as she breathed a kiss across her clitoris, barely touching the ultrasensitive tip. Reese whimpered at the fleeting contact. Tory kissed it again, then drew away.

"Let me feel your mouth. Please. *Please,* Tory," Reese begged. Her eyes were cloudy, her neck taut with strain as she looked down her body to where Tory lay nestled between her thighs. "Kiss me... until I come."

Reese's need produced an answering surge of excitement that nearly pushed Tory to orgasm. She had to fight to keep from pressing herself against Reese's muscled thigh and riding the smooth skin until her own aching clitoris exploded. Ignoring the warning twitches of an impending climax, Tory ran her tongue over the soft skin of Reese's inner thigh. "Not yet, sweetheart, not yet."

Only when Reese sobbed her name again, almost incoherent, did she take Reese into her mouth. She sucked gently, tonguing the underside of the stiff shaft. She expected it to be fast, but she wasn't prepared for the force of the contractions that exploded under her tongue. Grasping Reese's hips and clinging fast, she accepted each forceful thrust like a gift, absorbing the essence of Reese's passion with all of her senses. For long moments, she knew nothing but the strangled cries, the quivering flesh, the taste of love. Only when she felt the tension ebb did the awareness of anything other than the pounding of her own heart penetrate her consciousness. She hadn't even been aware of her own orgasm until she felt the lingering spasms throughout her pelvis.

"Reese?" she questioned gently as she moved upward. Reese was so still, one arm flung over her face, that Tory was frightened. "What is it?"

The breath caught in her throat when Reese turned to her with an expression so pained that Tory thought she had hurt her. She gathered her close, cradling Reese's face against her breasts. "Oh God, sweetheart, what's wrong?"

"I never imagined this," Reese murmured, her voice breaking. "I never imagined anyone touching me this way." She turned away, afraid of what need might show in her face. For the first time in her life, she felt exposed and disoriented. Almost inaudibly, she whispered, "Now, I can't imagine you *not* touching me."

Tory pressed her face against Reese's hair, holding her firmly. She could feel her tremble, and it nearly broke her heart. This warrior woman, who would face death without a qualm, was suddenly so vulnerable that Tory was overwhelmed with the terrible power of their passion. It frightened her, and thrilled her, more than anything she had ever known.

"It's all right, Reese," she whispered, stroking her softly. "I won't hurt you."

Reese lay silent, knowing that Tory was the one person on earth with the power to destroy her. All Tory need do was send her away, and she would be lost. The desire, the need, which had exploded between them could never be met by another. As clearly as Reese knew this, she knew that she wanted Tory, regardless of the cost, for the rest of her life. Placing her fate in Tory's hands, she rested her head against Tory's breast and slept.

CHAPTER EIGHTEEN

Two nights later, Tory returned from the clinic close to eleven p.m. Reese's Blazer was parked in the drive. Tory stared at it, a mixture of fury and fear warring in her mind. She knew Reese had been fretting with boredom since her injury, but she still had sutures in, and Tory had told her specifically that she was not ready to drive.

Cath heard the front door slam and steeled herself. Jed scuttled behind the couch.

"Where's Reese?" Tory asked by way of greeting, her voice like flint.

"Uh, upstairs, I think," Cath uttered. *This is going to be worse than I thought.*

"Did you get her truck for her?"

"No, Marge did," Reese replied, walking into the kitchen. She had her badge pinned to the pocket of her denim work shirt and wore a pair of blue jeans. As she spoke, she eased into the shoulder strap of her holster. She smiled softly at Tory in welcome. "Hi."

Tory ignored the greeting, too angry to acknowledge how much she had missed Reese during the day. "Are you seeing a physician I don't know about?"

"Of course not," Reese responded in surprise.

"Then who cleared you to work?"

"I'm not working. I'm just going to drive around the dunes for a few hours, unofficially."

"With a gun, in the middle of the night?" Tory's hands were clenched, and she fought down the urge to throw things. Reese just stared at her, clearly astounded by her reaction.

"Did Nelson approve this?" Tory asked harshly.

"Didn't ask him. I'm doing it on my time."

"The *hell* you are," Tory responded curtly, walking toward the phone. "If you won't follow my orders as your physician, I'll have Nelson suspend you. You can see another doctor tomorrow."

"Tory," Reese said softly, resting a gentle hand on her lover's arm to stop her. "Just hear me out, and then if you don't want me to, I won't go out."

Tory turned from the phone reluctantly, her jaw clamped rigid. She nodded her head sharply for Reese to go ahead.

"Someone is after kids, Tory, *our* kids. Bri told me there have been other incidents of gay boys and lesbians being verbally hassled on their way to or from the dunes. Caroline has seen a black pickup cruising out there, and she thinks once or twice it's followed her home after she's been with Bri. The kids are in danger, Tory. I just want to be seen out there, and let whoever's doing this know that *I* know. Maybe that will be enough to put an end to this before someone gets hurt."

"It doesn't have to be you, Reese," Tory argued. "Not now, not when you're not even healed. Call Nelson. Tell him what's going on. He can have someone else patrol the dunes."

"I can't, not for a few more days. Bri promised me she would tell Nelson about her and Caroline. I told her I'd give her a week. And even if Nelson knew, he doesn't have enough personnel, without Smith and me, to cover the town and step up patrol in the dunes. Since we don't really have an official complaint, there's no way he's going to pull someone off the streets now. Neither would I." She squared her shoulders unconsciously. "There's no one else to do it. I'll only be out a few hours." It was so clear to Reese what needed to be done. Surely, Tory would see that.

"Damn it, Reese," Tory cried. "You're not fit for duty. The hole in your side is barely closed. How could you handle another dangerous situation? And if you're out there, anything could happen." She turned away abruptly, not wanting Reese to see the fear in her face. Wordlessly, she walked out onto the deck, leaving Reese staring after her. *How could I handle it is the real question.*

Cath spoke quietly from the corner of the room. "My sister isn't used to talking about her fears. She's gotten used to dealing with her terror and her pain alone. First she lost her Olympic career, and she nearly lost her leg. Then she lost the woman with whom she had believed she would spend her life. She can't take any more loss in her life, Reese. She was watching you through the night glasses during the rescue on the beach. When she saw you get shot, she thought you had been killed. Now, she's terrified. She's terrified of loving you, and she's terrified of losing you."

"Cath, I don't want to hurt her. It isn't a question of me just *caring* about her. She means more to me than I thought anyone ever could." Reese swallowed, forcing herself to say the next words. Eyes filled with torment, she looked at Tory's sister. "She's already been hurt too much. I'll leave her alone if you think I should."

"Oh, I can see why you scare her to death. You're beautiful." Cath shook her head, laughing softly. "You don't know much about women, do you, Reese?"

"I don't know anything about any of this," Reese responded quite seriously. "I only know what I feel for her. And it's everything that I have."

"I can see how much you care. She needs you, Reese. Just go to her and follow your instincts. They've been right so far."

Smiling her thanks, Reese walked outside and crossed to the woman highlighted in moonlight on the deck.

"Tory," she said, slipping her arms around the still figure from behind, cradling Tory's body gently against her. "I'm sorry I didn't talk to you first. I need a little practice at this. Forgive me?"

Tory grasped the hands that circled her waist, stroking the tender flesh of Reese's palms. "This is so damn typical of you. I know you believe you have to do this. I keep trying to tell myself you're right—"

"But?" Reese questioned, pressing her cheek to Tory's hair, sliding a kiss against the soft skin at her temple.

Tory shivered at the touch. "But my heart keeps saying it doesn't have to be you. Let someone else do it. Let someone else's lover be the one in danger. Let someone else get hurt." Her voice trailed off in a nearly inaudible sob.

Reese tightened her hold until there was nothing between them but the night. "It has to be me because that's what I do—that's who I am," she whispered with absolute conviction.

"I know that." Tory nodded imperceptibly, not wanting to disturb their union. "It's one of the reasons I..."

She stopped before she gave voice to feelings whose consequences she wasn't ready to accept. "I don't think I'm strong enough for this, Reese," she finished miserably, starting to move away.

Reese tightened her hold.

"I can't promise you I won't get hurt, Tory," Reese continued, unwilling to let Tory withdraw from her. "But I *can* promise you that I will never put myself in a situation I'm not trained for. And I can promise you that every day of my life, I'll be here for you, if you let me."

Tory turned in Reese's arms, reaching around her shoulders to clasp her close. She pressed her forehead into Reese's chest, clamping down on the desire that flooded her as she felt Reese along the length of her. "God, I could get used to that idea," she admitted reluctantly.

"Good," Reese said, lifting Tory's face to kiss her.

❖

"Can't sleep?" Cath asked when she joined Tory on the deck. It was two o'clock in the morning.

"Not while she's out there," Tory responded, tipping the glass to finish her drink.

"You'll have to learn to, you know," Cath said, lighting a cigarette, offering the pack to her sister. Tory accepted wordlessly, smoking in silence as the stars hovered overhead.

"I know I'm overreacting," she said at length.

"Probably," Cath agreed. "But it's been a hellacious few days, and you've been through as much as she has, maybe more. Give yourself some time."

"I'm not used to being so emotional," Tory confided. "I'm not proud of myself."

"Oh, God, Tor," Cath exclaimed. "If it were me, there'd be more screaming than you can imagine. Sometimes I think I might scream *for* you. I've never met anyone quite like her; she's so goddamned logical, and *right*, that it's hard to argue with her. If I didn't know her, I wouldn't believe it. But she loves you, Tor. I can see it when she looks at you."

"God, I hope so," Tory whispered fervently. "Because my defenses are in shambles, and she's inside of me now."

❖

Reese found them both dozing in deck chairs when she returned a little after three a.m. She bent to kiss Tory softly on the cheek, murmuring her name.

Tory reached for her sleepily, circling her arms around Reese's neck. "Anything?" she asked.

"No," Reese replied, lifting her into an embrace and kissing her again, more thoroughly. Once she had Tory fully awake and gasping, Reese just held her wordlessly, simply enjoying the feel of her. Heart pounding, Tory rested against her. Nestled in strong arms, she relished the slow swell of desire.

"I think I'll just toddle off to bed," Cath remarked, casting a glance at the two figures outlined in the dim light of the stars. She brushed her hand fondly across her sister's back as she passed.

"She's a good woman," Reese remarked.

"Yes," Tory agreed dreamily. "Are you ready to take me to bed?"

Reese laughed. "More than ready, although I had something in mind other than sleep."

"That's what I was hoping."

Reese led Tory upstairs to the bedroom, then urged her gently toward the bed. With infinite care, Reese removed each article of Tory's clothing, exploring the enticing landscape of her body with lips and hands, captivated by the sensuality of her delicate strength. "You're so beautiful."

"You feel so good." Tory quivered as insistent fingers traced her skin from her breasts down her legs and back up. "I love the way you touch me."

When Tory was completely naked, Reese quickly shed her clothes and pulled Tory down onto the bed with her, pressing fleeting kisses everywhere. Mouth to the soft skin where thigh met belly, she murmured, "I intend to touch every part of you."

"Don't hurry," Tory gasped as the teasing lips moved up her body to linger on her breast, coaxing her to ever higher peaks of pleasure. As every muscle clenched with the effort of containing her desire, Tory moaned Reese's name. She grasped Reese's shoulders and tightened her legs around a muscled thigh.

"I'm close," Tory whispered raggedly. "Touch me, Reese, please. You make me want to come so much."

Reese groaned, so inflamed by the wet heat of Tory's need against her skin that she had no other thought, only wanting. When she found Tory swollen with urgency, open and ready, she was driven by some deeply primal instinct to claim her. As if she had been born knowing how, Reese pushed into her, hard. In a single motion, her fingers entered Tory fully while her thumb rode against Tory's clitoris, igniting a chain reaction. Immediately, the velvet muscles spasmed around her hand.

"Oh, God!" Tory screamed, her body heaving, her mind melting with the instant orgasm.

Reese pressed deeper as the cataclysmic spasms gave way to small internal contractions. So consumed by the wonder of it, she was barely breathing. Slowly, she became aware of sobs.

"Tory," Reese gasped in panic, slipping from her, her withdrawal eliciting another sob. "Oh Jesus. Did I hurt you?"

"No," Tory whispered, her face pressed against Reese's shoulder, her body still shuddering.

"Are you sure I didn't hurt you?" Reese persisted fearfully. "I didn't mean to be rough. God, I don't know what happened. I just wanted you so much." She tilted Tory's chin, searching her face anxiously. "Are you all right?"

Tory nodded "yes," but her cheeks were streaked with tears.

Something twisted in Reese's chest, catching at her heart. "Tory," she choked. "Tory, I swear to you I never meant to—"

"You didn't hurt me, Reese," Tory managed, drawing a shaky breath. She had never been possessed like that before. She felt as if she had been devoured.

What frightened her was not Reese's passion, but how much she had *wanted* Reese to take her. If Reese hadn't claimed her when she did, she would have begged. What Reese was capable of awakening made her a stranger to herself. "You make me so damn helpless, I want you so badly. What you do to me..." *What it will do to me now if you leave me.*

Reese held Tory gently in her arms, hearing in the silence what Tory had not said. She remembered Cath speaking of all that Tory had lost, understanding the enormity of that pain as she contemplated what a life without Tory would be like. Barren and so lonely.

"Tory," she said, her voice soft but crystal clear.

"Yes?" Tory questioned as she lay listening to the strong, steady heartbeat beneath her cheek.

"I love you."

Tory was silent a long moment, hearing the words, wondering if she dared allow them inside her. *Reese has never held another woman, never made love to another woman. How can she be sure now?*

Reese had not expected an answer. Instinctively, she knew that it wouldn't be her words, but her constancy, that would eventually convince Tory of the truth of her love. She had spoken because she needed to, and as she said the words, something shifted inside of her. She felt peaceful in a way she never had before. Gently, she settled Tory even closer into the curves of her body, her hands gliding the length of Tory's back to her buttocks. "I love to fall asleep with you."

"You're not going to get any sleep tonight if you keep touching me like that," Tory murmured, wanting nothing more at that moment than their closeness.

"That's okay," Reese laughed contentedly, continuing her caresses. "I don't have to work tomorrow."

CHAPTER NINETEEN

Reese wasn't due to return to work for a few more days, so she stayed on at Tory's. To Tory's delight, Reese shopped and cooked dinner every night. Eventually, Tory reconciled herself to Reese's nightly sojourns through the dunes and even managed some restless sleep waiting for her new lover to slip into bed beside her in the dark. Some personal items of Reese's had also migrated to the closet and the bathroom during her stay. Neither of them discussed exactly what that meant.

Reese had only been back an hour one night when they were awakened by the phone. Tory reached for it with a sigh, thinking how much harder it was going to be to leave her bed with Reese asleep beside her. She didn't want to think about what it would be like when Reese returned to her own home. The sheriff had fast become a part of her life.

"Dr. King."

"Doctor," an unfamiliar male voice said apologetically, "this is Officer Jeff Lyons. Sorry to bother you, ma'am, but I'm trying to locate Sheriff Conlon. I've got a girl on the other line. She's hysterical, and she says she won't talk to anyone except Reese."

"Of course," Tory replied with concern. "She's right here."

"Conlon," Reese said tersely as Tory switched on the bedside light. As she listened to the call patched through to her, her body tensed. "Where are you now?...Where were you supposed to meet?...Go home. I'll call you as soon as I find her. I will. I promise you."

Reese replaced the receiver as she climbed out of bed. It was two o'clock in the morning.

"What is it?" Tory asked anxiously as Reese pulled on her uniform, her face a professional mask.

"Bri's missing," Reese said as she checked her automatic and holstered it on her hip. "She and Caroline had a date to meet in the dunes. Bri didn't show. That was two hours ago. I...what are you doing?"

As Reese was outlining the situation, Tory had started hastily dressing. "I'm going with you," she said, her tone leaving no doubt. "We'll find her faster with two of us looking. And if she's hurt, you're going to need me."

"You're right," Reese replied absently, her mind occupied formulating plans. "Get your Jeep, your medical equipment, and your cell phone. I'll swing by the station on the way and get a patrol car. We'll keep in touch that way. If we haven't found her in an hour, I'm going to have to call Nelson. I'm hoping it doesn't come to that."

"Where should I look?"

"I'm going out to Herring Cove where they were supposed to meet. Why don't you drive down Commercial, then out 6A and circle back to the beach on 6. Look for her motorbike. Maybe she was just late, missed Caroline, and she's hanging out somewhere in town."

Tory could tell by the set of her jaw that Reese did not believe that.

"Reese, promise me if there's trouble that you'll call for backup. Your wound isn't healed yet. Your reaction time will be slowed. I can't worry about both of you."

To Tory's relief, Reese nodded agreement. "I will. Call me every five minutes with your location."

Then, unexpectedly, Reese grasped Tory's shoulders and kissed her with bruising intensity. "Be careful. I don't want you hurt."

As Tory followed Reese downstairs, she was certain from the rigid cast of her lover's back and the closed expression on her face that Reese was more than a little worried. Once outside, Reese said nothing as she strode off to her Blazer, her attention clearly focused completely on her mission. Tory watched her go, knowing that this single-minded determination was the essence of the woman she loved. Knowing, too, that to love Reese Conlon meant she must accept what that dedication demanded of Reese, emotionally and physically. Tory doubted she would ever grow accustomed to the danger, but she would have to live with it, because it was no longer possible for her to stop loving Reese.

Tory drove the length of Commercial Street, slowly canvassing the narrow lanes and alleys that intersected it. Several times she stopped to glance into the few bars and late night hangouts still open. Bri was not in any of these secluded places.

Circling the end of town past the jetty to Long Point, she remembered her own perilous journey out onto the rocks and the way Reese had suddenly appeared at her side, offering assistance and security as only Reese could. She recalled with aching clarity how great her pain was that night and the comforting sight of Reese bending over her, administering to her bruised and swollen leg. That was the night she had fallen in love with Reese Conlon.

She was nearing the Provincetown limits when her cell phone rang.

"King," she responded tersely.

"It's Reese. Take 6 west toward Herring Cove. Look for my cruiser on the side of the road. I'm about a hundred yards in along the dune trail."

"Have you got her?" Tory asked, thinking that Reese's voice seemed strangely hollow.

"Yes. On the double, Tory."

Reese was waiting at the roadside, hastily stringing yellow crime scene tape across the mouth of a narrow path in the sand. Illuminated by Tory's headlights, Bri's motorbike lay on its side in the scrub by the side of the road. The front was twisted and dented. Tory's stomach churned when she saw it and what Reese was doing.

"My God, is she alive?" Tory called as Reese approached.

"Yes, for now," Reese replied grimly, helping Tory slide the portable stretcher from the back of her Jeep. "Follow me, and keep to the trail. I don't want to contaminate the scene any more than we have to."

Contaminate the scene? Tory stared at her in astonishment. *This is Bri, for God's sake. Doesn't she have any feelings?*

Reese saw the question in her eyes and read the silent criticism. It hurt, but she didn't have the time or the inclination to explain.

"You tend to her body, Doctor, that's your job. Mine is to catch the bastard that did this to her," Reese stated flatly, a dangerous finality in her voice.

"Of course." Tory nodded. "Lead the way."

Bri was lying unconscious in a shallow cleft between two brush-covered dunes. Tory lifted the blanket Reese had laid over the young woman and recoiled from the sight of the torn shirt and the jeans yanked down around Bri's ankles. For an agonizing moment, all she could imagine was Bri's terror. "Oh my God."

A soft touch on Tory's shoulder jerked her back to the present and her responsibility.

"Tory, we need to move her. Is her spine secure?" Reese asked evenly.

Tory knelt, making a quick assessment of Bri's vital signs. Her airway was clear, and her pulse was strong and steady. Her face was badly battered, both eyes already discolored and massively swollen. There was a stream of blood from her left nostril and a hematoma forming over the right side of her jaw. Even in the dim light from Reese's flashlight, Tory could make out bruises on Bri's throat. Blood crusted in patches over her neck and chest.

"She fought hard," Tory murmured, barely aware of speaking aloud as she continued her evaluation of the battered girl.

"Yes. She would."

Glancing up at Reese, who stood staring down at Bri's violated body, Tory shivered at the coldness in her eyes. Forcing herself to tend to the work, she then slipped a soft restraining collar behind Bri's neck, immobilizing her cervical spine. Running her hands over Bri's extremities, she noted no obvious deformities. The rest of the exam would have to wait until they moved her to the clinic.

"She's okay to transport. Just get your forearms behind her neck and under her shoulders when we lift. Keep her head midline and don't flex it," Tory ordered, her mind already busy planning what else needed to be done.

"Have you notified Nelson?" she asked as they maneuvered slowly through the sand.

"Lyons is on his way here to secure the scene," Reese replied. "I'll radio the chief en route to your place. I didn't want him to see her like this."

Tory nodded, wondering how she could have questioned Reese's sensitivity, regretting her initial reaction. Reese was only doing what she was trained and sworn to do. "Reese, I'm sorry about earlier. I didn't think about what you needed to do out there."

"It's okay. Why should you?" Reese responded evenly.

"No, it's not okay." *Because I know you better than that, and because I love you.*

Tory needed to tell her that, but now was not the time. Instead, she followed the flashing lights of Reese's patrol car as they led her through the dark.

❖

"What the hell is going on, Conlon?" Nelson Parker demanded as he shoved through the door of Tory's clinic. "I heard on the scanner that you ordered Lyons and Jameson to block off a section of 6. You're not even on duty."

He got a good look at his second's face, and he stopped short, his stomach churning. There was fury crowding anguish in her eyes, yet her hand on his arm was so gentle that he was suddenly afraid. He'd seen that look in cops' eyes before, when it was something bad. He steeled himself to hear it. "Tell me," he said softly.

"It's Bri. She's alive, but she's seriously hurt. Tory is with her now."

Nelson steadied himself with a hand against the wall. There seemed to be something wrong with his vision; he could hardly see Reese's face. He heard his own words but didn't feel himself speak. "Did she crash her motorbike?"

"Someone beat her, Nelson."

"I don't understand...why?" He felt as if he was gut shot. "How did you find her?"

"Caroline Clark called me. She told me Bri was missing, and I went to look for her. I found her in the dunes."

"Caroline?" Nelson looked at her in confusion. "Why did she call you? What's going on?"

Reese returned his questioning gaze steadily, a decision made. "Bri and Caroline are lovers. They've been trysting in the dunes.

My guess is that someone followed Bri, forced her off the road, and dragged her up into the scrub."

Nelson rocked back as if she had struck him. Then he leveled angry eyes on her. "You *knew* about them? That's why Caroline called *you?*"

"Yes. Bri told me she was going to tell—"

"What?" All of his terror was transformed into palpable rage. *This is Reese's fault. If she'd told me, I would've put a stop to this nonsense before Bri got hurt.*

"You son of a bitch." Nelson moved so unexpectedly that Reese didn't have time to counter, had she been so inclined. He grabbed her with both hands and slammed her into the wall. "You knew my daughter was fooling around with some girl, and you didn't tell me?" he roared. He punctuated his fury by pounding his forearm into her body. "You *let* it go on?"

Fire tore through her side. Reese never lifted a hand, though she was well equipped to defend herself. "Nelson—" she gasped. His elbow crashed into her again, and the pain was so blinding she thought she might black out. "Uhh."

When Tory came around the corner, she saw the pain in Reese's face. Nelson stood, one fist poised to strike, the other hand twisted in Reese's shirtfront, pinning her to the wall.

"No!"

Nelson was momentarily stunned as Tory's cane cracked down on his forearm, the curved handle catching around his wrist, preventing him from swinging into Reese's unprotected face.

"Let go of her, Nelson," Tory commanded in a deadly tone. "Now."

Reese sagged slightly in Nelson's grasp as he turned to Tory in confusion. Reese coughed, one hand pressed to her side, trying to catch her breath. Every inhalation felt like a knife stab. She slid down a few inches as her knees turned to jelly, but she finally managed to stop herself from falling.

"Take your hands off her." Tory's eyes never left Nelson's face as she shifted her weight, ready for the next strike. "Do it, Nelson, or I'll break your arm."

"It's okay, Tory," Reese gasped.

"He'd better pray to God he didn't hurt you," was all Tory said.

When Nelson finally dropped his hands to his sides, Tory relaxed slightly, but she kept her eyes on him. "The evac team is on its way for Bri. She's stable and intermittently conscious." She flicked her glance to her lover, who was white-faced and still slumped against the wall. "And she's asking for you, Reese."

"You stay away from her, Conlon," Nelson seethed. "If you weren't queer yourself, this never would have happened."

"I need a statement from her," Reese stated, forcing herself upright and working to keep her voice even. *And I need to see that she's all right.*

"Forget about a statement. You're fired."

"You can fire me tomorrow." Reese shrugged, setting off spasms in her side. She was in control now, and the pain didn't register in her voice or face. "Tonight, I'm going to catch whoever has been terrorizing the kids in this town. Tory, call Caroline, will you? I promised her."

"Go ahead, Reese, I'll take care of it. Then I need to look at you." Tory said these last words with a glare toward the chief.

Smiling gently, Reese brushed her fingers over the hand Tory clasped around the head of her cane. She drew as deep a breath as she could, determined not to reveal how much it hurt. "I'm really okay."

The she walked the short distance down the hall, pushed open a door, and entered the procedure room. Nelson followed, then stumbled to a halt just inside, paralyzed at the sight of his daughter.

Bri lay naked under a thin sheet, nearly unrecognizable from her bruises, needles in each arm hooked up to two IV bags. When he saw a clear plastic evidence bag filled with bloodied clothes on the counter, an open rape kit beside it, he had to fight the sudden urge to vomit. Then he looked again at the stretcher, expecting to see his little girl, but he saw a battered woman, someone he didn't know. *How can this be?*

He was afraid to go near her.

Reese pulled up a stool, taking Bri's hand in hers. Aware of Nelson coming to stand behind her, she pressed the torn and bloodied fingers to her cheek.

"It's Reese, Bri," she said gently. "You're all right now. You're safe."

Bri's eyelids fluttered, then the left opened a few millimeters. She tried to focus on Reese's face. Her throat was so dry that it was hard to form words. She found the blue eyes and let herself be held by the tenderness in them. "Carre?" she managed at last. "Is she...?"

"She's fine, Bri. She's on her way."

"Don't...let her see me...like this," Bri said with a struggle. "Please."

Reese smiled in understanding, brushing a lock of hair out of Bri's eyes. "She'll need to see you, Bri. She'll be more scared if she doesn't." She waited for a second, then continued with what she knew must be done. "Can you tell me who did this, Bri?"

Bri tried to turn away as tears leaked from the corners of her eyes. Reese caught them on the backs of her fingers.

"Did he rape me?" she whispered. Nelson choked back a groan as Tory moved from where she had been standing in the doorway.

"I don't think so, honey," Tory said softly. "I still have a few tests to run."

Bri closed her eyes with a sigh. Reese waited patiently, her entire being focused on the young woman before her. She gently stroked Bri's hair. "I'm going to get him, Bri. I promise. You fought well. Now help me get him."

Tory watched her lover, knowing that, at this moment, Bri was the most important thing in Reese's life. *How had I ever been naïve enough to think this was just a job for Reese?*

"Help me, Bri," Reese prompted softly.

"It was the black truck that's been following us. I don't know him, but I...I think I broke his nose. I punched him, when he was on top of me." Bri lapsed into silence again, shaking, clearly overcome by the events too fresh yet to be memories. "He had his hands..."

"Oh, Jesus," Nelson moaned.

"Give me something more, Bri," Reese pushed.

Bri gasped for breath as she tried to put words to her terror.

"Reese," Tory warned.

Reese ignored her. "Tell me, Bri. Help me get him."

Tory bit her lip, not wanting to interfere but vowing to stop it if Reese didn't.

"He hit my bike. I think it smashed his headlight," Bri said with a struggle.

"Good girl," Reese said.

Bri, fighting to remain conscious, looked up at her father. "I'm sorry, Dad. I wanted to tell you. I was scared..." Her voice trailed off as exhaustion claimed her.

Reese moved aside so Nelson could sit with his daughter, her mind already on the job ahead. To investigate, she had to get back to the field. She needed to check the motorbike for evidence and start looking for the perpetrator. Very likely, he would be seeking medical attention himself if Bri had really broken his nose. As she stepped out into the hall and pulled the door closed, she saw Tory forcefully interrupt Caroline's headlong dash down the hall.

"Wait a minute," Tory soothed, holding the struggling young woman. "It might be better if you see her tomorrow, Caroline. It'll be hard to see her like this."

Caroline fixed Tory with a contemptuous glare. "You're just like all the rest. You think just because we're young that our feelings don't matter. Last night right about now, she was making love to me. Do you think *that* doesn't matter either?"

"That's not what I meant, Caroline. I know you care about her."

"*Care* about her?" the young blond said coldly. "What if it were Reese in there, Dr. King? Just how long would *you* wait out here?"

Tory stared at her, knowing that it could easily be Reese under other circumstances. Just the thought made her ill.

"You're right. I'm sorry," Tory said softly. "Nothing on earth would keep me away. Go ahead."

Tory watched the pretty young woman, who now seemed so much older than her years, resolutely push through the door to her lover. Then she turned to her own lover, who was issuing orders into the phone.

"Call me with anything," Reese said. "I'm heading out now."

"Not until I take a look at you," Tory stated as Reese hung up the phone.

"Five minutes," Reese conceded.

"In here," Tory said, motioning to an empty exam room. "And I'll take as long as I need. Take off your shirt."

Reese complied with a sigh, trying to hide the pain that pierced her side as she shrugged out of her clothes.

Tory bent to examine the stitches. "Why didn't you stop him?" she asked as she cleaned the healing incision with peroxide. "You could have."

"He didn't know what he was doing," Reese grunted as Tory probed a tender spot along her rib cage. "Besides, he's my commanding officer."

"I'm going to pretend I didn't hear that, Reese. Because as much as I respect and admire your pigheaded dedication to your job, I cannot believe you would let him do that to you." There was a faint sensation of movement under her fingertips, and she felt Reese withdraw from the pressure.

"He would have come to his senses in a minute. If he had really endangered me, I would have stopped him."

Tory stepped back, furious. "Well, he broke at least one rib. Now, give me your goddamned gun. You're not working tonight."

Reese took Tory by surprise when she caught both her hands, pulling Tory against her body. *I'm going to frighten her again. How many times can I do this to her before it's too much?*

"Tory, I love you with everything in me. But I can't do what you want. Please, don't ask me to." Reese's embrace was so tight it was almost painful.

Tory pushed back in her grasp, searching the blue eyes that searched her own. There was honesty there and, shockingly, fear. *My God, she's afraid I'll leave her.*

"You'll need them taped," Tory stated, feeling the tension in Reese's body ease. "And I want your word of honor that you won't take any chances. Not one. If you love me, you owe me that, Reese."

"I do love you." Reese kissed her softly. "And I promise. Thank you."

CHAPTER TWENTY

Nelson stood back against the wall, watching Caroline Clark tenderly stroke his daughter's swollen cheek. With her free hand, Caroline brushed tears from her own face. The look she had given him when she entered the room had warned him he would have to forcibly keep her away. The steel in her gaze rendered him speechless.

"It's me, Bri. I love you," she whispered over and over. "I love you, baby."

At first, Nelson was embarrassed to hear her say such things to his daughter. But after a while, he found himself praying that the love of this slight blond girl would be enough to keep his only child holding on. God knew he hadn't offered her much reason lately.

Finally, Bri opened her eyes as much as she could, trying to smile when she heard Caroline whisper her name.

"Hi, babe," she said through cracked lips.

"Hi, baby," Caroline replied softly. "Dr. King says you'll be okay."

"You?" Bri croaked.

"Don't worry about me," she said tremulously. "Just get well."

"I knew he was following me." Bri squeezed her hand weakly. "That's why I didn't meet you. I went the other way...so he wouldn't find you."

Caroline was crying in earnest now. "I love you so much, Bri. I just want us to be together."

"Soon, I promise," Bri whispered as her strength faded. "Be careful. I love you..."

Nelson cleared his throat. "I'll look after her, Bri," he said, thinking he had finally found something he could do for his daughter.

Tentatively, he placed a hand on Caroline's shoulder. As Bri's eyes closed, Caroline turned unexpectedly into Nelson's arms.

"I'm so scared," she cried, clinging to him like the child she would never be again. "I don't know what I'll do if something happens to her."

"She'll be okay, honey. She's got her mother's grit." He led her around the table to a stool. "You sit here with her in case she wakes up. She'll need you then."

He looked back from the door at the stranger who was his daughter, thinking what a fine, brave thing she had done. Right now he didn't know her, but he swore that that would change.

Tory stood in the hall, giving a report to the team of paramedics who were there to transport Bri to the trauma center. When she finished, she looked at him coldly.

"Where's Conlon?" he asked, his voice gruffer than he intended.

"Out looking for the man who assaulted your daughter."

He nodded, intending to step past her. She moved purposely into his path.

"I have several messages for you, Nelson. The first one is from Reese. She wants you to stay with Bri. She said, and I quote, 'That's where you're needed. You'll taint the case if you're involved in any way.' She promises she won't rest until she gets him. I, for one, have no doubt she means that." She paused until she was satisfied that he agreed. "The next message is from me, and you can be *sure* I mean it. You broke her ribs tonight, Nelson. If you ever lay a hand on her again, you'll never wear a badge in this or any other place as long as you live."

The furious look she gave him caused Nelson to take a step back.

"Now get out of my clinic, and stay out of my sight."

"I'll resign tomorrow," Nelson said, his face gray.

"Reese wouldn't want you to do that," Tory said as she turned away. "And I'd rather you face her every day knowing that."

He stared at her retreating back, feeling smaller than he ever had. In the last hour, he had seen what love between women was made of, and he knew that he would never discount it again. He only hoped it was in him to love so well. He walked out to the ambulance holding his daughter's hand, praying she would forgive him.

❖

What happened, in the dark hours before dawn, was the stuff of which legends are made. And as this story was told and retold by every cop on the Cape and every person in Provincetown, the story grew. Only the two young officers who answered Reese's call for backup could really say for sure, and even they couldn't agree on what really transpired.

Certain facts were indisputable. In her patrol car, Reese waited in the dark on the edge of Route 6, watching the few vehicles leaving Provincetown. When a black pickup truck with a single headlight passed her going five miles over the speed limit, she flicked on her lights and siren and chased him to the outskirts of Truro. He finally pulled over, and Reese pulled her cruiser in front of him, angling onto the shoulder so that he could not drive off. She sat still momentarily, looking at the fresh dent in the right front fender of his truck. Remembering her promise to Tory, she radioed her position and requested backup. They were five minutes away. She did everything by the book, as she believed it should be done. Then she made a human error. For a brief instant, she stopped thinking like a cop and thought instead about Bri—of her brave, young spirit and her beautiful face, unrecognizable now. She thought about the finger marks on Bri's neck and her breasts, the gouges on her inner thighs. She thought about Bri's terror with him battering for entrance to the places only her lover had ever touched. She thought about Bri out there alone, bleeding into the sand, because some man did not like whom she chose to love. With these images of Bri haunting her mind, she stepped from the cruiser and unsnapped the strap that secured her gun.

❖

Hospitals in the dark hours of the night were places like no other. Hushed with unnatural silence, punctuated by the moans and murmurs of the ill and dying, they were places to pass through, not to linger. Lives were changed forever there, for the dead as well as the living.

Tory walked down the dim hallway toward the ICU carrying her third cup of coffee of the long night that promised to become a longer day. It was just after five a.m., and she welcomed the activity she knew the morning shift would bring. She'd had too much time to think the last couple hours, sitting with Caroline, waiting for word from Reese.

At the end of the hall, Caroline stared at the closed doors of the intensive care unit. She automatically wiped the tears that overflowed her eyes, longing for seven a.m. when she could see Bri.

Watching her, Tory reflected on the clear and simple passion connecting the young women. Untainted by disappointments, untarnished by the accumulated experiences of loves gone wrong, their devotion was unrestricted, their commitment complete. They were brave and fearless and so pure in their loving. They trusted in tomorrow, believing nothing could come between them. They were glorious in their innocence.

Sadly, Tory knew there had been a time when she had loved like that. She knew, too, as did all those whose first loves withered with change, that she could never love that way again. Some part of her would always be afraid. She wondered if she could ever truly give herself fully to love again. Even with Reese, she wasn't sure she could, or even that she wanted to.

She glanced into a small dark waiting room just down the hall from the harshly lit main sitting area. Reese stood at the window, her back to the room. The sky beyond was just lightening with the dawn. The tense stillness in Reese's figure signaled to Tory that something was wrong. She went to her, slipping her arms around Reese's waist from behind, laying her cheek against Reese's strong back.

"I'm glad you're here," Tory murmured against her.

"How is she?" Reese asked, folding her arms over Tory's.

"They're still running tests. Her head CT was clear, thank God, so it appears to be only a bad concussion. We should know the rest of the results within the hour."

Reese nodded, not turning.

"Did you get him?" Tory asked quietly.

"Yes."

"Are you all right?"

"I don't know," Reese answered hollowly. She took a shaky breath. "I couldn't stop thinking about her, lying alone out there in the night, what he had done to her for no other reason than she loved another woman. Jesus! She's just a girl."

Reese pulled away abruptly, sinking into a nearby chair. She stared at her hands, dangling between her knees. Tory went to her, stood between her legs, and placed her hands lightly on Reese's shoulders. Reese was trembling.

"Tell me," Tory said gently.

"I got out of my car intending to kill him," Reese admitted in a low voice. "I knew it when I walked up to the vehicle. If it was him, I was going to kill him."

Tory's chest constricted in fear, but her voice was steady. "What happened?"

"It was him." Reese laughed joylessly. "His nose was halfway over to his ear, and he had cuts on his face and hands from pulling Bri through the brush. Whoever he got to patch him up hadn't done a very good job. I asked him to step out of the truck. I could hear my backup coming, and so could he. He didn't put up a fight. As soon as he was out, I spun him down onto the hood. When the other patrol car pulled in, I had my gun against the back of his head."

Tory nearly stopped breathing, but she tightened her grip on Reese's shoulders. She would not leave her alone with this. "Keep talking, sweetheart," she whispered. "It's all right."

Reese drew in a long breath, then let it out slowly. "They just watched me. I knew they'd never say what happened. This was about the chief's daughter. I thought about this pervert ripping at her clothes, on top of her—oh, Jesus," she gasped, her voice breaking. "I could hardly see him any longer. My arm ached from *not* pulling the trigger."

When Reese lapsed into silence, Tory lifted her chin with a cupped hand and searched her tormented blue eyes. "What did you do, sweetheart?"

"I holstered my weapon," Reese said hoarsely, "and as I reached for the cuffs, he made his move. He came at me fast, but this wasn't Nelson, and I was ready. I broke his arm. But God, all I wanted was to kill him. I came so close, Tory, so close. What does that say about me?"

Reese reached out in her pain for Tory. Wrapping her arms around Tory's waist, she buried her face against her lover's breasts and wept.

"Oh, my darling," Tory whispered, pierced by Reese's anguish. She stroked her hair, ran her hands tenderly over her quivering shoulders, held her fast. Reese's need was so clear, her emotions so raw. In her own way, Reese was as innocent and vulnerable as those two girls down the hall. If ever there had been a barrier to Tory loving this woman, it was gone now. This was her chance at love again, the simple, fresh, untarnished love of the young. She had likened her frighteningly valiant, frustratingly honorable lover to an innocent, and in the uncompromising way she loved, she was.

"Oh, Reese," she sighed, her throat aching with emotion. "I love you. I love you so much."

Tory looked over Reese's bowed head to see Nelson standing in the shadows of the door, watching them. Wondering how much he had heard but not caring what he thought, she motioned him away. Reese would not have wanted him to see her this way.

Nelson turned away from the image of Tory cradling the sobbing woman. He had once foolishly thought that Reese had no more needs than a man. Now he understood what bravery it took to let the woman who loved you offer comfort. He walked back to join the young woman who loved his daughter.

"I'm sorry," Reese mumbled at last, her cheek still against Tory's breast.

Tory laughed shakily, lifting Reese's face, gently brushing away the tears. "Don't you dare say that. I so needed for you to need me."

"Need you?" Reese looked perplexed. "Didn't you know that I do?"

Shaking her head, Tory softly kissed Reese's forehead. "You do give the impression of self-sufficiency, my love."

"Tory," Reese said, anxiously, "it may seem as if I don't need any help because I never had anyone to ask. How I feel about you—what I feel since we've been together." She stood, pulling Tory close. "God, how I need you. You mean everything to me."

"I love you, Reese. I love your strength, and your integrity, and your beautiful sense of assuredness. I need that; it scares me how much I need that. But you don't have to be strong all the time, especially not for me. When you share yourself with me, I only love you more. Although God only knows how that's possible." She kissed her soundly, then stepped back, running her hands down Reese's arms. "I want to get you home. I'm not even going to ask about your ribs."

"They hurt like hell, and I'm beat." Reese smiled, slipping an arm around her. "I just want to check on the kids."

"I know. Me, too."

❖

After a few hours' sleep, Tory got up to go to the clinic. Reese stirred as Tory slipped from the bed and grabbed her hand, pulling Tory down beside her. "I'll miss you," Reese said softly.

"I don't want to go, but there are a few patients who can't wait. I won't be long." She kissed Reese, all too aware of her nakedness. "Besides, since you always seem to be recovering from some injury or another, it's just as well that I stay away from you." She smiled suggestively. "I can't trust myself to have any restraint."

Reese guided Tory's hand down over her taut stomach to the spot that ached to be touched. "Too late," she whispered unevenly as Tory's fingers brushed over her. She was already hot and hard.

"You can't know what you do to me or you wouldn't torture me this way," Tory groaned, instantly ambushed by the wet warmth of Reese's desire. Helpless to stop, Tory caressed her, gently sliding her fingers up and down her distended clitoris.

Reese rose against her hand, gasping. "Just for a minute," she pleaded, feeling the pressure mushrooming in her belly. "Just...for a minute."

"Who could stop?" Tory whispered, staring into Reese's half-hooded eyes. Rhythmically, watching the eclipse of color reflect her touch, Tory worked her higher. Reese's blue gaze grew hazy, her lips parting with a groan, as she blossomed into ripe fruition under skilled fingers.

"Tory, love," Reese sighed as release rippled through her. Eyelids fluttering, then closing, her neck arched with the final spasm. She smiled softly as the tension slowly subsided. "Ahh, God. Thank you."

Tory buried her face in Reese's neck, still holding her fast. "You break my heart, you're so beautiful."

Reese languidly slipped her fingers into Tory's hair, turning her face to breathe a kiss against her cheek. "May you always think so," she said drowsily.

"Don't worry about that." With the aftermath of passion still gripping her, Tory laughed shakily. "Now unhand me, or I'll never leave."

Reese smiled contentedly. "Hurry home."

❖

When next Reese awoke, most of the day had passed. Tory was moving quietly around the room as she undressed. Reese watched her in silence, her pleasure so acute it was almost agony.

"I always want to wake up and see you," Reese said into the still room.

Tory halted, catching her breath. "And I always want to be there when you do."

"Come here," Reese commanded gently, sitting up against the pillows.

"Aren't you tired?"

"I've been sleeping all day." Reese grinned. "Now I want to put *you* to sleep. In a little while."

"What about your ribs?" Tory cocked her head, smiling slowly. *God, she's sexy. How is it that no one ever claimed her before this?*

"*I* don't plan on moving very much." Reese held out a hand. "Come on."

When Tory leaned over the bed, Reese placed both hands on her waist, then silently guided Tory up and over her, one leg on either side of her body. With Tory gazing down at her, lips parted in anticipation, Reese lifted her head and took her gently with her mouth, dimly aware of the swift intake of breath followed by a soft whimper. Taking her time despite the insistent rhythm of Tory's pulsing hips, Reese alternated light kisses with circling caresses of her tongue. As Tory's movements became more frantic and her breathing harsh and irregular, Reese brought a hand between them, entered her, and sucked hard on the stiffening clitoris. With a cry, Tory dug her fingers into Reese's forearms and grew rigid.

"Oh Reese! Make me come, please...please...do it now!"

With a knowing brush of her lips, Reese ended the sweet torture. Even as Tory bucked against her, she held fast, only slowing her strokes when Tory slumped down, exhausted. Settling Tory beside her, Reese pressed her face to her lover's breasts. Supremely content, she drifted, listening to Tory's soft murmurs of satisfaction.

After long moments, Tory said brokenly, "If you ever leave me, I'll be lost."

Reese lifted her head, her face still faintly flushed from their passion, and met Tory's gaze. "Not as long as I live."

"That sounds just about right, then." Tory sighed, curling closer in Reese's arms. "Although if you keep this up, *I* may not live that long."

"Oh, I think you'll survive," Reese murmured, laughing softly before she closed her eyes and slept.

CHAPTER TWENTY-ONE

It was a clear Provincetown morning in August, with a bright blue sky punctuated by scattered wisps of clouds overhead. The waves on the bay broke gently against the sands at Herring Cove. Reese sipped her coffee, waiting. She smiled as a flicker of color far off to her left caught her eye. Her heart lifted as she followed the course of the red kayak cutting swiftly through the early morning sea. Tory's rhythm was so steady that the craft seemed barely to touch the water as she paddled toward the lighthouse at Race Point. When she could no longer imagine she saw her, Reese drove away, filled with peace.

Nelson glanced up when Reese entered the station, then shied his glance away uncomfortably.

"Morning, Chief," Reese said, tossing her hat on her desk and heading for the coffeepot. She grimaced in disgust, emptying the contents into the sink.

"Good to have you back," Parker said gruffly. "Did the doc clear you for duty?"

"You think I'd be here if she didn't?" Reese laughed, remembering the scene at Tory's just a few hours before.

Tory had first inspected the freshly healed wound on Reese's side, then professionally poked and probed her rib cage, before reluctantly approving Reese's return to work. While Reese dressed, Tory had watched her, then stood in front of Reese and straightened a tie that was already perfectly knotted. After running her hands over the razor-edge creases in Reese's shirtsleeves, she had smoothed down the collar of her shirt. With her hands pressed lightly against Reese's chest, she had whispered, "I love the way you look in this uniform. You won't do anything to get any holes in it, will you?"

Reese had pulled her close. "I won't. I promise."

Nelson Parker watched Reese's expression turn inward to some private thought he couldn't fathom, but he knew it was something powerful. She'd changed in the time she had been gone, and he figured he knew who had been the cause of it.

Remembering Tory King brought back images of the night that he wished with all his being he could have to do over. He recalled, too, the look on Tory King's face as she stared him down. He knew damn well that if he had struck Reese, Tory would have taken him apart.

Nelson cleared his throat, ready to say what he had been preparing to say since that night. "Elections are coming up in the fall, Conlon. I think you should run for sheriff."

Reese poured two cups of fresh coffee, placing one on his desk as she passed.

"We already have a sheriff," she said with finality, reaching for the stacks of paperwork that had accumulated during her absence.

"You're qualified, the people of this town already think you're a hero, and every lawman in the state respects you for how you handled Bri's assault. You're a shoo-in."

He swiveled in his chair to stare out the front window for a minute, but he forced himself to look at her when he spoke again. "You handled the police part of it as well as anybody could, and you handled the personal part better than I ever could. If it hadn't been for Bri and Caroline trusting you, Bri would have died out there." His throat tightened with sudden emotion, and he continued gruffly, "I failed her, and I repaid you by busting you up. I don't deserve my own daughter's trust, and I certainly don't deserve to be sheriff. Take the damn job, Conlon, you deserve it."

"I'm not interested," Reese stated again. "There's too much paperwork and too much politics. I like patrol. I like being out on the streets. I like community interaction." She leaned back and regarded him with a small smile. "Plus I plan on teaching more martial arts classes in the fall. I'm too busy."

"Is that what the pow-wow with the kids was all about last night?" he asked, curious.

"Yep."

When Reese had stopped by the Parker residence to check on Bri the previous night, she had found the young woman polishing the new motorbike Nelson had bought to replace the one destroyed in the accident. Bri's face was still swollen and discolored, but her eyes were clear and happy. Caroline, who had barely left Bri's side since her release from the hospital, was there with several of their friends. Bri was chafing at the bit to ride again and resume her martial arts classes, but her doctors had declared no contact sports for six weeks due to her concussion.

Three of Bri's friends, two young women and a boy, had expressed interest in taking self-defense classes. Reese knew it was mostly a reaction to Bri's assault, but they seemed genuinely interested, too. After talking with them, she had agreed to teach several evening classes a week. Tory endorsed the idea and planned to teach as well. This was truly the kind of cop Reese wanted to be, one who was part of the community, responding to the needs of the community in a personal way.

"You didn't fail Bri either, and she doesn't think so," Reese continued. "Sure, she was afraid to talk to you, but some of that fear came from what others had done to her or her friends. As it turns out, her fear was unwarranted. Jesus, Caroline is practically living at your place since her father threatened her."

"Yeah, she's pretty much moved in." Nelson looked pained as he remembered Caroline calling Bri in tears when her father swore he would beat "this queer bullshit" out of her. "But still, that *might* have been me saying something as stupid as that if Bri hadn't almost been killed. It took almost losing her to put things into perspective for me. I don't know that I'd be trying as hard as I am to understand it. Still, I look at those two girls, and all I see is a rocky road ahead."

Reese nodded. "That may be, but having you on their side will go a long way toward making their lives easier. And believe me, Nelson, you couldn't keep them apart without hurting them more than any prejudice ever could."

"The reason Caroline spends most of her time with us is because that hardheaded kid of mine tried to get up out of her sickbed to go after Caroline's old man." He grinned self-consciously. "Jesus, she's tough to handle. Kinda reminds me of you."

"Thank you. I'll take that as a compliment." Reese grinned back.

"You and Tory give them something to look up to," he said, to Reese's surprise. "I'm grateful for that."

"We both care about them, Nelson, but it's you they need."

"About that night, Reese. I...I don't know how to ask you to forgive me for that night. What I said about it being your fault, that was bad enough. But what I did...Jesus, there's no way to make that right," he said quietly.

"There's nothing to forgive, Chief. If anything ever happened to Tory, I'd—" Her voice cracked, and she looked away for a second. "I'd be no different than you. Forget it."

He shook his head, disbelieving. "I appreciate your saying that, but I know better. I know Tory King won't forget it."

"She was worried about Bri and scared for me."

"She was protecting you, Conlon. I can see what you mean to her. You're a lucky woman to have that."

"Yes, I know."

"Well, I guess I'll just have to prove to her that I know what you're worth, too." He cleared his throat again, busying himself with the papers on his desk. "So, why don't you get out of here and go patrol somewhere. Tonight's Carnival Night, so expect it to be crazy. We'll need every able body on duty."

"Yes, sir." Reese sighed with relief, more than ready to get back out on the streets. "I still need to hunt down leads on that piercing parlor, too. If they haven't pulled up stakes and moved on, I'll find them."

"I don't doubt it," he muttered to himself.

"You want anything while I'm out?" she called from the door.

"Donuts."

Reese smiled happily. "Roger that."

❖

An hour later, she pulled into the crowded parking lot of the East End Health Clinic and walked inside. As usual, Randy looked to be on the verge of a nervous breakdown. "Please, *please,* don't tell me you want to see her," he exclaimed.

Reese smiled. "No good, huh?"

"If she agrees to see one more walk-in without an appointment, I'll have to cancel the hottest date of my life," he wailed.

"Just tell her I stopped by," Reese laughed. Then she lowered her voice. "And Randy, try to get her to take a break once in a while. At least see that she gets lunch."

Randy's face softened for an instant, then he said in a martyred tone, "Like she wouldn't kill me if I sent you away. Go on back."

As Reese passed, he inquired seriously, "Are you all mended?"

"Good as new," Reese responded.

"That's good, Captain Marvel. A lot of people around here need you." He touched her shoulder lightly, then fixed her with a frown. "If it takes more than five minutes, I can't guarantee your safety."

Reese waited as she always did, studying the pictures of Tory's Olympic days, warmed by the images. She brushed her fingers lightly over Tory's face in one of the photos, a close-up that showed her alone in a racing scull, her head thrown back in the sunlight, smiling and triumphant.

Across the room, Tory stood silently in the doorway, chart in hand, watching Reese. The very sight stirred her, causing her breath to catch for an instant.

"Hello, sweetheart," Tory said, her voice husky, as she pulled her office door closed behind her.

Reese turned with a smile. "Hi, love." She went to her, sweeping off her hat as she leaned to pull Tory close. "I just stopped for a second. I missed you."

"Mmm. I missed you, too."

"Randy says it's a rough day."

Tory slipped her arms around Reese's waist, loving her solid strength. "Not anymore," she sighed. "You're just the kind of interruption I needed."

"I'm glad you don't mind."

"Never." Tory indulged herself with the feel of her lover for an instant longer, then stepped back to straighten Reese's tie and brush a stray lock of dark hair from her forehead. "Happy to be back at work?"

"Just happy," Reese said softly, smiling tenderly. "Randy warned me that I couldn't stay. I just wanted to see you."

"Stop in anytime," Tory murmured, her fingers resting lightly on Reese's chest.

"I plan to." Reese settled her hat low over her brows, kissed Tory swiftly on the lips, and stepped toward the door. "See you at home, Dr. King."

Tory called after her, the kiss still tingling on her lips, "You can count on it, Sheriff."

The End

About the Author

Radclyffe is the author of numerous lesbian romances (*Safe Harbor, Innocent Hearts, Love's Melody Lost, Love's Tender Warriors, Tomorrow's Promise, Passion's Bright Fury, Love's Masquerade, shadowland,* and *Fated Love*), as well as two romance/intrigue series: the Honor series (*Above All, Honor* revised edition, *Honor Bound, Love & Honor,* and *Honor Guards*) and the Justice series (*Shield of Justice,* the prequel *A Matter of Trust, In Pursuit of Justice,* and *Justice in the Shadows*), selections in *Infinite Pleasures: An Anthology of Lesbian Erotica,* edited by Stacia Seaman and Nann Dunne (2004) and in *Milk of Human Kindness,* an anthology of lesbian authors writing about mothers and daughters, edited by Lori L. Lake (2004).

A 2003/2004 recipient of the Alice B. award for her body of work as well as a member of the Golden Crown Literary Society, Pink Ink, and the Romance Writers of America, she lives with her partner, Lee, in Philadelphia, PA where she both writes and practices surgery full-time. She states, "I began reading lesbian fiction at the age of twelve when I found a copy of Ann Bannon's *Beebo Brinker.* Not long after, I began collecting every book with lesbian content I could find. The new titles come much faster now than they did in the decades when a new book or two every year felt like a gift, but I still treasure every single one. These works are our history and our legacy, and I am proud to contribute in some small way to those archives."

Her upcoming works include the next in the Provincetown Tales, *Distant Shores, Silent Thunder* (2005); the next in the Justice series, *Justice Served* (2005); and the next in the Honor series, *Honor Reclaimed* (2005).

Look for information about these works at www.radfic.com and www.boldstrokesbooks.com.

Other Books Available From
Bold Strokes Books

Change Of Pace: *Erotic Interludes* (ISBN: 1-933110-07-4) Twenty-five hot-wired encounters guaranteed to spark more than just your imagination. Erotica as you've always dreamed of it.

Fated Love (ISBN: 1-933110-05-8) Amidst the chaos and drama of a busy emergency room, two women must contend not only with the fragile nature of life, but also with the mysteries of the heart and the irresistible forces of fate.

Justice in the Shadows (ISBN: 1-933110-03-1) In a shadow world of secrets, lies, and hidden agendas, Detective Sergeant Rebecca Frye and her lover, Dr. Catherine Rawlings, join forces once again in the elusive search for justice.

shadowland (ISBN: 1-933110-11-2) In a world on the far edge of desire, two women are drawn together by power, passion, and dark pleasures. An erotic romance.

Love's Masquerade (ISBN: 1-933110-14-7) Plunged into the often indistinguishable realms of fiction, fantasy, and hidden desires, Auden Frost discovers a shifting landscape that will force her to question everything she has believed to be true about herself and the nature of love.

Beyond the Breakwater ISBN: 1-933110-06-6) One Province-town summer three women learn the true meaning of love, friendship, and family. Second in the Provincetown Tales.

Tomorrow's Promise (ISBN: 1-933110-12-0) One timeless summer, two very different women discover the power of passion to heal and the promise of hope that only love can bestow.

Love's Tender Warriors (ISBN: 1-933110-02-3) Two women who have accepted loneliness as a way of life learn that love is worth fighting for and a battle they cannot afford to lose.

Love's Melody Lost (ISBN: 1-933110-00-7) A secretive artist with a haunted past and a young woman escaping a life that proved to be a lie find their destinies entwined.

Safe Harbor (ISBN: 1-933110-13-9) A mysterious newcomer, a reclusive doctor, and a troubled gay teenager learn about love, friendship, and trust during one tumultuous summer in Provincetown. First in the Provincetown Tales.

Above All, Honor (ISBN: 1-933110-04-X) The first in the Honor series introduces single-minded Secret Service Agent Cameron Roberts and the woman she is sworn to protect—Blair Powell, the daughter of the president of the United States. First in the Honor series.

Love & Honor (ISBN: 1-933110-10-4) The president's daughter and her security chief are faced with difficult choices as they battle a tangled web of Washington intrigue for...love and honor. Third in the Honor series.

Honor Guards (ISBN: 1-933110-01-5) In a journey that begins on the streets of Paris's Left Bank and culminates in a wild flight for their lives, the president's daughter and those who are sworn to protect her wage a desperate struggle for survival. Fourth in the Honor series.